I0656976

Frederick W. (Frederick William) Briggs

Bishop Asbury

A biographical study for Christian workers

Frederick W. (Frederick William) Briggs

Bishop Asbury
A biographical study for Christian workers

ISBN/EAN: 9783742837530

Manufactured in Europe, USA, Canada, Australia, Japa

Cover: Foto ©Raphael Reischuk / pixelio.de

Manufactured and distributed by brebook publishing software
(www.brebook.com)

Frederick W. (Frederick William) Briggs

Bishop Asbury

BISHOP ASBURY:

A BIOGRAPHICAL STUDY FOR CHRISTIAN WORKERS.

WITH A PORTRAIT.

BY THE
REV. FREDERICK W. BRIGGS.

Published for the Author at the
WESLEYAN CONFERENCE OFFICE,
2, CASTLE STREET, CITY ROAD,
1874.

CONTENTS.

NOTE.

EXCEPTING the facts relating to the early life of Bishop Asbury, for the accuracy of which I must hold myself responsible, my principal authorities for the statements contained in this volume are the following :—

Asbury's Journal.

Wesley's Works.

Minutes of the Methodist Conference.

The Arminian and Methodist Magazines.

"History of the Methodist Episcopal Church," by Abel Stevens, LL.D.

"History of the Methodist Episcopal Church," by Nathan Bangs, D.D.

"Life of Dr. Coke," by Dr. Etheridge.

For the portrait I am indebted to my friend, Mr. W. E. Whitehouse. Asbury sat twice for his portrait, and each was engraved and published ; but I may safely say that that which I have the satisfaction of prefixing to this volume is a truer likeness than either of them. It is the work of a competent artist, who has spared no pains to gain a true appreciation of the character of his subject, who has the great advantage of being himself in moral sympathy

with that character, and who has thoroughly studied and
striven to faithfully reproduce the distinctive features as
represented in the engravings referred to, but with a more
natural expression.   That he has been successful cannot be
doubted.   Mr. Whitehouse has generously presented his
fine oil painting to the Trustees of the Asbury Memorial
Chapel, Handsworth.   I am under obligation to another
friend, Mr. W. H. Wilkinson, for the admirable photographs,
the originals of the engravings with which the volume is em-
bellished,—the one being a view of Manwood's Cottage,
near West Bromwich (at one time a noted centre of Methodist activity and influence), where Asbury preached his
first *authorized* sermon ; and the other a view of his parents'
residence, the home of his childhood and youth, and also a
preaching-place for half a century.

BISHOP ASBURY.

CHAPTER I.

INTRODUCTION.

The Writer's Purpose—Asbury's Character and Appearance—The single Aim of his Life.

AT the Methodist Conference of 1768 it was said, "In many places the work of God seems to stand still. What can be done to revive and enlarge it?" And one recommendation in reply to this momentous question was, "Let every preacher read carefully over the 'Life of Mr. Brainerd.' Let us be followers of him as he was of Christ, in absolute self-devotion, in total deadness to the world, and in fervent love to God and man." Had Mr. Wesley framed a similar answer to the same question in our time, he would have probably associated the name of Francis Asbury with that of Brainerd; perhaps still more likely he would have substituted the one for the other.

"I reckon him," said Dr. Dixon, in a letter to the Rev. Luke Tyerman, the latest biographer of Wesley, "the second man in Methodist history; and, in the extent of his labours, and the variety of incidents connected with them, he is not the second but the first man in our community." *

---

* "Life of Dr. Dixon," p. 416.

1

Mr. Tyerman's own estimate of him he expresses in these
words : " Among the self-denying, laborious Christian
ministers of the past eighteen hundred years, we believe
that Francis Asbury has no superiors, and but few that can
be considered equals. And yet, how little does the Church
Catholic—indeed, how little does the Methodist section of it—
know concerning this great and grand because good o d
man ! " *

In the confidence that no man of competent knowledge
and ability will dissent in opinion from these verdicts, and
acting on the principle of the above-quoted advice, I put
forth this biography as a fit " study for Christian workers."
Yet I am not without good hope that it will be found attractive
and useful to Christian readers generally, whether they are in
a position to be specifically designated *workers* or not. The
fault must certainly lie with the writer or reader, if, in any
case, the contemplation of so noble a character as that which
I have undertaken to delineate,—one of the noblest that the
Church of Christ, the most fertile nursery of noble characters,
has ever produced—is not found to be gratifying, stimulating,
and improving.

But I venture, with sincere respect, to commend the study
particularly to recognised workers in the Church of Christ;
to ministers, preachers, Sunday-school teachers, and all
others who in any sense " watch for souls," and in any form
" labour in the word and doctrine." If I may mention any
class of persons whose thoughtful attention I am most of all
anxious to secure, it is that of young men who are preparing
for ministerial service. If they are sincere in their profession
of a belief that they are called of God to the office they hope
to fulfil, and real in their desire to discharge its duties with

---

* " Life of Wesley," iii. 248.

efficiency and success, they will find the study of so genuine an example of ministerial fidelity helpful to them in a variety of ways. It must have the effect of strengthening their sense of responsibility. It will serve to impress them with the value of time by shewing them how much successful work for the benefit of the world may be crowded into a single devoted life. It will reveal to them the true secret of success. It will teach them how well and safely a man whose purposes and motives are right may guide himself through the folds of tangled difficulties and snares, and how nobly he may bear up and acquit himself under formidable tests and trials. It may serve to convince them also that spiritual experiences, sympathies, and ends, do not tend to contract the mental powers, but to expand and develope them. One of the greatest thinkers of our age has recorded with commendation that his father, who was his sole instructor and educator, was "fond of putting in his hands books which exhibit men of energy and resource in unusual circumstances struggling against difficulties and overcoming them." Such a man, and much more than this description includes, was Francis Asbury; and I cannot think that any active Christian can ponder his history without deriving from it, not instruction only, but suitable guidance, encouragement, and a fresh quickening of all his best powers of thought and feeling.

In person, Asbury was tall, slender, and sinewy, and his constitution, though not robust, was healthy, remarkably elastic, and happily had never been impaired by vice or evil habits. He had a lofty forehead, an open and benignant countenance, and a clear, full voice which he could modulate at will from tones of tenderness and pathos to those of the most thundering declamation. His most characteristic endowments were firmness of will, and the capacity of prompt,

guarded, and sustained exertion. He was emphatically a
man of action. His intellectual gifts were not of the highest
order, and his educational advantages were but few and
meagre. What he became is to be ascribed chiefly to his
possession of that which every other man may possess in an
equal degree—not genius, not showy talents ; but strength,
constancy, and consistency of religious principle. But for
his early conversion, his complete surrender of himself to
the sway of truth and duty, and, it may be added, the providential concurrence of favouring circumstances which he
was prompt to use, he probably would have lived and died
in his native parish, respected it may be for his good sense,
discretion, and steadiness of conduct, but otherwise undis-
tinguished from his humble neighbours; and his name would
have been rarely heard beyond a limited circle. No man
could have appropriated to himself more truly those words
of St. Paul: "By the grace of God I am what I am, and
His grace which was bestowed upon me was not in vain, but
I laboured more abundantly than they all ; yet not I, but
the grace of God which was with me."

Greatness of character is usually attained through the
predominant force of a single principle or passion. A man
becomes great by his enthusiasm of devotion to *one thing.*
A single aim or end commands the approval of his understanding, captivates his feelings, and engrosses the energies
of his soul ; then, as carried out into practice, it takes a
deeper and firmer hold on his whole moral nature, and
eventually subdues every opposing motive, and becomes the
fixed, ever-present, guiding, and ruling passion of his life.
The result is the moral heroism which we admire in the
world's greatest benefactors. In the case of Asbury, this
ruling passion was an enthusiasm to save men by the power
of the Gospel. From the moment when the Divine impulse

toward this end was first imparted to him in the surrender of himself to Christ, to the very close of his marvellous career, his all-absorbing aim was to bring sinful men into union with Christ as their Saviour, and to keep them beneath His yoke. It was under the promptings of this noblest passion that he began to instruct and discipline his mind, and to devote himself to spiritual service, first, in his own neighbourhood, and afterwards in the stations to which he was appointed by the Conference in his own country; it was this which urged him, when the occasion offered, to go out to labour in behalf of his countrymen settled in America; and, as we shall be frequently reminded, it was this which impelled him there to encounter and overcome all but insuperable obstacles, to undertake and accomplish all but impracticable tasks; and to go steadfastly forward from year to year "in weariness and painfulness, in watchings often, in hunger and thirst, in fastings often, in cold and nakedness," till in age and feebleness he was carried into the church to preach Christ with almost his last breath. From day to day,—morning, noon, and night,—he might have heard whispered to his soul one of those "Rules of the Helper" which he had eagerly accepted for the guidance of his life: "You have nothing to do but to save souls. Therefore spend and be spent in this work; and go always not only to those who want you, but to those who want you most."

CHAPTER II.

YOUTH AND EARLY MANHOOD.

Scantiness of Material—Place of Asbury's Birth—His Parents—His Mother's Conversion—Her solicitude for his Spiritual Welfare—His churlish Schoolmaster—His Apprenticeship—Fitness of his Training by means of Manual Labour—His Spiritual Awakening—The "Evangelicals" at West Bromwich—The Methodists of Wednesbury—The old Barn—His godly Companions—Becomes a Local Preacher—Appointed to a Circuit—Offers himself for America—The Parting.

WITH reference to the early life of Asbury, I might almost adopt the words with which Izaak Walton introduces his "Life of Hooker" : "Though I have undertaken it, yet it hath been with some unwillingness, foreseeing that it must prove to me a work of much labour to inquire, consider, research, and determine what is needful to be known concerning him. For I knew him not in his life, and must therefore, not only look back to his death (now sixty-four years passed), but almost fifty years beyond that." But I have this advantage which quaint old Walton had not, that the subject of my biography has left a concise account of his parentage and early history, which, although evidently written in haste, and contained within little more than a page of his Journal, suggests the facts to be sought out, and indicates sources of information concerning them. The following account is that of Asbury himself, with such superadded details, associated facts, and illustrations as I have been able to gather up by careful personal research in the localities familiar to his youth.

"I was born," he says, " in old England, near the foot of Hamstead Bridge, in the parish of Handsworth, about four miles from Birmingham, August 20 or 21, 1745." Some of the aspects of this locality have been changed since Asbury's time ; but the spot he describes may be easily identified by any person who visits it, when the changes that have taken place are pointed out. The domain of Hamstead, or Hamstead Hall, the seat of the ancient family of Wyrley, lies at the north-east of the extensive rural parish of Handsworth, and is intersected by the pleasant old road between Birmingham and Walsall. At a distance of about two miles to the north-west of the spot referred to, is the town of West Bromwich, at present spread out over what was then Bromwich Heath ; and a mile or two further on in the same direction, and in the very heart of the " Black Country," is the old Saxon town of Wednesbury. Through the broad and beautiful valley of Hamstead winds the river Tame, which at that time was crossed by the bridge which Asbury indicates ; but half a century ago it was turned into a new and straighter channel, the public road being also diverted, and a new bridge built, to which the name of Hamstead Bridge has been transferred. The former bridge, however, still remains, with the vestiges of a river beneath it ; but its only use is to connect the road with the coal-wharf adjoining the Hamstead and Great Barr Railway Station,—and to mark the spot where the great evangelist was born. At the point where the present old Walsall road (for there is a newer one still) diverges from the older one, and at the south end of the old bridge, is a rather large ivy-clad house, with its front towards the former road ; and, in a corresponding situation across the bridge, stood the house where Asbury first saw the light.

His parents, he informs us, who " were people in common

life, were remarkable for their honesty and industry, and had all things needful to enjoy. Had my father," he adds, "been as saving as he was laborious, he might have been wealthy. As it was, it was his province to be employed as a farmer and gardener by the two richest families in the parish." His mother belonged to a Welsh "family, ancient and respectable, of the name of Rogers." She was "an ardently affectionate," quick-witted and strong-minded woman, perfectly contented with her lowly social condition, and only concerned to fulfil its duties wisely and well. The death of her only daughter, Sarah, in infancy, plunged her "into deep distress, from which she was not relieved for many years." This event, however, was the means of leading her to give such attention to her spiritual interests as "terminated in her conversion." Under a profound conviction of sin and of her spiritual helplessness, "she sought religious people" who might afford her sympathy and guidance, and became distressingly conscious that she lived "in a very dark, dark, dark day and place." Then she betook herself to religious books; and "many were the days she spent chiefly in reading and prayer." This arrested his attention as a child, and filled him with surprise. It was "strange," he thought, that his "mother should stand by a large window poring over a book for hours together." Shortly after she had "found justifying grace and pardoning mercy," she removed with her family' to a house in Newton Road, Great Barr, just over the parish boundary of Handsworth, where "for fifty years her hands, her house, her heart, were open to receive the people of God and ministers of Christ." This house still stands, its immediate surroundings but little altered; and the memory of Mrs. Asbury, one of its earliest occupants, is lovingly cherished by a few old people who knew her personally, and by many others to whom her excellencies of character have been often told. About the time of her death a chapel was built "within two or three hundred yards of her dwelling," to which the congregation and class she had been the means of forming were transferred; and "thus a lamp was lighted up in a dark place." A sermon on the occasion of her death was preached by the Rev. Samuel Bradburn. Both parents lived to a good old age, the father to his eighty-fifth, and the mother to her eighty-eighth year; and they sleep together in the quiet burial-ground which surrounds the Great Barr Church.

After her own conversion Mrs. Asbury, by a natural instinct of piety, sought the conversion of her husband, and "strongly urged him to family reading and prayer." She also became the more earnestly watchful over Francis, her only son, guarding him especially against forms of insincerity, and impressing him with the solemn obligation of being always simply truthful. This had the restraining effect upon him which she prayerfully laboured to produce; so that, although "the love of truth is not natural, the habit of telling it" he "acquired very early." He "abhorred mischief and wickedness" such as the boys of his age were addicted to, and frequently "returned home" from their company "uneasy and melancholy." "Sometimes" he "was much ridiculed, and called *Methodist parson*, because" his "mother invited any people who had the appearance of religion to her house."

He was early sent to school, and "began to read the Bible between six and seven years of age, and greatly delighted in the historical part of it." But unhappily his "master was a great churl and used to beat him cruelly." "My father," he says, "having but the one son, greatly desired to keep me at school, he cared not how long; but in this design he

was disappointed, for my master by his severity had filled
me with such horrible dread that with me anything was
preferable to going to school."

He was allowed to leave it—with what effect upon his
after life cannot be conjectured. But when only "about
thirteen years and a-half old," he was apprenticed, by his
own "choice," to a laborious trade. Within a short distance
of his father's house was a famous forge, the only one ever
built in that neighbourhood, and one of the first in the whole
district. At night, the lurid flames flashed up from its fur-
naces cast an unearthly glare over the whole valley. Its
ponderous machinery, worked by four huge water-wheels,
he thought of with wonder and eager curiosity; and the
skilful and active energy displayed within its precincts, con-
trasting so strongly with the tame and quiet plodding of his
father's employment, captivated his boyish fancy. Some of
the youths engaged in it had become his personal friends,
and they seemed to him to have acquired by their manly
toil a strength of character which had raised them to a higher
level than his own. The work, he knew, was hard; but
this rather strengthened his desire to have the satisfaction
of doing it.

Forge-operations then, as now, were carried on in several
associated departments. Besides the process of *smelting*,
there was that which is now called *puddling*, the agitation
of the liquid mass with rods till it has got rid of its foreign
matters, and is formed into spherical balls called blooms;
there was the process of flattening out these blooms by sub-
jecting them to the blows of the heavy forge-hammer, now
more effectually accomplished by the rolling-mill; there was
the process of *slitting*, by which the iron when made malle-
able was cut into bars suitable for the use of the smith; and
there was also the smith's department where tools required

by the forgemen were made and repaired. At the head of
this department was a godly man named Foxall, who had
recently come from Monmouthshire, where he and his wife
had been converted to Christ under the preaching of Mr.
Wesley. Between Mrs. Foxall and Mrs. Asbury there had
begun to grow up an intimate friendship, which originated
where so many pure friendships take their beginning—at
some homely religious gathering. On these grounds it was
specially satisfactory to the parents of Francis, when he had
declared his desire to work within the forge, to find that Mr.
Foxall was willing to take him as an apprentice. An arrangement was made with this result, and for "about six years
and a-half" he exercised, developed, and strengthened his
muscles, expanded his chest, and hardened his whole bodily
frame, by learning and practising the honourable craft of
smith. "During this time," he says, gratefully, "I enjoyed
great liberty, and in the family was treated more like a son
or an equal than an apprentice."

No better training of its kind for his great future work
could have been given to him. Had he been called to
found, organize, and direct the Methodist Societies in the
conditions of social life in England, he might have needed
for his task the erudition, dialectic skill, and courtly refinement which John Wesley acquired under the influence
of his extraordinary mother, and at the university of Oxford.
But the work that Asbury was to accomplish in America
called for qualifications of a different kind. It demanded
practical good sense, a love of method, and an active and
well-balanced mind; and this Asbury had in common with
Wesley. But it required also a muscular frame, fortified by
early discipline against exposure to the power of the churlish
elements, ability and readiness to contrive on sudden emer-
gencies, and the capacity of sustained bodily exertion and

endurance; and he could have been placed in no better school to be trained for all this, than the blacksmith's shop of that *Old Forge*. Modern improvements in machinery, and the substitution of steam for water-power, have caused that once noted forge to be removed from the locality; and the very "cinder-field," where its *scoria* were deposited, is now as green as the meadows which surround it; but the anvil on which Francis Asbury wrought is still reverently preserved as a precious memento of his providential early training.

But a fitness for spiritual work of another and higher kind was necessary,—more necessary than physical training, or even a liberal education. A successful evangelist lives and acts in fellowship with Christ and under His guidance. In order to do this he must be *converted, and become as a little child*. The life and experience of a true disciple of Christ must be a matter of personal consciousness to him.

A boy of right natural sensibilities necessarily feels the time when he is first put to a business to be a serious crisis in his history; and a word of spiritual counsel judiciously spoken to him then, may leave an impression for good which is never afterwards effaced. Asbury at the time of his apprenticeship did not lack the prayerful advice of his mother; but it happened also that a godly man, previously unknown to her, had just come to reside in the neighbourhood, and was beginning to pay occasional visits at Mrs. Asbury's house. She quickly discerned in him a power of spiritual usefulness to her son, and enlisted his sympathies and co-operation in his behalf. It was arranged that he should call at times when Francis could meet him; and it was not long before he had won his confidence and succeeded in putting great and stirring thoughts into his mind. "By his conversation and prayers," says Asbury,

" I was awakened before I was fourteen years of age. It was now easy and pleasing to leave my company, and I began to pray morning and evening."

Gradually, as his knowledge, insight, and earnestness increased, he grew dissatisfied with the ministrations of the " dark priest " who officiated at the church which the family attended (the church at Great Barr, at that time a chapel-of-ease to Aldridge), and went on Sundays to *All Saints'*, the old parish-church of West Bromwich. Here he found something more suitable to his spiritual wants. The rector, the Rev. Edward Stillingfleet, M.A., had participated in the Methodist revival, and, together with his like-minded curate, the Rev. Mr. Bagnall, was preaching with almost Methodist plainness, fidelity, and fervour. Besides these, the youthful inquirer now heard " esteemed Gospel ministers," whose occasional services were procured by the Earl of Dartmouth. This nobleman, who was Stillingfleet's parishioner, was a friend of the Countess of Huntingdon, and Sandwell Hall, his seat, was the frequent resort of the Evangelical clergymen whom the good Countess had gathered around her as earnest fellow-labourers. The rector was a member of this elect circle, and welcomed them to his pulpit.

Amongst others whom Asbury now heard, and whose fervid discourses remained fresh in his memory in mature life, he enumerates " Ryland, Talbot, Mansfield, Hawes and Venn." Under the light and guidance and holy influence which came to him from this varied spiritual agency, his mind was exercised more and more respecting his personal relations to God. He " became deeply serious ; reading a great deal of Whitefield's and Cennick's Sermons, and every good book he could meet with." These sermons had probably come into his hands through the Calvinistic clergyman he so gratefully mentions, or as having been put in circulation by the Dartmouth family. Their theology was not altogether of such a character as he would have accepted in after life ; but they contained the essential truths of the Gospel, their earnestness of tone and directness of appeal harmonised well with his state of feeling, and they no doubt strengthened his longings for spiritual realities. In some sense also they were the productions of Methodists on whose labours, sufferings and sayings he was daily hearing favourable or contemptuous and jeering. comments.

All this, and the affection he was beginning to acquire for his Methodist master, made him eagerly curious to know by personal observation what Methodism was. He says, "I began to inquire of my mother who, where, what were the Methodists. She gave me a favourable account, and directed me to a person that could take me to Wednesbury to hear them." The Society at Wednesbury, as Mrs. Asbury must have heard, was large, active and full of life and energy ; and she must have been able to give him accounts of its history since the time when the Wesleys had first preached to assembled thousands " in a large hollow not half a mile from the town," which would naturally create in his mind feelings of interest and wonder. He and his guide set off buoyantly together ; and he says that he was impressed with everything he witnessed. " I soon found this was not the church —but it was better. The people were so devout—men and women kneeling down—saying *Amen*. Now, behold ! they were singing hymns—sweet sound ! Why—strange to tell— the preacher had no prayer-book, and yet he prayed wonderfully ! What was yet more extraordinary, the man took his text, and had no sermon-book : thought I, this is wonderful indeed ! " But he experienced something more than a sense of surprise ; for there suddenly passed into his soul an inspiration from the Holy One which filled him with a deep and stirring consciousness of his spiritual relations to an unseen world. It was not yet, however, that he could say, "Being justified by faith, we have peace with God." He continued to attend the Methodist services at Wednesbury with his young friend, whose name, I believe, was William Emery; but he did not obtain the spiritual satisfaction he sought until some time during the summer of 1760, when he was in his sixteenth year. Alexander Mather had then come fresh into the Staffordshire Circuit, and was holding prayer-meetings at Wednesbury, at which he urged penitents with his characteristic fervour "to believe *now*; to come to Christ *now*; without any other qualification than a sense of their own sinfulness and helplessness."* Asbury was roused by these enthusiastic exhortations to increased earnestness; and when he and Emery were praying together in his father's barn he was brought, he says, "to Jesus Christ, who graciously justified my guilty soul, through faith in His precious blood." That old barn thus became invested for him with an attractive sacredness. It appears to have been in a tumble-down condition; and Asbury so regularly resorted to it for personal communion with God that, as I have been told by an aged person who knew his mother, neighbours were wont to say gaily, but not flippantly, that it was kept standing by young Asbury's prayers.

From this time he was a decided and happy Christian, ready to be in any way in which he was competent a "worker together with" Him who came to seek and to save the lost. In a month or two, youth as he was, he began to hold meetings for prayer, Bible-readings, and exhortation, in his father's house,—in a house which he opened for these purposes at

* "Lives of Early Methodist Preachers," ii. 179.

Sutton Coldfield, and elsewhere; and he records gratefully that "several souls professed to find peace through my labours." * His "friend and father," Mr. Mather, became inspired with so much confidence in his good sense and stability, that before the completion of his seventeenth year he gave him authority to form and lead a Society-class at Bromwich Heath, where a house had been recently opened for public worship. Thus sanctioned, he obtained additional influence over youths of his own age, and he soon became the centre of a group who clung to him with sincere and warm affection, and not only looked to him for guidance at the weekly meeting, but were his chosen and constant companions. One of them, recalling in his old age those days of youthful fervour, says in an autobiography written for the gratification of his family : "In 1761 my father and mother came to live at Barr, where I soon became acquainted with Francis Asbury; and he, I, and three or four more used to go to Wednesbury in the morning of the Lord's-day to the preaching at eight o'clock, and, when that was over, twice to West Bromwich Church and at five in the evening to Wednesbury again."

The writer of this account was Thomas Ault, a fellow-apprentice of Asbury and of exactly his own years. He lived to the mellow old age of eighty ; was identified with the West Bromwich Society from its first beginning under Asbury to the time of his death, when it had become large and influential ; was for twenty years the clerk of the parish-

---

* The occupier of this house at Sutton was Edward Hand, an ancestor of the Sunderlands, an estimable family now resident in Birmingham, several branches of which are attached friends and supporters of Methodism. Mr. Hand was violently persecuted for his religious earnestness by his ignorant neighbours : twice they set fire to his house. He and Asbury were fast friends through life. They are said to have spent together in prayerful conversation the last evening before Asbury finally quitted home.

church, and he sleeps beneath a stone in the parish grave-
yard on which affection inscribed the lines now scarcely
legible :—

> "Here lies the body of Thomas Ault,
> Who, to human ken, was without a fault."

Another of the youths referred to in the extract was Jabez
Ault, the brother of Thomas, whose son, the Rev. William
Ault, was one of the six devoted young men who sailed with
Dr. Coke to Ceylon, and the first of that distinguished band
to pass from the Mission field to the rest and reward of
Heaven. Two others were James Bayley and Thomas
Russell, whose names are gratefully remembered as those of
ardent youths associated with Asbury in the erection and
subsequent enlargement of the room on Bromwich Heath, in
which the West Bromwich Methodists worshipped till 1806,
and another, of whom more particular mention may be made,
was Henry Foxall, Asbury's master's son.

Henry, who was three years younger than Asbury, was
taken specially under his care and watched over by him with
the solicitude of a loving elder brother. Whether he ever
became a member of his class I have not been able to ascertain, but he certainly accompanied him to public services both
at All Saints' Church and the Methodist preaching-houses,
paid him frequent visits at his mother's house, and was
deeply influenced and affected by his consistent piety. Some
years after Asbury had quitted the neighbourhood, Foxall
undertook the superintendence of extensive ironworks in the
North of Ireland. There "one Lord's day, while riding out
on horseback, he saw a number of people gathered together
under some trees in a field. Curiosity induced him to
approach the assembly, when he found a preacher of Mr.
Wesley's Connexion calling sinners to repentance. He

2

listened with deep attention.   The words reached his heart ;
he was convinced of sin."   The religious impressions of his
youth were revived, and for some months his mind was in
a state of great agitation and distress.   He at length found
peace in believing ; became an active member of the Methodist Society ; and, eventually, "a highly respectable local-
preacher."   After a year or two he removed to America, and
fixed his residence in George Town, near Washington.   There
he amassed considerable wealth, a portion of which he
appropriated to the erection of a Methodist Church in the
city of Washington, which, in 1810, his intimate, and then
venerable, friend, Bishop Asbury, had the satisfaction of
dedicating to the worship of God.   This church—in allusion
to the Old Foundry, the cradle of Methodism, in Finsbury, and
also to the iron business by which Foxall had acquired his
wealth, and at which the now hoary-headed friends had spent
their youth together,—they agreed to call *The Foundry*, and
to this day the " Foundry Church " of Washington is known
throughout American Methodism.   Foxall finished his mortal
career at Handsworth.   " Five days before his death," says
the Rev. Joseph Entwistle, from whose account some of these
details are taken, " he took a ride in his carriage to shew his
now disconsolate widow the house in which Mr. Asbury was
born." *

   But the most noteworthy of all Asbury's youthful associates was Richard Whatcoat, whom we shall meet again as
an ordained companion of Dr. Coke on his mission to America
to constitute and organize the Episcopal Church, and who
was eventually raised to the office of Coadjutor-Bishop with
Asbury.   Whatcoat came to reside in Wednesbury in 1757,
joined the Methodist Society there in 1758, was moved and

---

* *Methodist Magazine*, 1824, pp. 69 and 505.

guided to the attainment of more abundant life in Christ under the same earnest preaching which was the means of Asbury's conversion, and they were employed together as leaders of Society-classes. He is spoken of with reverent affection as one of the most saintly men that ever lived. The American Methodist Conference say of him in their published *Minutes* for 1807 :—" We will not use many words to describe this almost inimitable man. Who ever saw him light or trifling? Who ever heard him speak evil of any person ? Nay, who ever heard him speak an idle word ? He was dead to envy, self-exaltation and praise ; sober without sadness ; cheerful without levity ; careful without covetousness ; and decent without pride. He died not possessed of property sufficient to have paid the expenses of his sickness and funeral, if a charge had been made ; so dead was he to the world."*

What degree of intimacy subsisted between him and Asbury can only be a matter of reasonable conjecture ; but that they often met as fellow-labourers and as friends, is certain ; and it may be well supposed that the influence of so holy a man, who also was the senior of Asbury by nine years, contributed much to the formation of his character.

When eighteen years of age, Asbury was raised to the rank of an authorized local-preacher. The first occasion of his conducting a public service in this capacity, or perhaps rather in the usual way of *trial*, with reference to the office, is spoken of by descendants of some members of his little congregation to this day. The place was *Manwoods Cottage*, at Bromwich, a lonely and antique dwelling, standing in subordinate relation to an old ecclesiastical building a short distance from it, known by the name of *Manwoods*, which at that time was the residence of the Earl of Dart-

---

* "Lives of Early Methodist Preachers," v. 319.

mouth's steward. Standing behind a chair in the spacious living-room of that—

> "Quaint old gabled place,
> With church stamped on its face,"—

to be henceforth invested with an interest of which the founders of *Manwoods* never dreamed, on account of the mighty issues dependent on that "trial sermon"—with many of the workmen at the neighbouring forge, or members of their families present, as hearers,—he delivered his message with agitated feelings, but with a full heart and a hopeful spirit, and with an impressive simplicity, directness, and force which has never been forgotten. Some words of commendation or encouragement must have been spoken, which he modestly attributes to a want of "knowing how I had exercised elsewhere." "Behold me now a local-preacher," he continues, "the humble and willing servant of any and of every preacher that called on me by night or by day; being ready with hasty steps to go far and wide to do good, visiting Derbyshire, Staffordshire, Warwickshire, Worcestershire, and indeed almost every place within my reach, for the sake of precious souls; preaching generally, three, four, and five times a week, and at the same time pursuing my calling."

In 1766 he was called to quit home and manual work, and for nine months he "went through Staffordshire and Gloucestershire in the place of a travelling preacher" whose health probably had failed. The next year (1767) he was regularly "admitted on trial" for the itinerant ministry, and appointed to the Bedfordshire Circuit; the year following (1768), having acquitted himself satisfactorily, he was "fully admitted," and appointed to Colchester; in 1769 was re-appointed to Bedfordshire; in 1770 he travelled in Wiltshire; and at the Conference which began in Bristol, on the 6th of August, 1771, he was accepted as a volunteer for what was to be the work of his life in America. It was the first Conference he ever attended, and he went to it fully resolved, under a deep sense of obligation, to offer himself for that trying mission. For six months previously "strong intimations" that it was his duty to do so had occupied his thoughts day and night; and he had earnestly sought definite Divine guidance with reference to it. Profoundly moved, as he sat reverently in the large room in the Horsefair, with the venerable leaders of the Methodist agency before him, he listened to statements freshly received from America respecting the encouraging success of efforts already made in behalf of that vast continent; and, when the words were pronounced, " Our brethren in America call aloud for help,—who are willing to go over and help them?"—he rose with a palpitating heart, but with a composed and unfaltering mind, to proffer his services. The trial of five years in laborious circuits in England had sufficiently attested his fitness for the enterprise, and, with the concurrence of the whole Conference, the appointment was given to him. With a disburdened mind, he returned to Barr to communicate the tidings to his parents. This was a difficult and painful task, for both father and mother clung to him, their only child, with the utmost strength and tenderness of affection. He " opened " the matter to them "in as gentle a manner as possible;" and they, being " blessed," as he believed, "in the present instance with Divine assistance," consented to " let him go." The moment of final severance from them must have presented a scene peculiarly affecting. His father, whom, he says, " I seldom if ever saw weep," was " overwhelmed with grief and tears;" his great-hearted mother, on the

contrary, being calm and self-restrained. How he manifested or subdued his own swelling emotion he does not
intimate, but a fact which my investigations in the neighbourhood have disclosed speaks all that needs to be told concerning this. He wished to leave with his mother a keep-
sake, a token of his deep, admiring, and grateful affection for
her. What should this be? His earthly treasures were few ;
but there was something—his large silver watch, the dear
companion of his solitary travels in circuits at home,—the
thing which he could least conveniently spare when going
abroad, but which would afford, for this reason, if freely
given, the best proof of the reality and strength of his love.
Might he not ask his mother to accept and retain this as a
perpetual remembrancer of him ?   No ; he would not request
this favour—he would not give that considerate mind the
opportunity to speak its refusal or remonstrance ! Sobbing
out his last farewell, he thrust his watch impulsively into his
mother's hand, and fled ! *   A day or two later he found himself again in Bristol, in a state of readiness for his voyage.
He had " not one penny of money; but," he says, " the Lord
soon opened the hearts of friends, who supplied me with
clothes and ten pounds."

Wesley expected his lay-preachers to think of themselves
" as learners, rather than teachers—as young students at the
University, for whom, therefore, a method of study is
expedient in the highest degree ; " and he advised them to
rise early, to devote the whole of the forenoon to systematic
study, and to read, in particular, a selection of works which

---

* This watch is preserved with reverent care by an aged couple now
living, from whom I heard the above, no doubt oft-repeated, tradition
concerning it.

he enumerates, "in order, slowly, and with much prayer." So faithfully did Asbury follow this advice during the five years in which he laboured in English circuits, that, although when he first entered upon his work he felt himself to be "exceedingly ignorant of almost everything a minister of the Gospel ought to know," by the time of his embarkation for America he had not only mastered the books recommended by Wesley and many other choice theological works, but had acquired a fair knowledge of Latin, Greek, and Hebrew.

CHAPTER III.

THE PLANTING OF METHODISM IN AMERICA.

The "Palatines" in Ireland—Embury and Mrs. Heck in America—First
Methodist Sermon—Captain Webb—The Sail-loft—Wesley Chapel—
Webb in Philadelphia—Strawbridge in Maryland—Appeal to Wesley
—Boardman and Pilmore—Mary Redfern—First Missionaries in New
York—George Whitefield.

FRANCIS ASBURY was not the first Missionary whom
Wesley sent to America; and it may be convenient, at
this stage of our history, to trace from its origin the progress
of the work which he was appointed to promote.

In the beginning of the eighteenth century there settled
in Ireland, in the county Limerick, a colony of about fifty
families of refugees from those so-long-distracted provinces
on the Rhine called the *Lower Palatinate*. Mr. Wesley discovered these persecuted people during his visit to Ireland
in 1756, and lingered with them some days. His labours
among them were attended with unusual success; he formed
many of them into a Society, and left them pleasantly impressed with the evidences of their artlessness and sincerity.
In 1765, however, he writes, sorrowfully, "I preached at
Ballygarane to the small remains of the poor Palatines.
As they could not get food and raiment here, with all their
diligence and frugality, part are scattered up and down the
kingdom, *and part gone to America.*"

How different would have been the tone of this record if
its writer could have foreseen the future issues of this

lamented dispersion! One of the " poor Palatines " whom he missed on this occasion was a young carpenter, named Philip Embury, who had been approvingly engaged in his connection with the Society as a local-preacher and leader. He had emigrated to New York in company with two of his brothers and a few other friends, including his cousins, Paul and Barbara Heck. They had all gone out under the pressure of want, and, unhappily, on their settlement in the new country, they made worldly success their absorbing aim, and suffered spiritual declension and loss. At the time of Wesley's visit to " the town of Palatines " in 1765, as just stated, another party of them was preparing to join Embury and his relations. Some of these, also, were Methodists ; but, after settling at New York, they, like their predecessors, lapsed into a state of spiritual carelessness. One of them was Paul Ruckle, the eldest brother of Barbara Heck. Whether or not he had made profession of godliness before his departure from Ballygarane is unknown, but in America he gave himself up, without restraint, to worldly frivolities and amusements. One day, when on a visit to his house, Barbara found him engaged in a game of cards. Suddenly she was seized with compunction of conscience. The ruinous spiritual state in which the whole company were living, flashed startlingly upon her recollection. She grasped the cards and dashed them into the fire ; then, vanishing out of the apartment, she ran down to the house of her cousin, Philip Embury, and, reminding him of happier times when, as a consistent Christian and an approved local-preacher, he had laboured for their spiritual benefit, she said, as if consciously speaking by Divine authority, " You must preach to us here, or we shall all go to hell, and God will require our blood at your hands." Roused by this abrupt and earnest appeal, he confessed his unfaithfulness,

and admitted his responsibility; but urged a variety of pleas
in his excuse, which she promptly repelled. In compliance
with her resolute entreaty, he ultimately consented to hold
a religious service in his own house. She persuaded three
or four persons to attend it with her; and probably the first
Methodist sermon ever preached in America was addressed
to that congregation of not more than five persons, including
a black servant, *Betty*, by that penitent local-preacher, re-
awakened to a sense of obligation and accountableness, in
his own dwelling. When the sermon was ended the hearers
formed themselves into a Society-class, with Embury as their
leader. *This was the germ of the Methodist Episcopal Church
of America.*

From week to week Embury preached and his congregation multiplied. In a short time the class was divided into
two; and, the congregation having outgrown the dimensions
of the apartment in his house, a larger room in the neighbourhood was hired for their purposes. This was situated
near the barracks; and three members of the military band,
John Buckley, James Hodge and Addison Low, attracted
by the singing, came and heard words whereby they were
saved. All of them were eventually associated with Embury
as leaders.

A month or two later, in February, 1767, a strange
military officer in full uniform joined the congregation after
the service had begun. His presence naturally attracted the
attention of all assembled. The unwelcome surmise passed
quickly into every mind that he had come with authority
from the governing powers to scatter them, and prohibit a
continuance of their meetings. But they were reassured in
a moment; for, on entering the room, he knelt reverently in
silent prayer; then he united in their singing, responded
audibly and heartily to their petitions, and conducted him-

self throughout the service in a manner which convinced them that he felt at home with Methodist worshippers. Before the congregation dispersed he introduced himself as a soldier of Jesus Christ, and a spiritual son of John Wesley, and gave an account of his religious history by which all were deeply affected and encouraged. They thankfully received him into their fellowship, and his name, *Captain Thomas Webb*, honourably associated as it is with stirring and important events in our national history, will be always still more honourably connected with the planting of Methodism in America.

The facts by which this remarkable man surprised and interested his new friends were of no ordinary character; and we are able to state them "in almost his own words," as one of his oft-repeated recitals of them was heard by the late venerable Joseph Sutcliffe, and reported by him in a paper contributed to the *Methodist Magazine* for 1849. "He had sailed with General Wolfe for the conquest of Canada," in 1759. "The fleet having anchored near Quebec the general called the crew on deck, and apprised them that the French, aware of their coming, had so pointed their guns as to be able to destroy both ships and men, in case they attempted to land near the batteries. He then asked them, ' Can you drag my cannon up those steep heights ? ' The voices being all ' Ayes ' the army landed during the night ; and next morning when Montcalm, the aged French general, was told that Wolfe had gained the Heights of Abraham, he was heard to say, ' that boy has outwitted me ! ' The battle followed in the open ground near the city. There was very severe fighting. Wolfe was twice wounded without being obliged to leave the field ; but he next received a wound in his chest, which closed his career. He only lived to hear the first shouts of ' Victory ! '" Webb was near him when the heroic man fell, and was himself wounded in the arm; but, as the wound was not serious, he was soon afterwards engaged with the detachment sent to reduce the fortress of Louisburg, where a shot struck his right eye and burst the eye-ball. "His only recollection was a flood of light which accompanied the destruction of the eye. The wounded were put into a boat, and, having crossed the water, all were assisted to land, excepting Webb, of whom one of the men said, 'He needs no help; he is dead.' His senses had returned, and he was just able to reply, 'No; I am not dead!'" For three months he was under surgical treatment, then he returned to England, and was taken by some Methodists in Bristol, with whom he had business transactions, to hear Mr. Wesley, under whose ministry he was spiritually awakened and converted. This great event had taken place two or three years previous to this visit to New York. At that time he was residing at Albany, where he was stationed as barrack-master; and, having heard of the labours of Philip Embury, he had come over to help him.

Such was in substance the story with which Webb interested his hearers on that memorable Sunday night; and, producing his credentials, he told them further that Mr. Wesley had authorized him to exercise his gifts as a local-preacher: henceforth he was associated with Embury as a recognised fellow-labourer.

Through the combined efforts of these godly men,— Embury preaching with increased earnestness, as encouraged and sustained by his gallant helper; and Webb preaching in his turn, with characteristic simplicity, power, and feeling,— dressed in military uniform, his sword girt by his side or placed on the desk before him, a green shade over the destroyed eye, and his face radiant with benignity,—the

congregation grew so rapidly that it was found necessary
to procure a much larger room, and a " rigging-loft," sixty-
four feet long, was rented and fitted up for their accommodation. This place became immediately crowded with
attentive hearers ; and the necessity of procuring something
still more commodious impressing itself on many minds, it
was agreed, on the suggestion of Mrs. Heck, to apply themselves forthwith to the erection of a regular meeting-house.
A suitable site was obtained in John Street ; money, time, and
labour were cheerfully contributed ; and a chapel was built,
—which has since given place to the more stately John
Street Methodist Church,—which its projectors lovingly
called *Wesley Chapel*.

Never was the building of a sanctuary undertaken with
more joyous and self-denying zeal; never was a " head-
stone " brought forth with more devout and gladsome shout-
ings of " Grace, grace, unto it! " Webb gave thirty pounds
towards it, and lent upon it three hundred pounds without
interest ; Embury devoted to it his strength and skill as a
carpenter ; Mrs. Heck white-washed the walls with her own
hands ; Thomas Bell, a hearty Yorkshire Methodist, who
arrived while the work was in progress, told his friends at
home, to whom he sent an account of it, that he found every
member working with a steady good will and strength of
determination which astonished him. He says, " They
made several collections about the town ; they went to
Philadelphia and got part of the money there ; I," he adds,
with satisfaction, " wrought upon it six days." * At length
on the 30th of October, 1768, the chapel was ready to be
opened for the sacred purposes of its erection ; and Philip
Embury, who had constructed the pulpit, himself preached

---

* *Methodist Magazine* for 1806, p. 46.

from it the first sermon to as large a congregation as could find accommodation.*

During the time that this building was in hand, Captain Webb took a house in Long Island, which he opened for preaching, and paid occasional visits to Philadelphia, where he gathered a good congregation into a sail-loft and formed a small but prosperous Society. "The Captain," as Mr. Wesley said a year or two later when he had had the opportunity of hearing him, "was all life and fire; therefore, although he was not deep or regular, yet many who would not hear a better preacher flocked together to hear him. And many were convinced under his preaching; some justified; a few built up in love." † About the same time Robert Strawbridge, another Irish emigrant, and an Irishman of the true type,—generous, impetuous, and full of energy,—began to preach in his own house in a new settlement called Sam's Creek, in Maryland. He also was encouraged with success, and his house being soon found to be too small to accommodate the numbers who desired to hear him, they built, a short distance from it, a curiously constructed " log meeting-house."

At New York the fast-increasing Society felt more and

---

* "The chapel was built of stone, faced with blue plaster. It was sixty feet in length, forty-two in breadth. Dissenters were not yet allowed to erect 'regular churches' in the city; the new building was therefore provided with 'a fireplace and chimney,' to avoid 'the difficulty of the law.' Though long unfinished in its interior, it was 'very neat and clean, and the floor was sprinkled over with sand as white as snow.' "—Stevens's Women of Methodism, p. 175.

† Wesley's Journal, Feb. 2, 1773. He had previously described him in a letter as "a man of fire. The power of God constantly accompanies his word." Charles Wesley hit off his character exactly when he told Mr. Benson that he was " an inexperienced, honest, zealous, loving enthusiast."

more deeply the need of having placed over them some regular and responsible preacher ; and resolved to lay the matter before Mr. Wesley, with the hope that he would sympathize with their solicitudes and send them one. The most active part in this measure was taken by Thomas Taylor, who came over from England shortly after Embury and Webb had began to preach in the rigging-loft. On the 11th of April, 1768, he addressed a long letter to Mr. Wesley, in which he gave him a clear and concise account of the work from its beginning, and implored him, " not only in his own name, but also in the name of the whole Society," to send them " an able and experienced preacher ; one who has both gifts and grace . . . a man of wisdom, of sound faith, and a good disciplinarian ; one whose heart and soul is in the work ; " adding, " with respect to money for the payment of the preacher's passage over, if they could not procure it, we would sell our coats and shirts to procure it for them."

This letter Mr. Wesley read to the Conference which met at Leeds in 1769, " one of the most loving Conferences," he says, " that they ever had." The result is best described in the characteristic record contained in the published *Minutes* for that year :—

Ques. 13. " We have a pressing call from our brethren at New York (who have built a preaching-house) to come over and help them. Who is willing to go ? "

Ans. " Richard Boardman and Joseph Pilmore."

Ques. 14. " What can we do further in token of our brotherly love ? "

Ans. " Let us now make a collection among ourselves." (This was immediately done ; and out of it £50 were allotted towards the payment of their debt, and about £20 given to our brethren for their passage.)

How far these first volunteers, in response to an appeal
for so trying a mission, satisfied all the requirements of the
work as they are stated in Mr. Taylor's letter, is a question
which will unavoidably suggest itself as we proceed, but
which, with our scanty information, must not be met with too
absolute an answer.   In regard to the matter of experience,
there would be in the appointment all that could have been
looked for.   Boardman was about thirty years of age and
had been in the work six years ; and Pilmore, who had the
advantage of an education at Kingswood School, had laboured
successfully for about four years.   They were also without
doubt " able preachers and of sound faith," and they seem
to have had moral endowments suited especially to some of
the conditions of their work.   Wesley describes Boardman
in his Obituary (in 1783),—in agreement with all other testimonies concerning him,—as " a pious, good-natured, sensible
man, greatly beloved by all that knew him."   So far he was
eminently qualified for his position as superintendent of the
hastily and loosely constituted, and heterogeneously composed,
Societies of New York and Philadelphia.   But we shall find
reasons to think that in administrative capacity he was not
equal to his position.   He had not the firmness of will
necessary to a " good disciplinarian," and both he and
Pilmore were probably more prudent than enterprising.

They embarked together from Bristol at the end of August.
Boardman, whose last circuit was in the Dales of Yorkshire,
travelled to that city through the Peak of Derbyshire ; and
an incident occurred in that part of his journey which would
have been sufficient in itself to immortalise his name.
Arrived at the village of Moneyash, he inquired whether there
were any Methodists there, and was directed to a cottager
who gladly proffered him entertainment for the night.   In
the evening he preached.   He was a widower, and his choice

of a text was probably dictated by his depressed state of
feeling under the consciousness of his recent loss, as well as
by its suitableness to his great undertaking.   The words he
selected were these :—" And Jabez was more honourable
than his brethren ; and his mother called his name Jabez,
saying, Because I bare him with sorrow.   And Jabez called
on the God of Israel, saying, Oh ! that Thou wouldst bless
me indeed, and enlarge my coast, and that Thine hand might
be with me, and that Thou wouldst keep me from evil that it
may not grieve me !   And God granted him that which he
requested."   (1 Chron. iv. 9, 10.)

One of his hearers on this occasion was Mary Redfern, an
intelligent and earnest girl, who had previously felt her need of
a Saviour, and to whom the sermon afforded the guidance she
sought; soon afterwards she found " peace in believing."   Ten
years later Mary Redfern became the wife of William Bunting,
and when William and Mary Bunting presented their only
son for baptism, they gave him the name of *Jabez*, in grateful
remembrance of this casual discourse which had been made
the means of his mother's conversion.*   Thus remarkably
was this earliest mission to America connected with one of
the greatest preachers, one of the most distinguished
missionary advocates, and by many degrees the most eminent
legislator and ruler, that Methodism ever produced.

On their arrival in America the missionaries took charge
at once of the Societies already formed, Pilmore remaining
for the present in Philadelphia, and Boardman, who was to
act as " assistant," or superintendent under Wesley, going
forward to New York.   Both were gratified with what they
saw of the state of the work, and were encouraged by the
immediate success of their own labours.   Pilmore, writing to

---

* " Life of Dr. Bunting," i. 9, 10.

Mr. Wesley on the 31st of October (six days after their
landing), informed him that he had found at Philadelphia a
Society of about a hundred persons ; that he had already
preached several times to large congregations ; and that on
the Sunday evening he had preached from the Grand Stand
on the Race-course to, he thought, " between four and five
thousand hearers, who heard with attention still as night."
Boardman also wrote soon after (November 4th, 1769) from
New York, stating that the new preaching-house would hold
about seven hundred people, but was much too small.
" About a third part of those who attend get in ; the rest
are glad to hear without."   And he adds, with a consciousness of obligation with reference to one branch of his work,
which probably was not always thereafter equally fresh and
undim :   "They have no preaching in some parts of the back
settlements."

These first regular preachers from England were followed,
shortly after their departure, by Robert Williams and John
King, two earnest local-preachers, who, the next year, were
received and duly recognised by Wesley as "helpers," with
their names entered on the published *Minutes*.

Five weeks after the arrival of Boardman and Pilmore at
Philadelphia, George Whitefield landed for the last time (his
thirteenth passage across the Atlantic) at the same port.
He met Mr. Pilmore and his friends there and "gave them
his blessing."   On the 21st of February following, Mr.
Wesley wrote the last letter he ever addressed to him.
Referring to rumours which originated in tidings of his
tempestuous voyage which had reached this country, Mr.
Wesley says,—"Mr. Keen informed me some time since of
your safe arrival in Carolina ; of which indeed I could not

doubt for a moment, notwithstanding the idle report of your being cast away, which was so current in London. I trust our Lord has more work for you to do in Europe, as well as in America. And who knows, but before your return to England, I may pay another visit to the New World? I have been strongly solicited by several of our friends in New York and Philadelphia. They urge many reasons, some of which appear to be of considerable weight; and my age is no objection at all, for I bless God, my health is not barely as good, but abundantly better in several respects, than when I was five-and-twenty. But there are so many reasons on the other side, that as yet I can determine nothing; so I must wait for further light. Here I am: let the Lord do with me as seemeth Him good. For the present I must beg of you to supply my lack of service, by encouraging our preachers as you judge best—who are as yet comparatively young and inexperienced—by giving them such advice as you think proper; and, above all, by exhorting them, not only to love one another, but, if it be possible, as much as lies in them to live peaceably with all men." Six months after Whitefield received this letter (September 30, 1770), he entered triumphantly into the joy of his Lord.

CHAPTER IV.

INITIATION OF ITINERANCY.

Arrival in America—Philadelphia—Staten Island—New York—No arrangements for Country Work—Asbury disappointed—First Preaching Tour—Second Tour—Staten Island—Third Expedition—Fourth Tour—Falls unwell—New York Circuit formed—Philadelphia—His Example begins to be followed—Philadelphia Circuit formed.

THUS the good work had been well begun before it came under the fostering care of Asbury. It had reached indeed just that stage of progress which required for its further successful prosecution the leadership of a man of his never-failing good sense, quick and true discernment, sound discretion, steadfastness of purpose, and ardent devotion. Accompanied by Richard Wright, a young man who, after the experience of a year or two, returned to England and retired into private life, he landed at Philadelphia on the 27th October, 1771.

Full of quiet enthusiasm,—grave, calm, dignified, self-possessed, eager for action, deeply conscious that his sufficiency was only of God, and looking every moment to Him for wisdom and strength,—he finds himself at length on that vast continent which had so long occupied his thoughts, with his work immediately before him, and his eye fixed directly upon it, or the indications of his Divine Master's will concerning it. On the evening of his arrival he heard Mr. Pilmore preach in "a large church" which the hopeful Society at Philadelphia had lately bought of Reformed Germans. He felt encouraged by the affectionate greeting with which he was welcomed ; by evidences of spiritual prosperity which he witnessed ; by the freedom and comfort which he experienced in preaching ; and he wrote in his Journal, " The Lord hath helped me by His power, and my soul is in paradise."

On Tuesday, Nov. 6, he says, " I preached my last sermon before I set out for New York." On his way thither he preached at Burlington, " in the Court-house, to a large, serious congregation," where he also felt his " heart much opened." Setting out thence the next morning for his destination, he " met with one Peter Van Pelt, who had heard me preach at Philadelphia. After some conversation he invited me to his house in Staten Island ; and, as I was not engaged to be at New York on any particular day, I went with him and preached in his house." The day following was Sunday, and he preached morning and afternoon to as large a congregation as could find accommodation in Mr. Van Pelt's house, and in the evening " in the house of Justice Wright, where " he had also " a large company to hear " him. " This was probably the first Methodist preaching in the beautiful island, and opened the way for it to become one of the garden-spots of the denomination, with its six Methodist churches of our day, though it is only fourteen miles in length, with but from two to four in breadth. Peter Van Pelt and Justice Wright continued to be steadfast friends of the infant cause, and their houses were long favourite homes of Asbury and his fellow-labourers. Benjamin Van Pelt, the brother of Peter, became a useful local-preacher, and one of the founders of Methodism in Tennessee, then the furthest West." *

Asbury arrived at New York on Monday, November 12,

---

* Stevens's " History of the Methodist Episcopal Church," i. 124.

"and found Richard Boardman there in peace, but weak in body." The next evening he preached to a large congregation on a text which might have been taken as the motto of his life. "I determined not to know anything among you, save Jesus Christ and Him crucified." He was gratified with his reception by the people; was favourably impressed with what he saw of their spirit and character; was more thoroughly persuaded than ever that he was "in the order of God;" and was irresistibly drawn to Boardman, whom he found to be "a kind, loving, worthy man, truly amiable and entertaining, and of a child-like temper."

During the week he made himself acquainted with the condition and requirements of the Society, visited the people at their homes, preached to them with his "heart truly enlarged," and, having remained with them over the Sunday, was ready the next day to sally forth to appointments in the country. But no such "appointments" existed. No system of regular itinerancy had been introduced or deemed practicable. There had been an exchange of cities at stated intervals between Boardman and Pilmore, each labouring for a continuous term of three or four months at New York or Philadelphia, and at the end of this term taking each other's place; but this was the only form in which the Methodist principle of periodical change had been recognised. No attempt had been made to form a *circuit*, and, with the aid of local-preachers and exhorters, to do the proper work of an *evangelist*. Asbury was disappointed. He had not, he says, "the thing which he sought,—a circulation of preachers. I remain in New York, though unsatisfied with our being both in town together." He expostulated with the Society; but his pleas, instead of enkindling sympathy, and moving to the immediate use of effort to rectify the defect he pointed out, only provoked opposition. Calm and dauntless, he then declared himself "fixed to the Methodist plan," whether others rose to the level of his own conceptions and purposes or not. Filled with uneasy feeling, he wrote : "I am willing to suffer—yea, to die, sooner than betray so good a cause by any means. It will be a hard matter to stand against all opposition, 'as an iron pillar strong, and steadfast as a wall of brass ; ' but, through Christ strengthening me, I can do all things."

It would be unjust to the excellent men who had preceded him to omit to say that they had not been unmindful of the wants and claims of the scattered, outlying populations. When they first landed in America in 1769, they were no doubt animated with a similar zeal to that of Asbury on his first arrival, two years later. How could they, as trained and approved Methodist preachers, have been regardless of the spiritual destitution of the surrounding settlements, hamlets, and small towns ? Boardman, in his first letter to Wesley, had expressed his concern with reference to them, and his hope that " an effectual door would be opened among them ; " and Pilmore, writing subsequently from Philadelphia, had said,—" We are chiefly confined to the cities, and therefore cannot at present go much into the country, as we have more work upon our hands than we are able to perform. There is work enough for two preachers in each place." Not unlikely the attractions of agreeable society and of a quiet fire-side, as time advanced, and facilities for extending their labours into the rural districts were neglected, contributed unconsciously to the maintenance of the opinion that their strength was not equal to the work they saw it necessary to undertake ; but that they were sincere in holding and acting upon that opinion there can be no doubt. Nor can it be alleged against them that they were unemployed. Boardman, and probably Pilmore also,

"preached at least four sermons weekly, and met the Society
on Wednesday night. He had but two leisure evenings a
week."* Their mistake seems to have been that of reconciling
themselves to the omission or postponement of an irksome
duty, until they had acquired an unconquerable reluctance to
do it, and a readiness to evade it by specious but insufficient
arguments—perhaps, until they had lost a true and perfect
sense of its importance. So persuaded were they, at least,
that the time for it had not yet arrived, that they strove to
retain Asbury himself in New York, on the plea that, for the
present, he could most usefully employ himself in assisting
Boardman to consolidate and extend the work among the
fast-growing population of that thriving city, as a centre.

But Asbury could not see it his duty to yield to their
wishes. What they urged upon him, and had partially
established, was not Methodism. It was not that which had
made Methodism so mighty and efficient an agency in
England; it was not what he had been appointed to carry
out in America. Whatever force there might have been in
the plea that this was the only thing practicable so long as
the preachers were single-handed, or assisted only by their
local brethren, this plea was now taken from them; and
for two men regularly set apart for evangelistic and pastoral
work to remain together in the same town, seemed to him
an incongruous and inexcusable waste of power. "I am
dissatisfied," he writes again; "I judge we are to be shut
up in the cities this winter. My brethren seem unwilling
to leave the cities; *but I think I shall shew them the way.*
I am in trouble." There was no possibility of restraining
him. He was resolved; he would forthwith begin, despite
the protest of those whose friendship he most desired to

---

* Stevens's "History of the Methodist Episcopal Church," i. 104

win. "Whomsoever I please or displease, I will be faithful to God, to the people, and to my own soul."

Accordingly, on the second Saturday after his entrance into New York, he took with him two friends as guides, and started for West Chester, a distance of about twenty miles. Arriving there in the evening, they waited upon the mayor to solicit "the use of the Court-house, which was readily granted; and," he says "on the Lord's-day morning, a considerable company being gathered together, I stood up in the Lord's power. . . . Seriousness sat on the faces of my hearers, and the power of God came on me and them. . . . In the afternoon the congregation was increased both in number and seriousness; some of the chief men of the town, the mayor and others, were present. . . . In the evening I preached at one M——'s, at a place called West Farms, to many persons, on the love of God. The next day I preached at West Chester again to a large company, and felt the presence and favour of God, and much love to the people. Being detained another day by the roughness of the weather, I preached another sermon on this text: 'Knowing, therefore, the terror of the Lord, we persuade men.' In the evening we went to the mayor's, where we lodged that night; and the next day at noon set out for New York."

The next Sunday he preached in the city, and had "much liberty, both in the morning and evening." His report to Boardman of his bold and encouraging attempt to initiate itinerancy, failed to persuade him to follow his example; but, as he was willing to be still left in sole charge of New York, Asbury set out again at the end of the week on a second tour. He returned to West Chester, and "lodged at the house of one Dr. White." The next morning he preached in the Court-house; but was disturbed by riotous boys and "the ill-behaviour of the unhappy, drunken keeper." In the afternoon he was "informed that the door of the Court-house was shut against" him. " I felt myself at first a little troubled; but soon after a tavern-keeper gave me the offer of an upper-room in his house, where I spoke on those words, ' If we confess our sins, He is faithful and just to forgive us our sins, and to cleanse us from all unrighteousness.' The power of God was with us, and many of the vilest of those present will, I trust, remember it as long as they live. In the evening I made another visit to West Farms, and preached there; and my heart was there also touched with the power of God. I lodged that night at the house of Mr. O--y. After supper I asked the family if they would go to prayer. They looked at one another and said there was need enough. The next morning, when I asked a blessing before breakfast, they seemed amazed." In the evening of Monday he preached at East Chester; on Tuesday " rode to New Rochelle, and was received with great kindness by Mr. Devoue and his family, and preached there to a few. The next day also I preached to a large company, and found liberty, and believed the power of God was among us. From thence I rode to Rye, where a few people were collected together to hear the word; and the next day preached to them again. On Saturday, 14th, I rode back to East Chester, and preached to a large company. On the Lord's-day I preached at New Rochelle in the church. . . . I published myself to preach again in the afternoon, and those who had most opposed me before came to hear, and behaved well. In the evening I preached in the house of my friend, Mr. Devoue. The next evening I preached again at Mr. Devoue's, and on Tuesday went to Rye, where I had many to hear, and felt some freedom of spirit. The next day I preached at Mairnock, to a company

of people who at first took but little notice of the worship
of God ; but I trust some of them felt the power of truth in
their hearts. On Thursday I returned to New York."

Sunday and Christmas-day he spent in pleasant labours
in the city, and on Friday started in another direction. We
have just seen that on his way to New York, on his first
arrival in America, he was induced to tarry and preach in
Staten Island, about six miles distant from the city. With
the certainty of finding a welcome and a congregation there,
he now paid it a second visit. " On the 28th, we arrived at
Justice Wright's, where we were entertained with the best his
house afforded. From thence I went to my old friend Van
Pelt's, who received me with his former kindness, and collected a congregation in the evening, to whom I preached ;
but had a violent pain in my head. After service I went to
bed and was very ill. However, the next day being the
Lord's-day, I preached in the morning and also in the afternoon, with some freedom of mind. In the evening I returned
and preached at Justice Wright's. Having received an invitation to preach at the house of one Mr. W—d, at the east
end of the Island, I visited that place on my return to
New York," where he assisted in holding "a very solemn
Watch-night" service, at which "many felt the power of
God."

The next day, January 1, 1772, he made a further
attempt to persuade Boardman, and the recognised local-
preachers in the city, to work with him on "the Methodist
plan" of itinerancy. He shewed them, by an account of his
own labours and successes, how possible it was to establish
a regular system of circuit-preaching which might be developed and extended as they had additional means and opportunity ; he urged this as an obligation imposed upon them
by considerations of consistency, by the spiritual destitu-

tion of families scattered abroad as colonists on that wide
continent from the centres of Christian life, and as necessary
to keep those centres themselves living, prosperous, and
forceful. But they were still unmoved by either his arguments, or his statements of experience. They admired his
zeal, they could not deny the desirableness or necessity of
his self-denying mode of procedure ; but they continued to
plead their inability, as yet, to adopt and carry it out efficiently. Their objections seemed to him to be dictated by
their preferences rather than their unfettered judgment, and
he wrote in sadness, " The preachers have their friends in
the city, and care not to leave them."

Once more, however, he would " shew them the way."
The next evening he preached his " last sermon for a time "
in New York, and the following day set out on his fourth
expedition. In the evening he preached again at West
Farms, where a person who acknowledged that he had led a
godless and wicked life, and that the Word came home to
his conscience, shewed him much kindness, "favouring him
with a man and horse all the time he was there." In that
village, and in neighbouring places, he preached three times
on the Sunday and every evening in the week, and " many
people felt the power of truth." Thence he proceeded to
Rye, where at first the people were indifferent, and raised
against him the cry of " The Church—the Church ;" but where
eventually he had " a large company " of hearers, and " felt
the Master near." There he " was taken ill of a cold,"—notwithstanding, the next morning, he pushed forward to New
City Island, where " a congregation was assembled to receive "
him. " During the whole night I was very ill. My friends
behaved very kindly, and endeavoured to prevail on me to
stay there till I was restored ; but my appointment required
me to set off for East Chester, where I preached, and rode near

eight miles in the evening to New Rochelle. On the 19th, the Lord's-day, I preached three times, though very ill. Many attended, and I could not think of disappointing them."

In a state of increasing pain and weakness he continued to travel and labour until he was completely prostrated by a severe quinsy, by which he was all but suffocated. But God, he says, "ordered all things well"; and not only did the doctor do "all that he could for me *gratis*," but the friends in whose house he was entertained, stranger though he was, "treated me as if I had been their own brother." By Sunday, February 10th, he had returned to New York, feeble in health, but able to preach.

Thus, by his firm and independent action, he had, as he purposed, shewn his brethren a way which it was impossible they should much longer decline to pursue. Before the expiration of the term for which he and Boardman were to be associated as fellow-labourers at New York, he had formed around the city an extensive circuit. Preaching-places had been opened, homes for the preachers had been procured, and people of all classes had been prepared to come together under approved guidance, as stated congregations and Societies. The preachers were, as yet, too few in number to visit these places—some of them remote from the city, and widely apart from each other—very frequently; but it was not necessary that any of them should be wholly neglected, and their requirements, if duly kept before the Society, would call forth and develope latent ability for their suitable supply. Already several young men, fittingly equipped for this work, were waiting to be commissioned to undertake it. John Mann may be mentioned as an example. He was attracted to Wesley Chapel, in the first instance, by the fervid preaching of Captain Webb. There, under a sermon preached by Mr. Board-

man he obtained "peace in believing"; and on Asbury's
arrival was already employed as a leader and occasional
exhorter. He was now, through the representations and
appeals of the earnest evangelist, added to the band of
accredited local-preachers, and soon became a valuable helper
in the aggressive work which Asbury had initiated. This
again prepared him for greater services, at that time unfore-
seen. For a considerable period during the Revolutionary
War, when the regular preachers had forsaken the city, Mr.
Mann took charge of the Society and kept the chapel open
for worship. Ultimately he and his brother were ordained
elders together by Dr. Coke and Bishop Asbury, and appointed
to labour as missionaries in Nova Scotia.*

On the 2nd of April the preachers met by arrangement at
Philadelphia, for prayer and conference, and the re-distribu-
tion of their work. "Brother Boardman's plan was, that
he should go to Boston; Brother Pilmore to Virginia;
Brother Wright to New York, and that I should stay three
months in Philadelphia. With this I was well pleased."
Settled in this new sphere, he immediately irradiated from
the city to the surrounding towns and villages, preaching in
taverns, court-houses, private dwellings, or in the open air,
to congregations large or small, serious or "wild" and
irreverent, as the case might be, and thus constituted the
Philadelphia Circuit. On his return to head-quarters, after
his first expedition of a fortnight, he was comforted with
the tidings that his example and earnest pleadings were
beginning to tell on the conduct of his brethren, and that
they too had, in several instances, extended their labours
into the country districts, and were encouraged with decisive
signs of success. No announcement could have been more

---

* *Methodist Magazine*, 1818, p. 641.

welcome. Full of satisfaction he wrote, "I humbly hope that before long about seven preachers of us will spread over seven or eight hundred miles, and preach in as many places as we are able to attend." With similar feelings shortly afterwards he wrote again, "Received a letter from Mr. Pilmore, replete with accounts of his preaching abroad, in the church to a large congregation, and the like." At last he saw the initiation of what he had so earnestly longed and laboured to establish,—a regular " circulation of the preachers." Methodism, with its essential plan of itinerancy, —the simplest, mightiest, and most rational engine for the spread or revival of religion,—was at length fairly introduced into the country, where at that time especially it was most urgently required.

The importance of this achievement it would be almost impossible to overstate. The preachers had every induce- ment, on personal grounds, to confine their labours to the large towns, and might have put forth good and substan- tial reasons for continuing to do so. They were never wholly without solicitude on behalf of the outlying popula- tions ; but their sense of duty towards them had not been up to this time sufficiently strong and clear to make a post- ponement of effort for their benefit unendurable. Had Asbury shewn the same spirit of timid adventure, how different a thing might have been the Methodism of America at this day from that widely-extended and mighty agency it is ! How different also must have been the moral and spiri- tual condition of the whole country ! The tendency of the human mind to ignore its noblest relations and destinies, and to become absorbed in worldliness, is sufficiently powerful even where it is subject to the restraints of religious ordi- nances ; and, left without them amidst the corroding anxieties incident to a settlement in a new country, its natural results must be a state of mere moral heathenism. Proofs of this were found by Asbury in distressing abundance : " Congregation about sixty people : very dead ; their minds and mouths were full of the world ;" " Found about thirty people, and they quite dead ; " " Had an insensible people, full of the spirit of the world ; " "I never felt more in earnest, and hardly a person moved." " I had about three hundred people ; but many of them were wicked whiskey-drinkers, who brought with them so much of the power of the devil that I had but little satisfaction in preaching." " Went to a place called *Hell Corner*, and so named because of the desperate wickedness of the people ; yet even here hath God brought many poor souls to Himself." " Oh, how many thousands of poor souls have we to seek out in the wilds of America who are but one remove from the Indians in the comforts of civilised society ; and, considering that they have the Bible in their hands, comparatively worse in their morals than the savages themselves ! " Left to themselves, these people, already sunk down into a state of semi-barbarity, must, in the nature of things, have degenerated more and more ; yet, sought out and rescued by an itinerant ministry, many of them became the brightest examples of spiritual excellence.

In the formation of the Philadelphia Circuit, Asbury passed through experiences similar to those which attended his previous travels around New York. No time was lost before entering upon the work. Beginning on the Sunday in the city, by first preaching " to many poor mortals in the Bettering-house " (House of Correction), and afterwards to " a very large audience in the church," he is off the next morning to Bohemia, and, making arrangements for preaching there on his return, pushes forward to Wilmington, and thence to Newcastle ; comes back to Bohemia, where he finds that " some mischievous persons have thrown the people into confusion," then departs to Chester, and returns " through a heavy rain to Philadelphia." He is a few days there; preaches repeatedly "with freedom;" meets the Society, and reads "Mr. Wesley's epistle to them;" then starts afresh, first to the Jerseys, next to Trenton, to Burlington, to Greenwich, to Gloucester, and has "serious thoughts of going to Baltimore; but the distance, which is ninety miles, seems too much at present." At one place he preaches to "a few people," but meets with opposition; at another to "the wildest congregation he has seen in America;" at other places to "a serious people," or "a few simple people," and falls in with a company "so stupidly ignorant, sceptical, deistical, and atheistical, that I thought, if there were no other hell, I should strive with all my might to shun that." Then he is filled with gratitude to God, "who opens the hearts of the people to receive him, and his heart to deliver His counsels to them." He is "heavily afflicted;" rides in "great pain;" finds himself unwell; preaches "twice at New Mills with great liberty and life, but was very ill that night." He is entertained at one place by "a tavern-keeper;" at another, he finds it difficult to procure lodgings anywhere; and at a third, is so well and hospitably treated that he writes involuntarily, " I admire the kindness of my friends to such a poor worm as I. O my God, remember them!" At Chester he visits prisoners under sentence of death. He found them penitent, "and two of the four obtained peace with God, and seemed very thankful. I preached with liberty to a great number of people under the jail-wall. The sheriff was friendly and very kind. The executioner pretended to tie them all up, but only tied one, and let the rest fall. One of them was a youth about fifteen." Again at Burlington he visits a condemned prisoner, and trusts that, "through

4

the mercy of God the poor man was humbled." In another case he first preaches under the jail-wall, then "for the benefit of the prisoner attends him to the place of execution," and, having seen him "tied up," he steps "on a wagon," and warns the crowd "to flee from the wrath to come, and improve the day of their gracious visitation." Amidst all this sustained exertion of mind and body, he diligently watches over his own soul, is troubled at times that he is not "more devoted," and longs "to do the will of God with all purity of intention, desire, and thought; that in all things God may be glorified through Jesus Christ."

CHAPTER V.

ESTABLISHMENT OF DISCIPLINE.

Influence over others—Importance of Discipline—Asbury begins to enforce it—Opposed, but unmoved—New York again—Richard Wright spoiled—The Society placed under improved Regulations—Long unsettled—Asbury appointed "Assistant" to Wesley—Princeton—Maryland—Success of Strawbridge—Watters—Williams—King—Gatch—Garrettson—Willing Hearers—Clerical Opposition—The Question of the Sacraments—Difficulties involved in it—Baltimore—Happy and Successful Labour—More Anxiety—The Character of a Quarterly Meeting—Mission of Rankin.

ASBURY'S influence over his brethren during this period increased, naturally, more and more. Had they been less sincere and earnest than they were, they might have rebelled against the restless energy of a man,—the last to come into the field with them,—which would let neither himself nor them have a moment's repose. But they, happily, surrendered themselves to its sway, and were moved at last to enter upon work from which they had so long timorously shrunk as irksome, hard, and perilous ; and to devote themselves to it with a hopeful enthusiasm like his own.

But he had now to grapple with difficulties of another kind. Next in importance to the preaching of the Gospel, was the gathering of awakened and converted men into well-regulated and disciplined Societies. Mr. Wesley, speaking of the comparative failure of Whitefield's labours in America, says : " What wonder ? for it was a true

saying which was common in the ancient Church, ' The soul
and the body make a man ; and the spirit and discipline
make a Christian.'   But those who were more or less
affected by Mr. Whitefield's preaching, had no discipline at
all."   Asbury, who had given his intelligent and hearty
adhesion to the form of godly discipline which Mr. Wesley
had instituted, as " simple, natural, and entirely founded in
common sense ; "—who felt its importance as deeply as he,
and whose zeal was equally practical,—was distressed to
find that in America it had been greatly and generally
neglected.   This grave defect he now most resolutely
laboured to rectify.   He says, April 25th, a few days after
his appointment to Philadelphia :   " Preached with some
sharpness.   In the evening I met the Society, and kept the
door."   A day or two later he writes :   " Many were
offended at my shutting them out of the Society-meeting, as
they had been greatly indulged before.   But this does not
trouble me.   While I stay the rules must be attended to ;
and I cannot suffer myself to be guided by half-hearted
Methodists."   It was not without much harassing opposition, and many painful symptoms of those usual accompani-
ments of wounded pride, when flaws of character are pointed
out, and efforts are made to remove them—jealousy, insult,
and detraction,—that he persevered in carrying out his
purpose.   But he never swerved from duty through considerations of self.   He was required, as a Methodist
preacher, not only to preach the doctrines of the body to
which he belonged, but also to enforce the observance of
its discipline ; he approved the one as conscientiously as he
believed the other ; and he would do his duty.   " I have
nothing to seek but the glory of God ; nothing to fear but
His displeasure. . . . and I am determined that no man
shall bias me with soft words and fair speeches ; nor will

I ever fear (the Lord helping me) the face of man, or know
any man after the flesh, if I beg my bread from door to
door." The result of this fidelity was that many half-
awakened hangers-on to the Society were separated from
it ; and thus, though its numbers were reduced, its strength
and purity were increased, and its influence on the outside
world intensified.

In July he was transferred again to New York. On his
re-arrival in that city he found that Richard Wright, whose
place he had to take there, had not only preached the usual
" farewell sermon," at the expiration of his term of labour,
but had " told his congregation that he did not expect to see
them any more. I have always dealt honestly with him,"
Asbury adds, " but he has been spoiled with gifts ! " He is
said to have had pre-eminently " the art of pleasing." No
doubt he was social, genial, and sprightly ; and therefore
sought after, petted, and flattered. Thus he came under
influences which, as he yielded to them, predisposed him to
self-indulgence, until the discomforts and hardships incident
to the life of a faithful Methodist preacher had become
intolerable to him. Within a few months of this time, he
not only withdrew from the continent, but retired altogether from the itinerant ministry. Asbury does not fail to
note that the selfishly indulgent people who had spoiled this
young man were the first to condemn him !

During his former connection with New York Asbury was
associated with Boardman, who was the responsible head of
the Society. He was now himself put in charge of it, and
began immediately to enforce the observance of its rules.
This task severely tested his piety, temper, and judgment ;
for, through the short-sighted forbearance and compliances of
Boardman, and the carelessness of Wright, he found the
Society in a state of depressing disunion and disorder. He

had much to endure from occasional outbursts of pettishness
on the part of opposers; but records his determination by
the grace of God to keep on in the way of duty, even if it
should be his lot to stand alone. "My business is, through
the grace of God, to go straight forward, acting with honesty,
prudence, and caution, and then leave the event to Him."
It was long before the Society was raised into what he
considered a healthy and prosperous condition. Continually
on his return to the city, after a few days' absence to visit
the country parts of his circuit, he discovered some new
cause of anxiety; but he always found comfort in the consciousness "of having acted uprightly before all men, and
having no by-ends in view."

On the 10th October (within the year since he first
stepped on shore at Philadelphia), he records: "I received
a letter from Mr. Wesley, in which he required a strict
attention to discipline; *and appointed me to act as Assistant.*"
He was thus placed in charge of all the American Societies,
—the office of an Assistant being "to feed and guide, to
teach and govern the flock;"—and also placed over all the
preachers, even Boardman himself. This may seem extraordinary, considering how short a time he had been in
America, and that he had only just completed the twenty-
seventh year of his age. But, in our ignorance of the immediate cause of his elevation, it is enough to say that
Wesley made appointments to office with a simple regard to
what he believed to be the requirements of the work which
he and his agents were prosecuting; that if, on the trial, it
seemed to him that a change was necessary, he never
hesitated to make it; and that, if this failed, he as readily
changed again, or reverted to former arrangements. He
had not lost his confidence in Boardman, as "a pious, good-
natured, sensible man;" but he had probably ascertained

that, as a superintendent, he wanted energy and a spirit of adventure. His change of relations between him and Asbury, however, made no difference in their affection for each other. They met shortly afterwards, took counsel of one another with reference to it, and, says Asbury, "we agreed in judgment about the affairs of the Society, and were comforted together."

This meeting took place at Princeton, a place which he says he had "long wished to see for the sake of the pious Mr. Davis, late President of the College there." He was then on his way to Maryland, where, in agreement with his wishes, Boardman had appointed him to labour during the ensuing winter. He had received encouraging accounts of the prosperity of the work in that colony, and was eager to witness, guard, and promote it. And he found it to exceed his expectations. "Men who neither feared God nor regarded man, swearers, liars, cock-fighters, card-players, horse-racers, drunkards, and others, are now so changed as to become new men ; and they are filled with the praises of God ! "

Maryland, it will be remembered, had been the scene of the labours of Robert Strawbridge, a strong-willed, somewhat eccentric, but right-hearted, and devoted local-preacher, who emigrated from Ireland shortly after Embury, had settled as a farmer in Frederick County, and may be regarded as the founder of Methodism in the South, as Embury was in the North. "He became virtually an itinerant, journeying to and fro in not only his own large county (then comprehending three later counties), but in Eastern Maryland, Delaware, Pennsylvania, and Virginia; preaching with an ardour and a fluency which surprised his hearers, and drew them in multitudes to his rustic assemblies. His frequent calls to preach in distant parts of the country required so much of his time that his family were likely to suffer in his absence; so that it became a question with him, ' Who will keep the wolf from my own door, while I am abroad seeking after the lost sheep ? ' His neighbours, appreciating his generous zeal and self-sacrifice, agreed to take care of his little farm, gratuitously, in his absence."*

In Asbury's records of his first labours in Maryland, we find ourselves introduced to names with which the student of the early history of Methodism in America is familiar, as those of men who became distinguished for their zealous activities and successes.   He says, "We proceeded to Henry. Watters's, whose brother is an exhorter and now gone with Mr. Williams to Virginia."   Mr. Williams has been already mentioned as having gone out to America about the same time as Boardman and Pilmore.   He had Wesley's authority to labour as a local-preacher before he left England, and in 1773 his name was inserted in the *Minutes* as regularly appointed to the American work, with that of John King, who also went out as a local-preacher shortly after him. Henry Watters and his brother William, "an exhorter," were both brought to a knowledge of the truth under the preaching of Strawbridge, Williams, and King.   William Watters has the distinction of being the first native convert to enter the itinerant ministry in America.   Others on this part of the Continent who had been converted and raised into the rank of preacher or exhorter before Asbury's arrival, were Richard Owen, the first native local-preacher, and Philip Gatch, "one of the most admirable characters in early Methodist history."   These names Asbury also mentions at this time : " At friend Gatch's the family were called together ;" "Friend Gatch treated me with great kindness;" " Many people attended the word at Mr. Gatch's ; and after

---

* Stevens's "History of the Methodist Episcopal Church," i. 73.

preaching John King came in. The next morning I returned
to J. C.'s, where the congregation was large, at twelve
o'clock. This man's friends have rejected him on account
of his religion. The family seem very serious; and I hope
there will be a great and good work here. Then rode to
Richard Owen's, where some people came to see me, with
whom we sung and prayed."

Another name connected with Asbury's first visit to Maryland which he does not mention, but which must not be
omitted, is that of Freeborn Garrettson, a man whose "memorable ministerial career," says Dr. Stevens, "was to
extend over half a century, and to leave historical and
ineffaceable traces on the Church, from North Carolina to
Nova Scotia." * We learn from a narrative written by himself, and reprinted in the *Arminian Magazine*, that he was
under deep religious concern before Asbury came into his
neighbourhood. " One day, as I was riding home," he says,
" I met a young man who had been hearing the Methodists.
He stopped me in the road and began to talk so sweetly
about Jesus and His people, and recommended Him to me
in such a winning manner, that I was constrained to believe
there was a reality in religion, and that it was time for me
to think seriously on the subject. . . . Some time after Mr.
Francis Asbury came into our county, and I went to hear
him. The place was much crowded; but I got to the door
and listened with attention. The Word was sweeter than
honey or the honey-comb; I could have tarried there till
the rising of the sun. I followed him to another preaching-
place, where the discourse came to my heart and I was ready
to cry out, 'How does this stranger know me so well?'"†

---

* " History of the Methodist Episcopal Church," i. 352.
† *Arminian Magazine* for 1794, pp. 4, 5.

After passing through a variety of experiences, he, one day, while riding on horseback, seemed to come suddenly under an extraordinary Divine influence. He involuntarily threw the bridle upon the horse's neck, and, clasping his hands, cried aloud, "Lord, I submit," and became consciously reconciled to God.

An incident which Asbury records at this time will show the eagerness of the people to hear him, and some of the inconveniences to which they and the preachers willingly submitted: "Dec. 6, 1772:—Went about five miles to preach in our first preaching-house. It had no windows or doors: the weather was very cold, so that my heart pitied the people when I saw them so exposed. Putting a handkerchief over my head, I preached; and, after an hour's intermission, the people waiting all the time in the cold, I preached again."

But there were also many adversaries. "A poor unhappy man abused me much on the road; he cursed me and threw stones at me." And some of the clergy became his open opponents. "Before preaching, one Mr. R., a Church minister, came to me and demanded who I was, and whether I was licensed." He then denounced him, "in great swelling words," as a needless intruder; charged him with creating a schism in his parish, and with drawing the people away from their work; laughed at him in the presence of a gathering crowd, and sneeringly called him a "fine fellow!"— then followed him into the house "in a great rage," as if determined to put him down.

Nor were these the only or most serious difficulties with which Asbury had to grapple at this time. Outward opposition and persecution gave him no anxiety; and, so long as he found willing hearers profiting under the ministration of the Word, he was content to endure any form of unavoidable exposure and hardship. But the people converted under his preaching and that of his fellow-labourers naturally thought of themselves as a charge committed to them by Christ Himself, and looked to them for pastoral oversight, and for all the rights and privileges which appertain to a Christian flock. And in many respects they were not disappointed. Unlike Whitefield, who had preached in these parts with his usual effectiveness, but had made no provision for the religious fellowship of his converts, the preachers commissioned by Mr. Wesley were required to invite those who evidenced a desire to flee from the wrath to come, and to save their souls, to combine together in regularly organized and disciplined Societies, and, as one body, to " have the same care one for another." But these Societies were to regard themselves as subsisting within the Episcopal Church, and were expected to attend its ordinances, and to receive the Holy Communion at the hands of its clergy. This, to some of their members, was intolerably repugnant. Why, they asked, should they be required to place themselves in a relation so peculiarly sacred to men who had been utterly regardless of their spiritual welfare, between whom and themselves there was so little sympathy, and whose personal character they could so little respect ? It was vain to plead their authority as " a special order consecrated unto the service of the Most High in things wherewith others may not meddle." The ready answer was that " orders " may be conferred upon men whom God has not authorized. Was the Church of Christ a mere human and political institution ? and was the validity of the Sacraments dependent on authority as pertaining to office ? It was not pretended that this extreme view was tenable ; but it was replied that neither did the validity and blessing of the Sacraments depend on the character of those who administered them ; and that, from a necessary regard to

ecclesiastical order and propriety, for the avoidance of strife
and contention, and in deference to the authority of Wesley
and the English Conference, the requirements of Methodist
rule should be faithfully observed.

This was Asbury's position ; but how was he to maintain
it in the peculiar circumstances of the people of America ?
In England he could have allowed no compromise. As a
Methodist superintendent he must have enforced a strict and
definite compliance with rule on this as on all other points.
But in America,—particularly in Maryland, and one or two
other colonies,—the circumstances of the people were essentially different from those of Methodists in England, and
seemed to him to give rise to different and conflicting obligations. Besides, he found that the rule had been already
infringed. The people whom Strawbridge had brought to
Christ demanded the sign and seal of their union with Him,
and Strawbridge had complied with this demand, and was ready
to maintain his right to do so. Moreover, Boardman himself
had, three months ago, quietly conceded the same right.

How was Asbury to deal with these elements of com-
plexity ? He was distressed, but not in despair. To indulge
silent regret would be useless and enervating ; to protest
without acting would be a perilous declaration of weakness ;
and to put down the practices it was his duty to disapprove,
by an arbitrary exercise of his authority, would be to provoke violent opposition, which would probably issue in a
disastrous disruption. He would therefore see what could
be done by a calm appeal to the Christian judgment and
conscience. He would introduce the subject at the approaching quarterly meeting, and endeavour to secure for it a calm,
orderly, and deliberate consideration.

This meeting was held on the 24th December. It was
numerously attended, many of its members having come

from distant places. Asbury preached at the opening, from Acts xx. 28: "Take heed therefore unto yourselves and to all the flock over which the Holy Ghost hath made you overseers, to feed the church of God, which He hath purchased with His own blood." Matters of routine were quickly dispatched; the appointments of the preachers for the next three months were agreed to; and the question was then solemnly proposed: "Will the people be contented without our administering the Sacrament?" Every person was encouraged to speak freely, as having no private ends to serve, and the preachers were appealed to severally for their decision. The result was unsatisfactory. "John King was neuter; Brother Strawbridge pleaded much for the ordinances; and so did the people, who appeared to be much biassed by him." Asbury told them plainly that it was contrary to "the Methodist plan," and that he could not agree to it; but he wisely forbore to coerce them. He thought it right "to connive at some things, for the sake of peace." His strength was to stand still. His account concludes thus: "Brother Strawbridge received £8 quarterage; brother King and myself £6 each. Great love subsisted among us in this meeting, and we parted in peace."

His own appointment was to Baltimore. Starting for it the next morning (Christmas-day) he preached at various places on his way thither, and first entered the city on the 3rd of January, 1773. This was Sunday, and, though in feeble health, he preached "to a large congregation at the house of Captain Paten, at the Point," in the morning, and in the afternoon and evening, in the town. "The house," he says, "was well filled with people, and we have a comfortable hope the work of the Lord will revive in this place." Nor was he disappointed. The arrival of Asbury at this particular juncture is said to have been "the happiest event

which could have occurred to Methodism in Baltimore, as
well as to the cause of religion generally." A preparatory
work had been carried on there by King, Pilmore, and
Boardman, and in the surrounding country by Strawbridge
and Williams; but its extraordinary prosperity from that
time to the present is unhesitatingly ascribed by competent
authorities to the impetus and right direction which was
given to it at this early period by Asbury.*

" *Mon.*, 4*th*. Rode to S. S.'s, and was much affected in
preaching to the people. I then met and regulated the
class. *Tues.*, 5*th*. They were kind enough to offer me the
court-house in the town; but, judging it unfit, I preached in
another house; then met the Society and settled a class of
men. *Wed.*, 6*th*. We had a pretty good gathering at N.
Perrig's about six miles from the town; I then rode back
to town, and, after preaching with comfort in the evening,
I formed a class of women. *Thurs.*, 7*th*. Rose with a determination to live more to God. Preached twice in the country, met two classes, and settled them as well as I could."
This is a sample of the records from day to day, for the
next three months. Sometimes he " suffers a little " through
" lodging in open houses," and from the cold, which was at
one time so severe that " a friend said the water froze as it
came from his eyes; " but " this was a very small thing,"
and he found an ample recompense in the readiness of the
people to hear him, and " the life and power he felt in dis-
pensing the Word among them." Never previously had his
influence been so powerful; never had his congregations
been so large and attractive; never had he found more satisfaction in " settling the classes," and meeting the Societies;
and he was never happier in his work.

---

* Stevens's " History of the Methodist Episcopal Church," i. 134, *seq*.

But, in his office of "Assistant," or General Superintendent, he was required to care for the Societies at a distance, and some of them continued to give him cause for anxiety. He says (Thursday, February 25th) : "Two letters came to hand to-day; one from New York, and one from Philadelphia. They entreat me to return, and inform me that trouble is at hand. But I cannot fear, while my heart is upright with God. I seek nothing but Him, and fear nothing but His displeasure."

It was clear that he required the aid and sympathy of other and experienced fellow-labourers, untrammelled by American prepossessions. This he had fully set forth in a letter to Mr. Wesley, which Captain Webb had gone to England to support by his earnest personal pleadings. Asbury's hope was, that Wesley would be induced to come over himself, and judge, from his own observation, what it was right and expedient to do. Iu this hope,—or that he would at least commission some man of sound judgment and weight of character to take the work under his guidance,—Asbury delayed his departure from his present prosperous sphere of service, notwithstanding the calls he had received simultaneously from New York and Philadelphia. But the unwelcome tidings from those great centres never ceased to harass him. "Satan," he writes shortly after, "has assaulted me very much of late, but hitherto the Lord hath helped and delivered me." And again, a few days later, " To-day my mind was depressed in such a manner as I hardly ever felt it before. In my journey my heart sank within me ; and I knew not why."

The next quarterly meeting was held on the 30th March ; and, to show the character of such meetings at that early period, I transcribe Asbury's account of it. He says : " *Monday*, 29th. Rode twenty miles to the Susquehanna ; and just got in, almost spent, time enough to preach at three o'clock. Hitherto the Lord hath helped me. Praised for ever be His dear and blessed Name! *Tuesday*, 30th. Our quarterly meeting began. After I had preached we proceeded to business; and in our little conference the following queries were propounded, namely—1. Are there no disorderly persons in our classes? It was thought not. 2. Does not dram-drinking too much prevail among our people? 3. Do none contract debts without due care to pay them? We found that this evil is much avoided among our people. 4. Are the band-meetings kept up? 5. Is there nothing immoral in any of our preachers? 6. What preachers travel now, and where are they stationed? It was then urged that none must break our rules, under the penalty of being excluded from our Connexion. All was settled in the most amiable manner. Mr. Strawbridge preached a good and useful sermon from Joel ii. 17 : 'Let the priests, the ministers of the LORD, weep between the porch and the altar,' &c. Many people were present at our Lovefeast, among whom were some strangers; but all were deeply serious, and the power of God was present indeed. Brother Owen preached a very alarming sermon, and Brother Strawbridge gave a moving exhortation. The whole ended in great peace. And we all went, in the strength of the Lord, to our several appointments."

Asbury then went back to Baltimore to preach and make arrangements for his absence; and, leaving John King in charge, at length set out for New York. On his way through Philadelphia he was relieved to find that there "all seemed to be in peace." In what state he found the Society in New York he does not mention. But, after spending a few days there in preaching, meeting and giving suitable advice "to the people," and "regulating" the classes, in all which his "mind was clear, his heart was fixed on God, and Christ was precious," he revisited some of the country places, and then returned to Philadelphia.

Here he writes on the 6th May: "This day a letter from Mr. Wesley came to hand, dated March 2nd, in which he informs me that the time of his coming over to America is not yet, being detained by the building of the new chapel." Instead of the personal visit, which he, as well as Asbury, saw to be most desirable, he had decided to comply with the alternative suggestion of sending out a specially trusted Assistant, with full powers to act in his name. This elect man was Thomas Rankin, a strong-minded Scotchman, the senior of Asbury by seven or eight years, who had already superintended the work satisfactorily in several circuits at home, and had commended himself to Wesley by his earnest sobriety. Rankin chose as his companion George Shadford, who had laboured with him in more than one circuit, and approved himself by his singular devotedness and fervour. A few days before their departure, Wesley met Rankin by appointment at Birmingham, and gave him definite instructions with reference to his mission; and he, together with Shadford, Captain and Mrs. Webb, and another preacher whose name was Yearby, and who seems to have gone out of his own accord, though with Wesley's concurrence, set sail from Bristol on Good Friday, the 9th April.

Thus they were on their passage when Asbury received Mr. Wesley's letter, and on the 3rd June they landed at Philadelphia, where Asbury was in waiting to receive them. The relief to his own mind was unspeakable. "To my great comfort," he wrote, "arrived Mr. Rankin, Mr. Shadford, Mr. Yearby, and Captain Webb." Quietly but eagerly he cast his eyes towards the chief man of this welcomed group. With an intelligence which it is said never failed in such matters, he read the signs of character the new superintendent displayed; he heard him preach "a good sermon;" he scrutinized his carriage towards the Society, heard his questions, weighed his comments and observations; and then noted in his Journal, "He will not be admired as a preacher; *but, as a disciplinarian, he will fill his place.*" He would enforce Methodist discipline—that was evident; and, if he should do this wisely and considerately, he would effect a much-needed good. But how much depended on the manner and spirit! A coincident record occurs in the Journal of Rankin himself. He says, "From what I see and hear, and so far as I can judge, if my brethren who first came over had been more attentive to our discipline, there would have been by this time a more glorious work in many places of this continent. Their lovefeasts and meetings of Society were laid open to all their particular friends; so that their number did not increase, and the minds of our best friends were thereby hurt."

In a day or two they both set out for New York, where (on Saturday, June 12) they were met and welcomed by a body of hospitable friends. The next day they both preached. Asbury's text, which was no doubt taken with reference to the coming of his adviser, was Ruth ii. 4: "And, behold, Boaz came from Bethlehem, and said unto the reapers, The LORD be with you. And they answered him, The LORD bless thee." "Mr. Rankin found his spirits raised, and was much comforted." His own text in the evening was equally characteristic: "I have a message from God unto thee." The following morning at five o'clock Asbury expounded the text, "I have no greater joy than to hear that my children walk in truth," and then started for a fresh tour of evangelistic labour. On his return he wrote, "I found Mr. Rankin had been well employed in settling matters pertaining to the Society. This afforded me great satisfaction."

CHAPTER VI.

MODES OF ADMINISTRATION.

Object of Rankin's Mission—His Fitness—His personal Character—The first regular Conference—Its Minutes—The Sacrament Difficulty—Asbury's re-appointment to Baltimore—The Non-compliance of Strawbridge—Asbury's Toils and Illness—A memorable Quarterly Meeting—Review and Survey—Revelation of Character—Successful Efforts in behalf of Individuals—Moore and Rogers—Rev. W. Otterbein and "The United Brethren in Christ"—Trials at New York—Rankin's Imperiousness—Dempster and Rodda.

RANKIN'S mission to the Methodist Societies of America was similar in its object to that of Barnabas to the newly-formed Church at Antioch. He was sent with authority to investigate the state of the work as it had been begun and carried on at a distance from its governing centre; to check and rectify what he might find in it to be injuriously irregular; and to aid and guide its extension. And, in the most essential respect, he had the same personal fitness for this duty—for he was undoubtedly "a good man." But, in regard to personal character, there was one important point of dissimilarity between them. Rankin was not, like the apostolic envoy, liberal and large-hearted. He had too great a disposition to detect and magnify imperfections; and so, "when he came and had seen the grace of God," he was not "glad," but restrained and cold. He failed to make sufficient allowances for the unfavourable circumstances of the people; and, not finding among them the completeness of character he had inconsiderately expected, he became

depressed and unforbearing. From the first he was too
eager to assert and exercise his authority. His manner also
towards both preachers and people was harsh, dry, and un-
bending. He had come over, he said, " to spread genuine
Methodism with all his might ; " and by *genuine* Methodism
he meant simply a strict and literal compliance with Methodist regulations. The question which was always present
to his mind was not, How would Mr. Wesley apply the
discipline, in particular cases, if he had been there ? but, Is
the discipline *in all cases* rigidly enforced ? He was one of
that class of godly and well-meaning men who do excellent
service to an infant cause by giving it a true bent, and guarding it against hurtful and deforming ingrafts ; but whose
influence upon it beyond a certain point ceases to be beneficial,—tends rather to stunt and impoverish " the fruitful
bough," so that " the branches " do not " run over the
wall."

Rankin lost no time in calling the preachers together for
conference. This, which is counted the first regular Conference in America, was held at Philadelphia. It began on
Wednesday, the 14th July, 1773, and continued its sittings
for three days. Its members were Thomas Rankin, Richard
Boardman, Joseph Pilmore, Richard Wright, George Shadford,
Thomas Webb, John King, Joseph Yearby, Abraham Whitworth, and Francis Asbury, who, however, did not join it
till the second day. Its *Minutes* were published. They
were these :—

" The following queries were proposed to every preacher :—

" 1. Ought not the authority of Mr. Wesley and that Conference to extend to the preachers and people of America, as
well as to Great Britain and Ireland ?

" *Ans.* Yes.

" 2. Ought not the doctrine and discipline of the Methodists, as contained in the *Minutes* (*i.e.* of the English Conference), to be the sole rule of our conduct who labour in connection with Mr. Wesley in America ?

" *Ans.* Yes.

" 3. If so, does it not follow that, if any preachers deviate from the *Minutes*, we can have no fellowship with them till they change their conduct ?

" *Ans.* Yes.

" The following rules were agreed to by all the preachers present :—

" 1. Every preacher who acts in connection with Mr. Wesley and the brethren who labour in America, is strictly to avoid administering the ordinances of Baptism and the Lord's Supper.

" 2. All the people among whom we labour to be earnestly exhorted to attend the Church and to receive the ordinances there ; but in a particular manner to press the people in Maryland and Virginia to the observance of this *Minute*.

" 3. No person or persons to be admitted to our Lovefeast oftener than twice or thrice, unless they become members ; and none to be admitted to the Society-meetings more than thrice.

" 4. None of the preachers in America to reprint any of Mr. Wesley's books without his authority (when it can be gotten), and the consent of the brethren.

" 5. Robert Williams to sell the books he has already printed, but to print no more unless under the above restrictions.

" 6. Every preacher who acts as an Assistant, to send an account of the work once in six months to the General Assistant " (*i.e.* to Rankin).

Asbury records that he did " not find such perfect harmony as he wished for ; " which can be easily understood, when the nature of the questions in discussion is considered. Rule 2 arose out of the irregularities of Strawbridge, as already referred to. In Maryland and Virginia, where his success had been achieved, the English Church was established by law ; so that, in the judgment of that loyal little Conference, they were under the same obligation to attend its services and communicate at its altars there, as in England. Yet it was in those very colonies that Methodist rule on this point had been systematically violated. Asbury mentions that, in consideration of the peculiar circumstances of Strawbridge, leave was given to him to administer the Sacraments "under the particular direction of the Assistant ;" that is, with the consent of his Superintendent for the time being, as any case should be shown to be sufficiently urgent. The concession to him was no doubt obtained by the pleadings of Asbury himself. He adds : " There were some debates amongst the preachers in this Conference relative to the conduct of some who had manifested a desire to abide in the cities and live like gentlemen. Three years out of four had been already spent in the cities. It was also found that money had been wasted, improper Leaders appointed, and many of our rules broken." Rankin refers in a similar tone to causes of dissatisfaction ; but concludes his comments with the statement, that " the preachers were stationed in the best manner we could, and we parted in love."

Asbury was re-appointed to the extensive circuit of Baltimore, as Assistant or Superintendent, with Robert Strawbridge, Abraham Whitworth, and Joseph Yearby for his colleagues. As soon as practicable after his return thither he assembled his Quarterly-meeting, in order to lay before it the decisions of the Conference with respect to the vexed question of the administration of the Sacraments. He had fondly hoped that Strawbridge would appreciate the effort he had made to conciliate him, and submit to the rule as specially modified in his favour. But it was not so: the resolute man would brook no interference or restraint of any kind. "He appeared to be inflexible," says Asbury; "he would not administer the ordinances under our direction at all. Many things were said on the subject, and a few of the people took part with him."

Asbury,—with his profound regard for his colleague, on the one hand, and his concern for the peace, unity, and continued prosperity of the Society, on the other, found his position to be one of painful anxiety. But he could not repudiate the force of Strawbridge's pleas, and he would not enforce discipline rashly. He would wait and forbear.

So, leaving the impracticable man to steer his own course for the present, he applied himself afresh to his evangelistic labours. The next day he is in the saddle, and off for the city. He is taken ill on the road, yet presses forward "though it was sometimes through hard rain and heavy thunder." Day after day he is travelling, preaching, visiting the sick, meeting the Societies, "settling" the classes and "bringing them to peace and order," encouraging godly young men to stir up the gifts that were in them for useful service, and giving "licences" to any whom, after due examination, he judged to be called and qualified to preach or exhort. He is leading the devotions of "a congregation assembled under a tree," when an unusual and overpowering Divine influence is felt; he is accompanied on his way from one place by a company of grateful people, and when "we came to the water-side we knelt down and prayed, recommending each other to the grace of God;" his "mind is much stayed on God," and he feels "but little weariness, though some days he preaches four times." But, in the midst of all this happy and incessant toil, and whilst rejoicing over many clear instances of success, he is again seized with a threatening illness. "Though exceedingly indisposed and in great weakness of body," he continued for a time to "go through the public duties of the day;" but at length was completely laid aside by quartan ague and fever. "I went to bed in great torture, and thought my frame could not long endure it. . . This is my greatest trouble and pain to forsake the work of God, and to neglect the people whose spiritual interest and salvation I seek with my whole soul . . . Felt some patience, but not enough. O that this affliction may answer the intended end! My will is quite resigned to the will of God, so that I cannot ask ease in pain; but desire to be truly thankful, and leave the disposal of all things entirely with Him."

He had scarcely recovered when the General Assistant came down to preside at the Circuit Quarterly-meeting, on the 2nd November. Rankin himself refers to this occasion in strains of exultation. He says, "I have not had such a season since I left my native land." But to Asbury the meeting was not a happy one. The position which he had seen it right to take in relation to his superior in office, on the one hand, and his colleague, on the other, and to their friends and sympathisers, exposed him to the assaults of both parties. "Some of my brethren," he says, "did not altogether please me. My hand appeared still to be against every man. Mr. Rankin," he adds significantly, "conducted the meeting."

It is impossible to misinterpret the meaning of these plaintive words—"*My hand appears still to be against every man!*" Strange, an inexperienced reader may think, that it should be so, in the case of a man so manifestly free from selfish ends, associated in spiritual service with fellow-labourers who might be supposed to be as earnest, single-minded, and self-renouncing as himself! Yet perhaps this ought not seriously to surprise us when our expectations from men are based on their character as we find it, and not as we fondly fancy it ought to be.

When men of various temperaments, casts of mind, and educational biases, are united as kindred spirits in the prosecution of the same important practical end, there must needs be diversities of opinion in regard to particular forms of action. And the more sincere and earnest they are *as workers*, the more sharply will their differences be defined. Too often earnestness produces narrowness and egotism; but where it exists, in combination with breadth of views and sympathies, with a readiness to attach due importance to the opinions of others, and with efforts to conciliate those from whom it is necessary to differ, by patience and forbearance, earnestness will always eventually attract their confidence and good will, and will frequently not only overcome their opposition but command their co-operation. The history of Asbury affords already decisive illustrations of this. He had been as yet but little more than two years in America; and what had he accomplished by his almost single-handed efforts? Where do we behold him?

1. He found his predecessors working on the safe and pleasant, but unaggressive, plan of an exchange of cities at stated intervals, where they had good congregations, hospitable friends, and many home comforts; rarely, if ever, visiting distant and small, but neglected, populations; taking no pains to call forth, train, and employ native talent; and making no attempt to establish a regular system of itinerancy. *All this he had changed.* Almost wholly through the force of his firm and independent example, and his importunate advocacy, the itinerancy was now in full and triumphant operation around six separate centres.

2. He found the Societies in a state of perilous disorder; but, under his wise and energetic management, they were now regularly constituted and disciplined; members were settled in suitable classes; leaders were appointed with a due regard to their relative and personal fitness; stewards were beginning to discharge their duties with comfort and efficiency.

3. He found one of his zealous fellow-labourers assuming and exercising, on his own authority, those ministerial functions to which Methodism at that early period made no pretension. He foresaw that this, if continued, would inevitably disturb the harmony, and destroy the unity, of the Societies, as well as create fresh obstacles to the spread of the Gospel through Methodist agency. He strove to dissuade and restrain this indiscrete man; but in vain. Strawbridge believed himself Divinely entrusted with all the prerogatives of the pastoral office, and refused to be withheld from their enjoyment.

4. Anxious to retain the services of so excellent and useful a man, but also to uphold the system to which he refused to yield a loyal allegiance, Asbury appealed to Wesley for guidance and help, and his appeal was answered by the mission of Rankin, whom Wesley invested with authority to superintend the whole work. But this arrangement, while it relieved Asbury of responsibility, increased his difficulty. For Rankin, with every disposition to execute his commission with conscientious zeal, was wanting in sympathy and considerateness, and too often repelled the best friends of the holy cause by his austerity of manner. He laboured hard to conserve and build up the Societies; but exercised his authority over them, unintentionally, with the "severity" which "breedeth fear," and even, in some cases, with "the needless roughness" which "breedeth hate."

5. At the first Conference which this faithful but exacting man held with his brethren, measures were proposed, which, if carried into effect everywhere, must have either coerced Strawbridge and his converts into conformity to Methodist rule, or driven them away from the Methodist body. Asbury succeeded in modifying those measures in their favour, and hoped to conquer the difficulty by mutual concession and compromise. But he found Strawbridge "inflexible." He would submit to no limitation of what he claimed as a Divinely-given right and trust. Asbury's conciliatory temper was thus sorely tried ; but his good sense and liberal spirit dictated the propriety of still forbearing to use force ; and, leaving the determined man to act for the present as he saw good, he exercised his influence to restrain others from following his example, and patiently left himself for the future to the guidance of Providence.

6. But this did not satisfy the vigorous General Assistant. Rules and resolutions had been adopted to be consistently carried out! In this determination he had come down into Maryland to preside at Asbury's Quarterly-meeting ; and it is clearly, with reference to certain hard speeches on both sides, and the attitude of apparent antagonism to both, which Asbury found it necessary to assume in the interest of peace, charity, and prosperity, that he saw himself a very Ishmael,— "his hand against every man ! "

We, in the review of this testing struggle and its issues, behold him in a different character. We see that at the very time when he seemed, to himself, to be standing defiantly alone, he was throwing a spell over the understandings and affections of his brethren, and drawing them irresistibly to himself.

After three months of persistent labour, carried on in great bodily weakness among the twenty-four places which at this time formed his circuit, Asbury again met his colleagues, local preachers, and others, in the Quarterly-meeting held on the 31st January, 1774, which he gratefully records was " all harmony and love." This was also the character of the meeting held on the 3rd May, with this drawback that, "when inquiry was made relative to the conduct of the preachers, there were some complaints of a few who had been remiss in meeting the Societies and catechizing the children."

Throughout his career Asbury was most remarkably successful in his efforts for the conversion of men taken individually. No man could have felt more deeply the importance of dealing with people separately ; no man had better opportunities of studying varieties of human character, and of understanding how to deal with particular cases ; and no man ever used more wisely and successfully the opportunities which Providence gave him. This may be said most especially with reference to the upper classes. " He had a notable power over them," says Dr. Stevens ; "and his personal influence probably brought more of them into the Church than that of all his ministerial associates together. His simple piety, his natural dignity and greatness of character, together with his fine conversational powers and cheerful humour, had a magical charm both to command respect and afford delight in any circle."*

Many examples of this will be presented in the course of this history ; but I here introduce two, as supplied by his own brief jotting at this period in his daily Journal. The persons concerned are William Moore and Mrs. Rogers and her son. It is unnecessary to amplify the records. I give them as the business-like notes of an observant, patient, painstaking man to whom the sacred calling was a reality.

---

* " Women of Methodism," p. 199.

William Moore is induced to open his house for preaching, which is "crowded with people who attend to hear the Word." Soon afterwards follows the natural statement, "I held a private conference with William Moore and Captain Stone, who both appeared to be convinced of sin." An active member of the Society, Mrs. Hurlings, introduces him to the family of *Mrs. Rogers*, who has expressed her willingness to entertain him ; and he is seized involuntarily with concern for her spiritual interests. "I have great hopes that my acquaintance with the family of Mrs. Rogers will be rendered a blessing to them ; and I expect to see mother and son bow to the cross of Christ." "On my return home, I had great hopes that Philip Rogers will yet become a disciple of Jesus Christ." "There is an apparent alteration in this family ; and I must conclude the Lord directed my steps among them." "William Moore and Philip Rogers seem to be in earnest about their salvation." A little later, when preaching, "a company of men, who would wish to support the character of gentlemen, came drunk, and attempted an interruption ; however, Philip Rogers, once their intimate associate in sin, had courage enough to defend the cause of God." "William Moore gave me a pleasing account of the unspeakable peace with which God has blest him." "While preaching at the house of Mr. Moore, his father and mother were moved by the word of God." Next, within about six weeks after his first introduction to them, we find them both heartily employed in chapel-building. "Was much pleased to hear of the success which William Moore had met with in raising a subscription of more than £100 for our building. Thus doth the Lord give us favour in the sight of the people. Mr. Rogers took up two lots of ground for the purpose of building ; and Mr. Moore seemed determined to prosecute the work at all events." And prosecuted it was with complete success. On Monday, April 18th, 1774, he writes: "This day the foundation of our house in Baltimore was laid. Who could have expected that two men, once among the chief of sinners, would ever have thus engaged in so great an undertaking for the cause of the blessed Jesus? This is the Lord's doing, and it is marvellous in our eyes. He hath touched and changed their hearts."

This was the Lovely Lane Chapel—to have an additional interest given to it, and to be rendered for ever memorable in the history of American Methodism, as the chapel in which the great Conference held its sittings ten years later which organized the Methodist Episcopal Church.

It was during this period that Asbury first made acquaintance with the Rev. W. P. Otterbein, a learned and eloquent Lutheran minister, who, under his guidance, became the founder of "The United Brethren in Christ," sometimes called "The German Methodists;" and to whose personal character he frequently refers in terms of esteem and affection. Methodism in America, as in this country, diffused the blessings of the Gospel indirectly and collaterally, as well as by its direct agencies. The history of Mr. Otterbein is a notable example of this. On the 4th January, 1774, Asbury writes, "Mr. Swoop, a preacher in High Dutch, came to see me. He appeared to be a good man, and I opened to him the plan of Methodism." The object of this visit was to submit to Asbury the desirableness of their uniting their efforts to bring Mr. Otterbein into Baltimore, who was at that time suffering persecution in Pennsylvania, on account of his distinguished devotion and zeal. It happened that a congregation of English-speaking Germans had been recently formed in the town, and Mr. Swoop was anxious to secure the services of Mr. Otterbein in its behalf.

Asbury saw, as by instinct, what a power for good this excellent man would be, especially if his great influence could be extended, by means of lay-helpers, beyond the limits of a single congregation ; and he took the opportunity of pointing out the advantages of systematic itinerancy. " We agreed to promote his settling here," he says, " and laid a plan similar to our own—to wit, that gifted persons amongst them who may at any time be moved by the Holy Ghost to speak for God should be encouraged." Otterbein came to Baltimore, the three conferred together on " the Methodist plan of Christian discipline, and," says Asbury, " they agreed to imitate our method as nearly as possible." Thus, without secession from another community, solely by means of combined evangelistic labour among the masses lying outside all organized Churches, originated " The United Brethren in Christ,"—a body which numbers at this day nearly a hundred thousand members.   Otterbein and Asbury were attached friends and mutual helpers till separated by death, the one surviving the other only about eighteen months.   " Great and good man of God," wrote Asbury, on hearing of his aged friend's departure, " an honour to his Church and country ; one of the greatest scholars and divines that ever came to America or was born in it ! "

At the next Annual Conference which was held at Philadelphia on the 25th May, 1774, Asbury had the satisfaction of reporting an addition to the Societies which had been under his care of 563 members.   The aggregate number in the American Societies was ascertained to be 2,073, being a total increase of 913 within a little more than ten months. Five preachers were " fully received," and seven admitted on trial : the circuits were multiplied into ten, the Baltimore circuit being divided into four.   Asbury was re-appointed to New York, which was still associated with Philadelphia, " to

change in three months" with Rankin. He says, "Our
Conference was attended with great power, and, all things
considered, with great harmony. All acquiesced in the
future stations of the preachers." But he had been, and
still was, under painful constraint. "If I were not deeply
conscious of the truth and goodness of the cause in which I
am engaged, I should by no means stay here. Lord, what
a world is this! yea, what a religious world!"

He started promptly for his former sphere, although with
many misgivings, and in a state of great bodily weakness,
praying that he might be prepared "to act and suffer in all
things like a Christian." The Society received him with
affection, and his "heart was warmed towards them." But
he soon discovered that "too much of the old party spirit
remained in a few." "Mr. C——, not content with his unkind
and abusive letter, is still exerting all his unfriendly force.
I feel myself aggrieved; but patiently commit my cause to
God." Strawbridge, also, continued to give him anxiety,
though now removed to a distance from him. Notwithstanding all his efforts to restrain him from the violation of
Methodist rule, he still remained stubbornly uncompliant.
"What strange infatuation attends that man!" he exclaimed,
on hearing that he was, as before, "officious in administering the ordinances; "—"*why will he run before Providence?*"
But, most harassing of all, was the continuance of discord in
his subordinate relation to Rankin. "Discipline, discipline,"
—perpetually cried the General Assistant—"see that the rules
are strictly kept; enforce our discipline!" Asbury, as we
have seen, did not require to have this duty harshly enjoined
upon him, for he was not less deeply impressed with its
importance than his chief. But he knew that the best and
nearest way to the attainment of a definite end is not always
that which at first sight seems the directest. He felt that

people in the condition and circumstances of the Americans ought to have a degree of consideration shown them which might not be due to Englishmen. He looked at things from *their* point of view, entered into *their* feelings, and realised in his own mind how forms of order presented themselves to *them;* and, as Rankin was indisposed or unable to do this, he was in constant dread of the work being marred and enfeebled at its foundation through his arbitrary rule.

So intolerable became the bearing of this good man in the course of this year that Asbury found it difficult to suppress the desire to sever his connection with him, and withdraw for a time from the continent. First he entertained the thought of going to Gibraltar, on being invited to visit that town as a promising sphere of labour; and he afterwards wrote : "I received a letter from Miss Gilbert, of Antigua, in which she informed me that Mr. Gilbert was going away; and, as there are about three hundred members in Society, she entreats me to go and labour among them. I feel inclined to go." Nor would Rankin have been unwilling to part with him. He not unlikely suggested to Mr. Wesley the expediency of his being recalled : he certainly complained of his want of co-operation. In a letter to Rankin, dated March 1, 1775, Mr. Wesley says, " As soon as possible, you must come to a full and clear explanation both with Brother Asbury (if he is recovered) and with Jemmy Dempster. But I advise Brother Asbury to return to England by the first opportunity."

James Dempster, a well-educated Scotchman, who was appointed to America by the Conference of 1774, could have scarcely entered upon his work there, when Rankin associated him with Asbury in some unfavourable representation to Wesley. He seems to have incautiously declared his sympathy with some members of the New York Society,

6

when they told him their grievances, and sought to induce him to join them in opposing Rankin's administrations. Wesley says to him, in a letter dated May 19, 1775: "That one point I earnestly recommend to Brother Rankin, you, and all the preachers,—by prayer, by exhortation, and by every possible means, to oppose a party spirit. This has always, so far as it prevailed, been the bane of all true religion." To Rankin himself he says, in a letter of the same date, assuming that Asbury would, immediately after his last, return to England,—"I doubt not that Brother Asbury and you will part good friends. I shall hope to see him at the Conference. He is quite an upright man." Happily and providentially, however, when the former letter came to hand Asbury was not within reach of its summons. Released from his duties in the New York Circuit by the arrival of Dempster and Martin Rodda, who were appointed with him, he had gladly gone back to Baltimore. Not long afterwards Mr. Wesley wrote again, "I am not sorry that Brother Asbury stays with you another year. In that time it will be seen what God will do with North America; and you will easily judge whether our preachers are called to remain there any longer."

Wesley's confidence in Thomas Rankin's integrity and earnest piety never faltered; but he was not blind to his characteristic failing. "My dear brother," he wrote to him, "nothing can hurt you if you are calm, mild, and gentle toward all men, especially to the froward." "Among our Societies," he admonishes him again, "we must enforce our rules with all *mildness and steadiness.*"

CHAPTER VII.

IN TROUBLOUS TIMES.

Conference of 1775—Advice from the Wesleys—The coming Struggle
—Asbury at Norfolk—New Schemes and Labours—Heroic Resolution
—Chaotic state of Society—The Preachers suspected—Wesley's "Calm
Address"—Death of Williams—Asbury with Shadford—Character of
Shadford—The great Revival—Rev. D. Jarratt—The miseries of War
—Asbury again Ill—Conference of 1776—Re-appointed to Baltimore
—Mr. Gough, of Perry Hall—His Conversion—Asbury with him at
the Virginia Springs—Returns to Baltimore—The States declared
Independent—Departure of Rankin and Rodda.

THE third Conference began at Philadelphia on the 17th,
and ended on the 19th, of May, 1775. It reported
an addition to the united Societies of 1,075 members, the
total being 3,148. Asbury records thankfully that all the
sittings were characterized by "great harmony and sweet-
ness of temper." Rankin says also, "We conversed together,
and concluded our business in love." He adds, "We wanted
all the advice and light we could obtain respecting our conduct in the present critical situation of affairs. We came
unanimously to this conclusion, to follow the advice that Mr.
Wesley and his brother had given us, and leave the event to
God." This advice was communicated in the following
letters which had just come to hand :—

"LONDON, *March* 1, 1775.

" MY DEAR BRETHREN,—

" You were never in your lives in so critical a situation as you are at
this time. It is your part to be peace-makers—to be loving and tender
to all ; but to addict yourselves to no party. In spite of all solicitations,

by rough or smooth words, say not one word against one or the other side. Keep yourselves pure ; do all you can to help and soften all ; but beware how you adopt another's jar.

"See that you act in full union with each other : this is of the utmost consequence. Not only let there be no bitterness or anger, but no shyness or coldness, between you. Mark all those that would set one of you against the other. Some such will never be wanting. But give them no countenance ; rather ferret them out, and drag them into open day.

"The conduct of T. Rankin has been suitable to the Methodist plan : I hope all of you tread in his steps. Let your eye be single. Be in peace with each other, and the God of peace will be with you.

"I am, my dear Brethren,

"Your affectionate Brother,

"JOHN WESLEY."

"March 1, 1775.

"MY DEAR BROTHER" (addressed to Rankin),—

". . . . As to the public affairs, I wish you to be like-minded with me. I am of neither side, and yet of both ; on the side of New England, and of Old. Private Christians are excused, exempted, privileged, to take no part in civil troubles. We love all, and pray for all, with a sincere and impartial love. Faults there may be on both sides, but such as neither you nor I can remedy ; therefore, let us, and all our children, give ourselves unto prayer, and so stand still and see the salvation of God. My love to Captain Webb when you see him, and to Mr. Bowden, to whom I owe letters, and much love. Shew yours for me by praying more for me and mine.

"Yours in the old love,

"CHARLES WESLEY."

The long-continued struggle between the Mother Country and her American colonies had reached at length its terrible crisis. Blood had been already shed in the skirmishes at Lexington and Concord, and a more serious engagement was then imminent at Boston. A portentous cloud was drifting over the whole continent, and men's hearts failed them for fear.

Asbury was appointed to Norfolk, Virginia, where a Society had been formed by Robert Williams, which, however, had not been regularly organized, and was as yet unconnected by circuit arrangements with contiguous places. Arriving there on the 29th May, after a disagreeable and fatiguing passage of seven days, he says, " I found about thirty persons in Society, after their manner ; but they had no regular class-meetings. However, there are a few who are willing to observe all the rules of our Society. Their present preaching-house is an old, shattered building, which has formerly been a play-house." He quietly subjoins, " My heart is filled with holy thoughts, and deeply engaged in the work of God." And again, " My body is weak, but my soul is in a sweet, pacific frame. May the Lord brace up my feeble bodily frame, and by His grace I am determined to use it for His glory and the service of His Church."

He was immediately occupied with fresh schemes of usefulness. Beginning with a sermon at five o'clock in the morning in Norfolk, he is off the same day to Portsmouth ; plunges " through such a swamp as he never saw before," to preach to a neglected people " of a simple heart " at the furthermost part of the parish ; preaches to a small congregation about six miles from town ; encourages the Society at Norfolk to subscribe for the erection of a chapel ; and labours there, and wherever he finds a few members, to bring them into conformity to Methodist rule ; " telling them that every civil society has its proper rules, and persons appointed to see them kept, and that every member forfeited his rights to membership if he wilfully transgressed them." " Without discipline," he notes, " we should soon be a rope of sand ; so that it must be enforced, let who will be displeased." Within a few weeks he had formed a circuit, including eight regular preaching-places.

On the 7th August he writes, "I received a letter from Mr. T. Rankin, in which he informed me that himself, Mr. Rodda, and Mr. Dempster had consulted, and deliberately concluded it would be best to return to England. But I can by no means agree to leave such a field for gathering souls to Christ as we have in America. It would be an eternal dishonour to the Methodists that we should all leave three thousand souls who desire to commit themselves to our care, neither is it the part of a good shepherd to leave his flock in time of danger; therefore, I am determined, by the grace of God, not to leave them, let the consequence be what it may."

The whole country was seething with political excitement. The discontent which the oppressive legislation of the Mother Country had created, but which had been long loyally smothered, or expressed only in respectful remonstrance and protest, was at last venting itself in one loud and general demand for *Home-rule*. Traffic with England was suspended; officers of the British Crown were publicly insulted and maltreated; preparations for an impending war were being hurried forward with enthusiasm, and society was in a state bordering upon anarchy, "Martial clamours," says Asbury, "confuse the land." Methodist preachers especially were in peril of their lives. The most eminent of them were Englishmen, with, it was naturally presumed, English proclivities; they were also the missionaries of John Wesley, who, it was well known, was a distinguished and warm-hearted Loyalist. For these reasons, even if they had conducted themselves on those principles of strict neutrality which they had agreed to adopt, they would have been suspected for a time. But, unhappily, one of them, Martin Rodda, had irritated the people by vaunting his attachment to the British Constitution and acting the part of an ardent partisan ; and through his indiscretion, not only he, but all his English brethren, and the native preachers associated with them, were indiscriminately denounced and proscribed as the foes of the country. Even Wesley himself unwittingly became the means of strengthening the popular prejudice against them by the publication of his " Calm Address to our American Colonies," in which he told them that they were the dupes of " a few men in England who were determined enemies to monarchy." It is true that this pamphlet, which consisted mainly of extracts from Dr. Johnson's "Taxation No Tyranny," was intended to influence the people of this country rather than the Americans ; * but that it soon found its way among the Colonists is certain from Asbury's lament that " that venerable man ever dipped into the politics of America,"—and its effects on the public mind, with reference to the Methodists, were most disastrous.

With his mind fully made up to brave all the consequences of his steadfastness in these threatening circumstances, Asbury steadily pursued his calling, notwithstanding frequent interruptions " by the clamour of arms and preparations for war." " My business," he says, " is to be more intensely devoted to God." A letter from Mr. Rankin informed him of his purpose to delay his return to England ; and another from Mr. Shadford told him " of about two hundred souls brought to Christ within the space of two months. Glory to God," he exclaims, " for the salvation of sinners ! "

On the 25th September he writes : " Brother Williams died. The Lord does all things well. Perhaps Brother Williams was in danger of being entangled in worldly business,

---

* " Need any one ask from what motive this was wrote ? Let him look round. England is in a flame ! a flame of malice and rage against the King, and almost all that are in authority under him. I labour to put out this flame."—*Journal*, Nov. 11, 1775.

and might thereby have injured the cause of God." At the
time of Asbury's arrival, he had retired from the itinerancy,
and was residing near Norfolk, where he opened his house
for preaching. When tidings of his death reached Asbury
he was himself "very ill with the fall-fever, and being able
to take but little nourishment was much reduced." However, he "ventured to preach a funeral sermon at the burial
of his friend," and records his belief that probably "no one
in America has been an instrument of awakening so many
souls as God has awakened by him." He was the first of
the English preachers to rest from his labours.

In October of this year Asbury was invited by his attached
friend, Mr. Shadford, to assist him to extend the work in
the Brunswick Circuit, where he was then stationed. Nothing could have been more seasonable, or more in accord-
ance with his wishes. "My heart rejoices," he said, as he
looked forward eagerly to this visit, "in hopes of seeing
good days, and many souls brought to God." On taking
leave of Norfolk he writes, "Some that had been displeased
with my strictness of discipline, were now unwilling to let
me go." It was not long after that he had to note, "We
have awful reports of slaughter at Norfolk and Great Bridge ;
but I am at a happy distance from them, and my soul keeps
close to Jesus Christ." A week later he says, with sadness,
"We are informed that Norfolk was burnt by the Governor."

November 2nd he writes : "By the good Providence of
God I entered Brunswick Circuit, and am now within a few
miles of dear Brother George Shadford. God is at work in
this part of the country, and my soul catches the holy fire
already." On the 5th he says, "Met Brother George Shadford. My spirit was much united to him, and our meeting
was like that of Jonathan and David. We had a large congregation, and I was much comforted among them." He

arrived on the eve of the Quarterly-meeting, concerning which he says, "There might be seven hundred people present. What great things hath the Lord wrought for the inhabitants of Virginia! At this meeting we admitted Francis Poythress, James Foster, and Joseph Hartley" (all of them to be thenceforward distinguished in the early history of American Methodism) "as travelling preachers. I had great satisfaction in preaching, and was much pleased with the manner and matter of the Christians' testimony in the Lovefeast, having a corresponding witness of the same in my own breast."

George Shadford was one of the most successful preachers that Methodism ever produced. For earnestness, singleness of aim, and directness of appeal, he may be compared to the better known John Smith ; but he was also characterized by a winning simplicity of manner, a frankness of disposition, and a tenderness of spirit, peculiarly his own. His autobiography, as included in the "Lives of the Early Methodist Preachers," is one of the most charming of that series. Wesley's estimate of him may be inferred from the laconic epistle he sent to him, as commissioned to accompany Rankin :—

"DEAR GEORGE,—The time is arrived for you to embark for America. You must go down to Bristol, where you will meet with Thomas Rankin, Captain Webb, and his wife. I let you loose, George, on the great continent of America. Publish your message in the open face of the sun, and do all the good you can."

The great revival which was being carried on at this time under his preaching had taken Shadford himself by surprise. "I was amazed," he says ; "for I seldom preached a sermon but some were convinced and converted—often three or four at a time." Rankin himself hastened down to witness it. He preached, and records that towards the close of his

sermon his " soul was so filled with the power and love
of God that he could with difficulty speak. Very soon,"
he adds, " my voice was drowned amidst the pleasing sounds
of prayer and praise. Husbands were inviting their wives
to go to heaven with them, and parents calling upon their
children to come to the Lord Jesus." A detailed narrative
of this movement was drawn up by the Rev. Devereux
Jarratt, a minister of the English Church, and was sent
through Asbury to Mr. Rankin to be forwarded to Wesley.
It is full of statements of the same remarkable character.
" The shaking among the dry bones," says Mr. Jarratt,
" was increased from week to week. Numbers of old and
grey-headed, of middle-aged persons, of youth—yea, of little
children, were the subjects of this work."

Much of the preparatory work had been accomplished
under the faithful ministry of Mr. Jarratt himself, who had
been trained for his duties by President Davis, and who now
not only sympathized with the movement, but directly aided
and encouraged it. He has been worthily called the American Fletcher. He always welcomed the preachers into his
parish, and to the hospitalities of his home ; and co-operated
with them heartily in preaching, prayer-meetings, lovefeasts, and in the visitation of the classes. Asbury first met
him on the 10th January, 1776, when he says, he " gave
me a long narrative of a great work under Brother George
Shadford." The same night they held a Watch-night service ;
" and," says Asbury, " Mr. Jarratt and I stood about two
hours each. There appeared to be a great degree of Divine
power among the people."

After having spent about two months in the Brunswick
Circuit in visiting and preaching at various places, partly in
company with Shadford or Mr. Jarratt, and partly unattended,
he returned to Philadelphia at the call of Rankin, having, he

says, "rode about 3,000 miles since I left it last. . . . Here I met with Mr. Rankin, in the spirit of love. I also received an affectionate letter from Mr. Wesley."

For the next two months his daily records of labour and personal experience are everywhere interspersed with lamentations over the miseries of war. "A friend from New York has informed us," he says in one place, "that troops were raised, and entrenchments made, in that city. ✎ O Lord, we are oppressed; undertake for us!" Before the ensuing Conference he was again seized with a perilous sickness, and carried to his lodgings. "My poor frame," he writes, "is much afflicted and shattered; but my mind is full of Divine tranquillity, ardently desirous to submit to the Providence of God with inflexible patience. How amazing is the goodness of God! He raiseth up the best of friends, such as love for Christ's sake, to show the kindest care for me in my affliction. My great desire to be at Conference induced me to make an attempt to travel; but, by the time I had rode three miles, I found if I travelled it would be at the hazard of my life, and was therefore obliged to decline it, though the disappointment was very great. Let it be, Lord, not as I will, but as Thou wilt."

This year the Conference was held for the first time in the city of Baltimore. It began on the 24th May, and reported an increase in the Societies—attributable almost wholly to the "revival" in Virginia—of 1,873 members, the entire number being 4,921. The circuits were eleven in number, and the preachers twenty-five. Asbury was re-appointed to Baltimore.

Here he came among people who not only received him with satisfaction as a messenger of good tidings, but many of whom welcomed him with affection and confidence, as his spiritual children. He met again with his "good friend,

Mr. Philip Rogers, and his wife," and rejoiced over their
continuance in the faith of the Gospel. He renewed his
intercourse with his reverend friend, Mr. Otterbein, with
whom he always found " so much unity, and freedom in
conversation ;" and he is treated "with the greatest affection in the family of Mr. Harry Gough." At the same time
he is made to feel the disquietude of the times, and in one
place in his circuit is " fined five pounds for preaching the
Gospel."

Mr. Gough had enjoyed the blessing of peace with God,
and a renovated heart for about twelve months. He was a
man of wealth. His wife was the daughter of Governor
Ridgeley, and his country residence—Perry Hall, about
twelve miles from the city—was one of the most spacious
and elegant mansions in America at that time. But for a
long period he was an unhappy man in the midst of his
luxury. His wife had been deeply impressed by the preaching of the Methodists, but he forbade her to hear them again.
While revelling with wine and gay companions one evening,
it was proposed that they should divert themselves by going
together to a Methodist assembly. Asbury was the preacher.
As they returned one of them exclaimed, " What nonsense
have we heard to-night !" But Gough replied sharply, start-
ling them with sudden surprise—" No ; what we have heard
is the truth,—the truth as it is in Jesus." " I will never
hinder you again from hearing the Methodists," he said, as
he entered his house, and met his wife. The impression of
the sermon was so profound that he could no longer enjoy
his accustomed pleasures. He became deeply serious, and
at last depressed and melancholy, under the awakened sense
of his misspent life. Riding to one of his plantations, he one
day heard the voice of praise and prayer in a cabin, and,
listening, discovered that a negro from a neighbouring estate

was leading the devotions of his own slaves, and offering fervent thanksgivings for the blessings of their poor condition. His heart was touched, and he exclaimed, "Alas, O Lord! I have my thousands and tens of thousands, and yet,—ungrateful wretch that I am,—I never thanked Thee as this poor slave does, who has scarcely clothes to put on, or food to satisfy his hunger." He returned home with a distressed and contrite heart. He retired from his table, which was surrounded by a large company of his friends, and threw himself upon his knees in his chamber. While there, imploring the mercy of God, he received conscious pardon and peace. In a transport of joy he went to his company, exclaiming, " I have found the Methodists'. blessing ; I have found the Methodists' God ! " " Both he and his wife now became members of the Methodist Society, and Perry Hall was henceforth an asylum for the itinerants, and a preaching-place. The wealthy convert erected a chapel contiguous to the Hall, the first American Methodist church that had a bell ; and it rung every morning and evening, summoning his numerous household and slaves to family worship. They made a congregation ; for the establishment comprised a hundred persons. The circuit-preachers supplied it twice a month, and local-preachers every Sunday." *

For more than two years Asbury had suffered under impaired health. The references in his Journal to attacks of fever, ague, and sore throat, are so frequent that we wonder how he could have continued in his trying labours. At length, however, he was persuaded by Mr. Gough to make arrangements for his temporary absence from his circuit, and to accompany him to the warm sulphur-springs of Virginia. "Perhaps," he says, as with difficulty he brought himself

---

* Dr. Stevens.

to the decision to try them,—"my strength may be thereby
so restored for future services that, upon the whole, there
may be no loss of time." On their way, "that no opportunity
might be lost," he lectured at the tavern where they tarried
for the night. On their arrival at this celebrated resort,
lodgings were found to be so scarce that he and his friend
were obliged to stay at different houses. His own accommodation was not such as we should deem most suitable to the
requirements of an invalid. The size of his room was
"twenty feet by sixteen; and there were seven beds and
sixteen persons therein, and some noisy children." Nor
should we judge his mode of spending this season of rest the
most conducive to the end he desired. His plan was, "to
read about a hundred pages a day; usually to pray in public
five times a day; to preach in the open air every other day,
and to lecture in prayer-meetings every other evening." But
he had his reward. "It clearly appears," he says, three
or four days after his arrival, "that I am in the line of duty
in attending the Springs: there is a manifest check to the
overflowing tide of immorality."

Within about six weeks he had returned to Baltimore
"with more health and perhaps more grace," praying,
"Now, O Lord, only make and keep me pure, and let me
be wholly and only Thine!" But he had come back to be
harassed everywhere by the baleful spirit of war. Two
months previous,—July 4, 1776,—the Congress of "Patriots"
had declared the thirteen colonies which it represented to
be *free and independent States;* and a thrill of delirious joy
had spread throughout the country. Loyalty to the British
Crown had suddenly become a crime. Every man who did
not declare himself in favour of a total disruption with
England was counted an enemy to the liberties and rights of
the State in which he lived. It was, therefore, impossible

for the clergy of the English Church to prosecute their duties, and almost equally impossible for Methodist preachers to carry on systematic itinerancy. Prayer for the King was forbidden on the penalty of imprisonment. No man could travel from place to place without a legal pass, and he could obtain no pass but by taking the test-oath, which pledged him to take up arms in defence of the national independence if called upon to do so by the authorities. What remained, then, to the preachers from England, but to make immediate arrangements for returning home?

So it was thought by all but *one*. At the close of a public service, a messenger from Rodda and Shadford, who were at the time the guests of Mr. Gough, informed Asbury that they were waiting to consult him with reference to this question. He promptly met them, as desired, and they told him that they had resolved to embark for England, and begged him to accompany them. But his simple reply was an appeal to his previous determination, "not to depart from the work on any consideration." Rankin was sent for, and the matter was earnestly and prayerfully reconsidered. Ultimately it was agreed that "dear George Shadford" should linger with his friend a little longer, and the other two prepare to return. They tarried till the next Conference,—"a season of uncommon affection," says Asbury, "many weeping, when the time of parting came, as if they had lost their first-born sons;" and soon afterwards they disappeared from the American continent. Rodda, whose indiscretion had culminated in his last circuit in the distribution of copies of the King's Proclamation, found it necessary to escape to the coast by the assistance of slaves, yet arrived safely at Philadelphia and took refuge in the British fleet; and Rankin "through divers dangers," as he states, succeeded eventually in reaching the same port.

CHAPTER VIII.

ALONE AND IN CONCEALMENT.

Conference of 1777—Position of Methodism—Providential Relation of
Asbury to it—Refuses to leave it—Jonathan and David—Asbury
alone—Declines to take the Test Oath—Retires into Delaware—Judge
White—He is taken Prisoner—Asbury's Usefulness at this Season—
His Hiding-places—Forms of Labour—Delaware becomes his Circuit
—Senator Bassett—Miss Ennalls—Methodism brought into Dor-
chester—Rev. D. McGaw—Judge Barratt.

THE Conference just mentioned (the fifth in order of
time) was held at Deer Creek, in Maryland, in May,
1777, and consisted of twenty preachers. The number of
members had risen to 6,968, being an increase in the year
of 2,047, and the number of preachers to thirty-six.

Thus had Methodism struck its roots deeply into American
soil, and grown to important dimensions. Its 7,000 members would represent many times that number of regular
hearers, and of others who occasionally attended its services ;
and it already included several families of extensive social
influence. It is clear that it had acquired powers and conditions for yet more rapid progress, and that its chief
requirement for this end was a wise and suitable leadership.
It was to be severely tested by the fearful storm which was
then sweeping over the land ; but the process of testing
would serve, under a judicious and fostering oversight, to
develope more fully its living energies and promote its
greater fruitfulness. How, then, was this necessary superintendence to be insured ? Who, of all the men of that trying

day, was there to whom the task could be safely entrusted of watching over, guiding and guarding, the holy cause when exposed, at so peculiarly susceptible a stage of its growth, to the influence of circumstances which so naturally tended to damp its enthusiasm, to corrupt its simplicity, and to thwart the purposes of its zealous promoters ?

If ever the agency of Providence is to be recognized in the events of history, is it not in the position assigned to Asbury at this time ? He came to America at the very moment when Methodism most needed the presence of a man of his peculiar gifts of mind and heart ; he was retained there, when Wesley, under misguidance, recalled him, simply in consequence of being out of reach of the summons to return ; and now, under an unfaltering conviction of duty, he abides there, when others depart, and is left in sole charge of the work when exposed to the disorders and convulsions of a protracted war. But what if he, too, had withdrawn, or if his place of responsibility had been taken by any of his English brethren ? What if the Methodism of America had been abandoned at that crisis of its history to the guidance of Boardman, who, with all his excellencies, seems to have been physically disqualified for sustained aggression ; or to Strawbridge, with zeal to extend rather than skill to consolidate ; or to Rankin, with his brusque and stern severity ; or to any man less earnest and conscientious than Asbury in the considerate enforcement of godly discipline ? It must be admitted that the conditions which combined so happily in him were such as do not often all meet in a single man ; yet they are such as most men may attain to whom the gifts and calling of God are felt to be a reality ; for are they not all traceable to the exercise of good sense, under the guidance of *faith that worketh by love ?*

7

Asbury at once resumed circuit work after the Conference, though amidst "great commotion on every side." Soon afterwards he was informed that the vestry of " Garrettson Church " had resolved to invite him to become their pastor ; but his prompt reply was, " I shall do nothing that will separate me from my brethren. I hope to live and die a Methodist." Shadford, who was still with him, and painfully disinclined to quit the continent without him, urged him again to consider whether it was not his duty to return home, and suggested that they should set apart another day for fasting and prayer together, with reference to this question. He readily acceded to this proposal, but the issue was not what Shadford so anxiously desired. " My convictions," he said, when appealed to for his decision, " are as clear and strong as ever, that it is my duty to remain." " I, however," rejoined Shadford, " believe my work in America to be done. I feel with as much certainty that it is my duty to return now, as I felt it to be my duty to come hither four years ago." " Then," said Asbury, tentatively, " one of us must be in error ! " " Not necessarily so ; " was the reply, and was it not right ?—" I may have a call to go, and you to stay." Asbury's affections clung with unwonted tenderness to " dear George Shadford," and he prevailed on him to delay his departure a few days longer ; and the friends then separated to meet no more. Barely three weeks had elapsed before the heroic man had to write, " George Shadford has left me ! " and the next entry shows how deeply he felt his bereavement : " I was under some heaviness of mind. But it was no wonder : three thousand miles away from home—my friends have left me—I am considered by some as an enemy of the country—every day liable to be seized by violence, and abused. However, all this is but a trifle to suffer for Christ, and the salvation of souls. Lord, stand by me ! "

The peril of life in which he laboured was indeed but too evident. Already his chaise had been shot through, and he was reminded continually of what might befall him any hour, by the reports which reached him of the ill-treatment by mobs, or by the prejudiced magistracy, of his brethren, although all of them now native Americans. The same day that Shadford left him (March 10, 1778), officers of the State of Maryland, where he then was, subjected him to the usual test of allegiance to the State authorities. As an Englishman and a preacher of the Gospel, he declined to pledge himself to take up arms in defence of American independence, and was, therefore, ordered to quit the State. He withdrew into Delaware. At first he says he was at a loss what to do, whether " to deliver myself into the hands of men, to embrace the first opportunity to depart, or to wait till Providence should further direct." Ultimately, he decided to tarry and wait. " It appears to be the will of God that I should be silent for a season, to prepare me for further usefulness hereafter ; therefore my time shall be employed to the best advantage. I am happy in the family where I stay, and my soul is fixed on God. I have a private chamber for my asylum, where I comfort myself in God, and spend my time in prayer, meditation, and reading."

His refuge was the house of Judge White, and, as he abode there, at considerable intervals, for nearly two years, it may not be unsuitable to give some account of this excellent man and his more remarkable wife. The following particulars, not found in the Journal, are from Dr. Stevens:—

Thomas White, Esq., was the Chief Judge of the Court of Common Pleas for the County of Kent, in the State of

Delaware. His devout wife, hearing the Methodists preach, was drawn to them as by a natural affinity, and soon induced him also to hear them. The preachers were invited to their mansion, which they opened for public worship, and which remained a preaching-place until they had erected a chapel in the neighbourhood, which is known to this day as White's Meeting-house. Mrs. White not only led her husband to "the Methodist Communion, but became his best guide to heaven. She was the priestess of the family,— a woman of rare talents, of remarkable but modest courage, and of fervent zeal."

Asbury records April 2nd (shortly after he had become a refugee in this godly dwelling): "This night we had a scene of trouble in the family. My friend, Thomas White, was taken away, and his wife and family are in great distress of mind. The next day I sought the interposition of God by fasting and prayer." He states in explanation that a body of light-horse patrol came to the house by stealth, seized the Judge on the absurd charge of being a Methodist, and, therefore, presumably a "Tory," and conveyed him to prison. Stevens says that when he was apprehended his wife "clung to him, defending him, and declaring to the ruffians, who brandished their swords over her, that she feared them not, until, overpowered by their numbers, he was borne away. She soon followed them, found out the place of his confinement, and rested not till she effected his restoration to his family."

On the review of this season of retirement thirty years afterwards, Asbury describes it as the "most active, the most useful, and most effective part of my life;" and adds that "the children and the children's children of those who witnessed my labours and my sufferings in that day of peril, now rise up by hundreds to bless me." A few extracts from his daily records may be sufficient to indicate the secret of this great success :—

"*Saturday, April 4th*, 1778. This was a day of much Divine power and love to my soul. I was left alone, and spent part of every hour in prayer; and Christ was near and very precious. The next day I preached with great solemnity at E. W——'s, on 2 Cor. vi. 2; and on Monday found freedom to move. After riding about fifteen miles I accidentally stopped at a house where a corpse was going to be buried, and had an opportunity of addressing a number of immortal souls. I then rode on through a lonesome devious road—like Abraham, not knowing whither I went; but, weary and unwell, I found a shelter late at night.

"*Tuesday, 7th*. My soul was kept in peace, and I spent much of my time in reading the Bible and the Greek Testament. Surely God will stand by me and deliver me! . . . At night a report was spread which inclined me to think it would be most prudent for me to move the next day. Accordingly I set out after dinner, and lay in a swamp till about sunset; but was then kindly taken in by a friend.

"*Thursday, 9th*. I felt strong confidence in God, that He would deliver me; being conscious that I sought neither riches nor honour, and that what I suffered was for the sake of His spiritual Church, and the salvation of my fellow men. I was informed that Brother John Hartley was apprehended last Lord's-day. May the Lord strengthen and support him, while he suffers for righteousness' sake! He shall be faithfully remembered by me in my addresses to the throne of grace. This evening I was called upon to visit a person in distress of mind; and the Lord gave him rest for his soul. Perhaps Providence cast my lot in this place for the assistance of this man.

"*Friday, 10th*. My heart was kept pure, and panting after God, though I was in some sense a prisoner. . . . My

practice is, to keep close to God in prayer, and spend a
part of every hour, when awake, in that exercise."

A little further on he says: "I purpose to spend ten
minutes out of every hour, when awake, in prayer. . . . I
am reconciled to my condition, and in faith and prayer commit all events to my Divine Protector. This is an excellent
season for dressing my own vineyard."

But it was impossible for him to be unemployed for others.
His "dumb Sabbaths" were but few, at the beginning
of this season of seclusion; and on Sunday and week-day
alike, when not engaged in spiritual exercises, or in reading
and study to prepare himself for greater usefulness in the
future, he catechized the children of the family; he stole
out after dark, and through the gloom of the woods, to visit
the neighbouring cottages, speaking words of instruction or
encouragement to the heads of households, and, taking their
children upon his knees, taught them the comprehensive
little lesson—

> "Learn to read, and learn to pray;
> Learn to work, and learn to obey."

He never left them without prayer; and, when he could
induce them to invite a few friends to hold with them a
quiet domestic service, he preached and exhorted:—"I met
a small congregation, and my soul was blessed in speaking
to the people;" "as a congregation was collected to hear
the Word, I ventured to preach;" "our family meetings
are attended with great power;" "the Lord favoured me
with great assistance in preaching three times to-day;"
"this week the Lord has given me two, as the children of
my bonds."

Gaining confidence by freedom from assault at these more
retired essays, he gradually extended his labours and made

them more public, until within a few weeks he had extemporized for himself a large circuit, which he systematically itinerated on the plan to which he had been accustomed. As early as July 18th he says: "I laid a plan for myself to travel and preach nine days in two weeks. This was one step towards my former regularity, in what appears to me as my duty, my element, and my delight."

This arrangement he carried out and exceeded, despite the difficulties of his situation, and notwithstanding perpetually-recurring attacks of fever and other forms of illness. Once, in a state of extraordinary depression, he wrote: "For some time it seemed as if I scarcely knew whether to fight or fly. My usefulness appeared to be cut off; I saw myself pent up in a corner; my body in a manner worn out; my English brethren gone, so that I had no one to consult; and every surrounding object and circumstance wore a gloomy aspect." Happily, however, seasons of gloom in his experience were but occasional, and never of long continuance. He was too busily occupied, even at this period, to dwell morbidly upon his ailments and sorrows; and was frequently cheered under them by tidings of the success which attended his own, or his brethren's labours. "Upon mature reflection," he says, when informed of "a gracious work" near him, "I do not repent my voluntary retirement; . . . the prosperity of the work far exceeds my expectation."

One instance of his usefulness at this time, remarkable in itself, and in its effects upon the subsequent history of Methodism in America, may be given in some detail. It is referred to in his Journal; but I am indebted for the interesting facts of the case to the same painstaking historian to whom I have had repeatedly to acknowledge my obligations.

Richard Bassett, Esq., a lawyer of note and influence, resident at Dover, Delaware, was travelling into Maryland

on professional business, and called at the house of Judge
White on his way, intending to spend the night there.   On
his arrival he unexpectedly found other guests present.
Passing a half-opened door of the room in which they were
sitting, he was surprised to see men "dressed in sable gar-
ments," and inquired of Mrs. White who her company were.
"Some of the best men in the world," was the ready reply;
"they are Methodist preachers."   "Then," he said, haugh-
tily, "I cannot stay here."   By a little adroit coaxing his
scruples were overcome; and he consented to remain over
night, as he had purposed.   Supper was announced, and
they all sat down together at the table.   Asbury, always
dignified, genial, and affable in society, impressed Mr. Bassett favourably; and before leaving the next morning he
invited him,—"more," he afterwards said, "from custom and
compliment, than from desire,"—to stay at his house when
next he came to Dover.   Asbury did not misunderstand the
character of this invitation; but he saw that he had gained
an influence over him, and determined to strengthen and exercise it for his spiritual benefit.   Not long after he was seen
in the streets of Dover inquiring his way to the lawyer's
house.   Mrs. Bassett had been told by her husband of his
unexpected interview with him, how much he had been
charmed with his nobility of spirit and his cheerful conversation, and that he had involuntarily invited him to become
their guest; but had assured her that it was most unlikely
he would come.   However, to their consternation, they saw
him wending his way towards their house.   Mr. Bassett
received and treated his visitor courteously, and his visitor's
desires were happily accomplished in the conversion of both
husband and wife.   Shortly after he first entered their house,
Asbury had the satisfaction of writing: "Mrs. Bassett is
under great distress; she prays much."   Within a few days

or weeks she rejoiced in God her Saviour, and her husband shared her consolations. "They became zealous and exemplary Methodists;" and "for nearly twoscore years Richard Bassett was Asbury's unfailing friend."

Mr. Bassett became Governor of Delaware; "he was also a member of the Convention which framed the Constitution of the United States, a senator in the first Congress, and a judge of the United States Court for the circuit comprising the districts of Pennsylvania, New Jersey, and Delaware. He often preached, and was the chief founder of Wesley Chapel in Dover. He had three residences: one in Dover; one in Wilmington; and another at Bohemia Manor, a famous locality in the early Methodist annals. All of them were favourite homes of the Methodist itinerants."

Growing out of this is another important and pregnant fact which I should not omit to mention. About the time of Mr. Bassett's conversion, his sister-in-law, Miss Ennalls, "niece of Judge Ennalls," came to his house on a visit, and was brought by him to obtain life in Christ. Her home was in Dorchester, in Maryland, a county which the Methodists had not yet visited. Returning thither in the fervours of her first love, her relations, who were strangers to spiritual experience, "thought her beside herself." Soon, however, she became the means of the conversion of her sister Mary; and Mary Ennalls, visiting a Mr. Airey, who resided in another part of the county, led him to the attainment of like precious faith. Mr. Airey—an educated, wealthy, and influential magistrate—began immediately to exert himself in behalf of his ignorant and godless neighbours. He communicated with Asbury and urged him to send a preacher into the county, and Asbury, in compliance with his request, appointed Freeborn Garrettson. "On the 10th February, 1780, Mr. Garrettson rose early in the morning and called upon God, and his soul was greatly strengthened; and, being commended to God in prayer by Asbury for this mission, he set out from Judge White's for Mr. Airey's. . . . For three days Mr. Garrettson laboured at Mr. Airey's, and the congregation were deeply affected. The work of salvation was begun." A persecution broke out shortly afterwards, and Garrettson was seized by ruffians who "lodged him in a prison, and took away the key, that his friends might not minister to him. He had a dirty floor for his bed, his saddle-bag for his pillow, and a cold east wind blowing upon him." With difficulty his friend, Mr. Airey, obtained his release at the expiration of a fortnight. But all this "turned out for the furtherance of the Gospel;" so that, "after two years' labour and suffering on the part of the preachers, they reported almost eight hundred Methodists in the county."*

Among the especial friends and helpers whom Asbury acquired during this period of comparative retirement, particular mention must be made of the Rev. Dr. McGaw, of Dover, a clergyman of the same devout and disinterested spirit as Mr. Jarratt; and also "the pious Judge Barratt." Both of them afforded Asbury protection, and greatly aided the extension of Methodism in Dover and the neighbourhood. Judge Barratt built a chapel in the outskirts of the town, which was called the "Forest Chapel." It was the first Methodist chapel erected in the State of Delaware, and was opened for worship by Dr. McGaw. Here, as we shall find, Asbury and Dr. Coke first met. Asbury frequently refers to it by the name of "Barratt's Chapel." April 26, 1809, he says, "At Barratt's Chapel I preached and baptized some children. I had powerful feelings of sympathy for the children and grandchildren of that holy man in life and death, Philip

---

* Stevens's "Women of Methodism," 214—218.

Barratt." And again, April 14th, 1815, a few months before his death, " I preached at Barratt's Chapel, in great feebleness of body. Must I needs dine with Judge Andrew Barratt ? 'Ah ! I know that my father and mother thought more of him than of any man upon the earth ; and well does it become their son to respect him.' And is this all ? God forbid ! "

CHAPTER IX.

FROM the beginning of the war, the question whether it
was not right and expedient for the preachers to
administer the Sacraments, and whether the Methodists were
not called to take an independent position as a Church, rose
more and more into serious dispute. The agitation which
originated in the assumption of pastoral functions by Strawbridge, as early as 1773, had been allayed, not because
either preachers or people were convinced he was in error,
but mainly through the influence of Asbury, and in deference
to the will of Mr. Wesley. They were persuaded to waive
for a time what they continued to believe to be their rights ;
and to wait, and watch the order of events.

Wonder has been expressed that Wesley so long delayed
to provide his American Societies with the spiritual privileges
they demanded. But those who condemn his "temporising"
or hesitancy in this matter, do not always give due consideration to the difficulties by which he was beset. Had he been
less deeply and conscientiously attached than he was to
the Church of England ; less loyal in his subjection to the

Crown and civil government; or less under the sway of prepossessions derived from his High Church education,—he might have allowed himself to sympathize with his people in their privations, and might have adopted some of the numerous suggestions made to him by his friends to provide for their requirements. But Wesley was too unambitious, and too true to his oft-declared determination not to secede from the Established Church, to give any serious thought to schemes which would have had the effect of placing his Societies in a position of isolation and independence. Nor could he have failed to see how directly any measure that he might adopt to supply the wants of his people in America would affect the relations of the Societies to the National Church at home. But we are called to recognize in the delay the operation of other than human motives and principles. Wesley was restrained from hasty legislation on this question by fidelity to his principles, and the strength of his attachments and prejudices; and his slowness to act was overruled to secure the more successful carrying out of his arrangements when they were at length completed. The Methodist Episcopal Church was constituted at precisely that stage in the progress of the great spiritual work of which it was the product, which was most conducive to its permanency.

The war-storm, as it swept over the Colonies, shook the Anglican Church to its very foundation. Its relations to them had been always anomalous and defective. In the North it had never been established by law; and in the South, " colonized to a considerable extent under Cavalier influence, it was indeed established, but it lacked one very important element of Episcopalianism,—the presence of a bishop. The whole jurisdiction of the thirteen colonies was vested in the Bishopric of London; but this supervision was merely nominal, and was not even persistently asserted ; the cautious Gibson refused, from doubts about his authority, even to appoint a commissary.   Two of the Stuarts, Charles II. and Anne, intended to supply the want; but the intentions of both were interrupted by death, and the Episcopal clergy had all to cross the Atlantic for ordination." *   Indeed the English Episcopacy, as planted in America, was little better than an untended exotic in an uncongenial soil.   The English clergy, as pledged upholders of the principle of Church and State, were compelled, after the declaration of American Independence, to withdraw from the country ; and, as natives could not obtain Episcopal ordination, adherents to the Episcopal Church, whether Methodists or non-Methodists, were left to a great extent without the sacraments.   " Of ninety-one clergymen of Virginia, twenty-eight only remained when the contest was over, who had lived through the storm, and these, with eight others, who came into the State soon after the struggle terminated, supplied thirty-six of the ninety-five parishes.   Of these twenty-eight, fifteen only had been enabled to continue in the churches which they supplied prior to the commencement of hostilities." †

It can be but little surprising that in these circumstances the question was raised with greater determination than ever —Why are the Methodist people to have the sacraments any longer withheld from them by their preachers and rightful pastors ?   At the Conference of 1777, the last which Rankin attended, this question was solemnly introduced and considered, but left undecided.   At the following Conference, held in 1778, which was attended by the native preachers only,—Asbury being in his retreat at Judge White's,—it was

---

* Wedgwood's " John Wesley," p. 385.
+ Hawks, quoted by Stevens, i. 276.

resumed, and debated with greater earnestness than ever; but, in the absence of Asbury, it was considerately agreed to let the question stand over for a year longer. The majority, who were in favour of the change, were with great difficulty persuaded to concur in this decision; and it was unanimously resolved that at the Conference of 1779, which was appointed to be held in Fluvanna County, Virginia, the important question should be finally settled.

In consequence of the continuance of the war and the inability of many of the preachers to assemble at Fluvanna as arranged, two Conferences were held this year, one of them, for the convenience of Asbury, at Judge White's. This section held its sittings a week or two in anticipation of the other. Asbury's account of it is as follows: " Our Conference for the northern stations began at Thomas White's. All our preachers on these stations were present, and united. We had much prayer, love, and harmony; and we all agreed to walk by the same rule, and mind the same thing. As we had great reason to fear that our brethren to the southward were in danger of separating from us, we wrote them a soft, healing epistle." Asbury was at this gathering formally recognized as General Assistant, and it was agreed that the power to determine questions, after a free discussion, should be vested in him as President. The decision on the sacramental controversy was that " by all means they must guard against a separation from the Church, direct or indirect."

Very different was the decision of the Fluvanna—and more regular—Assembly. Watters, who had been President of the Conference the preceding year, and was a member of Asbury's meeting at Judge White's, had been sent to attend the Fluvanna Conference, as the bearer of the " healing " letter referred to. But, despite his influence and the message of affectionate expostulation which he had brought from Asbury and their brethren in the North, it was determined that henceforth the two sacraments should be administered generally "to those who are under our care and discipline ; " and a committee, composed of Gatch, Foster, Cole, and Ellis, —these being some of the older preachers,—was appointed, "first, to administer the ordinances themselves ; and, secondly, to authorize any other preacher or preachers, approved by them, by the form of laying on of hands." They accordingly first ordained one another, and afterwards such of the preachers present "as were desirous of receiving ordination."

Thus a serious schism had occurred ; and, but for the godly tact and skill of Asbury, and the spirit of conciliation eventually shown by those thoroughly sincere and devout young preachers, that rent would probably have been permanent. And in that case what would have been the condition of American Methodism by this time ?

On receiving information of these proceedings Asbury wrote in sadness, " I learn that the preachers of the Virginia Conference have been effecting a lame separation from the Episcopal Church. I pity them. Satan has a desire to have us, that he may sift us like wheat." The matter was too serious to be disregarded. He at once addressed letters of remonstrance to all the leaders of the movement, freely admitting the purity of their motives, and the reality and strength of their pleas ; but condemning the action they had taken as premature and unauthorized, and such as he foresaw would be most damaging in its results to the cause which they had all so much at heart. It was his chief source of anxiety throughout the year ; and too soon his apprehensions began to be realised. November 13, 1779, he writes : " I received a etter from Mr. Jarratt, who is greatly alarmed ; but it is too late—he should have begun his opposition before. Our zealous Dissenting brethren are for turning all out of Society who will not submit to their administrations. I find the spirit of separation grows among them, and fear that it will generate malevolence and evil-speaking." "I am troubled," he says again, "about our separating brethren in Virginia. I tremble to think of the cloud of the Divine Presence departing from us : if this should be, I hope not to see it ; and, with Mr. Wesley, desire that God may rather scatter the people to the ends of the earth ! "

As the time for holding the next Conference approached, he naturally became growingly anxious with reference to its probable character and issues.

" *Friday, April* 14*th*. A day of fasting. I was employed in preparing my paper for Conference. I am under some apprehensions that trouble is near.

" *Saturday,* 22*nd*. Rode to Mr. Gough's, Baltimore County. My friends appeared very joyful to see me. Brother Glendenning has his objections to make, and pleaded some in favour of the Virginian brethren. I had cause to talk more than I desired . . . I am kept in peace through grace, and am casting my care upon the Lord. Spent some time in private, and prepared some conditions for a partial reconciliation, in hopes to bring on a real one, in Virginia. I prayed with my heart full."

It had been arranged by the Delaware Conference that its sittings for the year 1780 should be held at Baltimore in April ; the Virginia Conference had decided to re-assemble at Manakintown in May. Asbury determined to attend them both. Respecting the earlier one he says, "Our Conference met in peace and love. We settled all our northern stations ; then we began in much debate about the letter sent from Virginia. We first concluded to renounce them. Then I offered conditions of union : (1) that they should ordain

8

no more ; (2) that they should come no farther than
Hanover Circuit ; (3) we would have our delegates in their
Conference ; (4) that they should not presume to administer the ordinances where there is a decent Episcopal minister ;
(5) to have a Union Conference. This would not satisfy
them as we found upon long debate, and we came back to our
determination ; although it was like death to think of parting.
At last a thought struck my mind—to propose a suspension
of the ordinances for one year, and so cancel all our grievances, and be at one. It was agreed on both sides ; and
Philip Gatch and Reuben Ellis, who had been very stiff,
acceded to it, and thought it would do."

Two days afterwards he writes cheerily, "Myself and
Brother Garrettson are going to the Virginia Conference to
bring about peace and union." Blessed and noble mission !
By what means was its end to be attained ? Let those who
believe themselves similarly called to promote unity of
spirit and action among brethren, ponder this simple
record :—

" *May* 4*th*. Prepared some papers for Virginia Conference.
I go with a heavy heart : and fear the violence of a party of
positive men : Lord give me wisdom. 6*th*. We found the
plague was begun. 7*th*. I expect trouble, but grace is
almighty ; hitherto hath the Lord helped me. 8*th*. We rode
to Granger's, fifteen miles. Stopped and fed our horses.
These people are full of the ordinances ; we talked and
prayed with them. Went to friend Smith's, where all the
preachers were met. I conducted myself with cheerful
freedom, but found there was a separation in heart and
practice. I spoke with my countryman, John Dickins,
and found him opposed to our continuance in union with
the Episcopal Church. Brothers Watters and Garrettson
pleaded with their men, but found them inflexible.

" *Tuesday, May 9th.* The Conference was called. Brothers Watters and Garrettson and myself stood back, and being afterwards joined by Brother Dromgoole, we were desired to come in, and I was permitted to speak. I read Mr. Wesley's thoughts against a separation; showed my private letters of instruction from Mr. Wesley; set before them the sentiments of the Delaware and Baltimore Conferences; read our epistles; and read my letter to Brother Gatch, and Dickins's letter in answer. After some time spent this way it was proposed to me that, if I could get the circuits supplied, they would desist; but that I could not do. We went to preaching : I spoke on Ruth ii. 4, and spoke as though nothing had been the matter. In the afternoon we met. The preachers appeared to me to be farther off; there had been, I thought, some talking out of doors. When we,—Asbury, Garrettson, Watters, and Dromgoole,—could not come to a conclusion with them we withdrew, and left them to deliberate on the condition I offered—which was to suspend the measures they had taken for one year. After an hour's conference we were called to receive their answer, which was that they could not submit to the terms of union. I then prepared to leave the house to go to a near neighbour's to lodge, under the heaviest cloud I ever felt in America. Oh, what I felt! nor I alone, but the agents on both sides! They wept like children, but kept their opinions.

" *Wednesday, 10th.* I returned to take leave of the Conference, and to go off immediately to the North ; but found they had been brought to an agreement, while I was praying, as with a broken heart, in the house we went to lodge at ; and Brothers Watters and Garrettson had been praying upstairs, where the Conference sat. We heard what they had to say. Surely the hand of God has been seen in all this ! There might have been twenty promising preachers and three thousand people seriously affected by this separation ; but the Lord would not suffer this. We then had a Love-feast. Preachers and people wept, prayed, and talked."

Thus the dreaded separation, with what would have been its necessarily disastrous consequences at that early period of Methodist history, was happily averted. The concession speaks favourably for the whole Conference. It shows that in that assembly of earnest Christian workers, the prosperity of the cause of God asserted its supremacy over every other consideration. No longer disunited, they now re-joiced together as men rejoice when they divide the spoil ; and henceforth, as one closely-embodied host, devoted themselves to their warfare against the powers of evil, with redoubled zeal.

But Asbury's work was not yet complete. It was much to have brought about so perfect an amnesty within the Conference; but the disunited Societies had yet to be conciliated, and he felt it to be his duty to visit the most distracted of them, and strive to pacify them by his per-sonal influence. The very next day after his exhausting efforts at the Conference he rode to Petersburg, a distance of thirty-five miles, and preached the same evening, though so unwell that he found it difficult to speak. The next day he wrote an account of the whole transaction, in a letter to Mr. Wesley ; then set out afresh on his mission of pacification. He says, "There seems to be some call for me in every part of the work. I have travelled at this time from North to South, to keep peace and union ; and oh ! if a rent and separation had taken place, what work, what hurt, to thousands of souls ! " In some weeks subse-quently his records are interspersed with similar reflec-tions. In one place he says, " I find some left the Society here at the time of the division. It is a sorrowful day

with me ; " and, on the other side, immediately afterwards,
" Went to White Oak ; and spoke on Titus ii. 2—5 ; then
met the Society. Mr. Jarratt wept, and all the people,
at the joy of union."

The Conference of 1781, preceded by a preparatory
gathering under Asbury in Delaware, was held at Baltimore, and begun on the 24th April. It reported an increase during this year of restored internal harmony of
2,035 members, the entire number being 10,529. The
number of travelling-preachers was fifty-five. Forty of
them were present, and thirty-nine subscribed a declaration
of their purpose, " to preach the old Methodist doctrine,
and strictly to enforce the discipline as contained in the
Notes, Sermons, and Minutes published by Wesley "; also
" to discountenance a separation among either preachers or
people." Asbury's record is : " All but one agreed to return
to the old plan, and give up the administration of the
ordinances. Our troubles now seem over from that
quarter, and there appears to be a considerable change in
the preachers from North to South. All was conducted in
peace and love." He adds, "I am relieved in mind, and my
soul is kept in peace, whilst I feel power to trust the Lord
with all."

The Conference of 1782 was begun at Ellis's Preaching-
house, Sussex County, Virginia, on the 17th April, and
continued, by adjournment, at Baltimore on the 21st May.
At this Conference Wesley's appointment of Asbury as
General Assistant was unanimously re-affirmed. The
increase of members during the year was reported to be
1,246. The Virginia Session was attended by the Rev.
Mr. Jarratt, who assisted at many of the public services,
and administered to the preachers the Lord's Supper.
Asbury says, " As there had been much distress felt by

those of Virginia relative to the administration of the
ordinances, I proposed to such as were so disposed to
enter into a written agreement to cleave to the old plan in
which we had been so greatly blessed, that we might have
the greater confidence in each other, and know on whom to
depend. This instrument was signed by the greater part
of the preachers, without hesitation. Next morning I
preached on Phil. ii. 1—5. I had liberty, and it pleased
God to send it home. One of the preachers, James Haw,
who had his difficulties, was delivered from them all; and,
with the exception of one, all the signatures of the preachers
present were obtained." On the review of this session he
writes, "I am persuaded the separation of some from our
original plan about the ordinances will, upon the whole,
have a tendency to unite the body together; I feel abundant cause to praise God for what He has done." Respecting the Baltimore Session he says, "We had a full meeting.
The preachers all signed the agreement proposed at the
Virginia Conference, and there was a unanimous resolve to
adhere to the old Methodist plan."

In 1783 the Conference was again held, for the accommodation of the widely-scattered preachers, first, at Ellis's
Preaching-house, and afterwards at Baltimore. It reported
an increase of 1,955 members. Asbury's account of it is
especially satisfactory for its brevity. He says of the
Virginia Session, "Some young labourers were taken in to
assist in spreading the Gospel, which greatly prospers in the
North. We all agreed in the spirit of African liberty; and
strong testimonies were borne in its favour in our Lovefeast.
Our affairs were conducted in love." Respecting that held
at Baltimore, he merely notes that there was a full attendance, and that "we had a Lovefeast and parted in peace."

The year most memorable for its Conferences was 1784.

In the spring two sessions were held according to precedent. An increase of 1,248 members was reported, making a total of 14,988 ; and the number of preachers was eighty-four. The Conference held at the close of the year was exceptional and extraordinary. It must be considered separately.

CHAPTER X.

ESCAPED, AND ON THE WING.

Resumes Evangelistic Labour—Settlement of Families Inland—They are followed by the Methodist Preachers—Visited by Asbury—General Character of his Travels and Toils—Outline Sketches from his Journals—Old and New Clothes—Death of a Companion—Tampering with his Horse—The Eastern Slopes of the Mountains—Sleeps among the Rocks—Arrival of Dr. Coke.

IN the preceding chapter we have passed rapidly from Conference to Conference, with reference to the demands of a section of the people to be provided with the sacraments and constituted a complete church. We shall soon have before us the admirable scheme which Mr. Wesley devised for satisfying these demands, and for carrying forward efficiently the whole business of church extension and conservation. Here, however, we pause awhile to glance at the evangelistic labours which Asbury had resumed, and which, during this interval, he was prosecuting with unfaltering energy of will in scenes and circumstances of extraordinary difficulty.

The outbreak of hostilities with England had naturally tended to swell the tide of emigration to the West. Families, singly or in groups, travelled in close succession, inland, and settled in wildernesses, forests, valleys, and the recesses of the Appalachian mountains. The state of destitution of religious advantages in which many of these adventurers had to live weighed heavily on the minds and hearts of the Methodist preachers generally, and some of them cheerfully offered to brave the hardships and perils of labouring among them in the Gospel. It was impossible that Asbury should be indifferent towards them. He saw in a moment,—especially when told that some of the emigrants were local-preachers and class-leaders—that however difficult a task it might be to bring the extensive tracts over which they were scattered within circuit arrangements, this was not impracticable ; and that it was his duty to undertake it. This, therefore, after his release from confinement in Delaware, he made his immediate object. Equipped for his protection against military interference with a certificate of citizenship, and a note of recommendation from the friendly Governor of the State, he gave himself up to this most trying work with a sustained ardour of devotion which never has been, or can be, surpassed.

His first year of restored liberty (1780-1) was divided between Virginia and North Carolina ; and his efforts were directed to the accomplishment of two principal results—the extension of the work ; and, as we have seen, the pacification and re-establishment of the disturbed Societies. Laying it down at starting, as a never-to-be-forgotten principle, that he "ought always to be employed," and resolutely resuming the practice of " twelve times of prayer " daily, he is away—for congregations, large or small, brought together in cabins, barns, or woods,—over rough roads and bridgeless rivers, through swamps and pathless forests, riding ten, twenty, thirty miles at a stage. He is " much tried on the way, and his horse is lame," but he " lifts up his heart to God," and is refreshed and comforted ; he rides "through a steep dangerous place into the river, but, though it was frightful, comes safe over." He is taken ill, and is so distracted with intolerable pain that he " cannot read, write, think, pray, or speak much ; " but he reminds himself that it is "for souls he labours and suffers," and renews his strength. He preaches to an attentive audience of three hundred people, who, grateful for his services, offer him a small remuneration; but he declines to take it, lest his doing so should impair his usefulness.

His "soul breathing after the Lord at all times," he unfalteringly passes through toils, hardships, and sufferings, of which the following continuous but curtailed statements in his Journal afford a sample :—

"*Sun.* Rode six miles to the Tabernacle: about 400 people, rich and poor, attended. I spoke near two hours to little purpose; held a Lovefeast, then rode eight miles. *Mon.* Rose early; my legs so inflamed I cannot tell what to do. But we must bear all things. Preached at Turner's. Had liberty in the Word: the hearers were stirred up. *Tues.* Preached at Price's. Many came to hear. Rode to Haw-tree. Had great freedom, and held a Lovefeast. Was much refreshed : rode through the woods—a blind path, to a friend's. *Wed.* Rode to Todd's, six miles. About seventy people, but very insensible. Laboured in public, and hope some will take it home. *Thurs.* Rode to widow Pegram's ; had about sixty people. Then rode to Capt. Burrows's. The people in many places are but children in understanding. Preached at Burrows's : about sixty people. Came off to the widow Ellis's, and found the Lord was there. *Fri.* Rose with a deep sense of God. Met with Henry Jones, a serious young man, and believe he is called to the work of the ministry. I advised him to go with me. *Sat.* My soul pants after God more and more. Preached—had liberty, and spoke as searchingly as I could to saints and sinners.

"*Sun.* Rode to Lindsey's, a rough road ; had about seventy people. *Mon.* Set out for Tar River. After riding about five miles I was told that I could not cross Bear Swamp; but, by the guidance of a Baptist friend, came through that and two very deep creeks. Rode three miles further and was stopped by what was called Ben's Creek. The bridge was gone, and a man said it was ten feet deep. Then made for Falcom's bridge; but the low ground was covered, and no bridge to be seen. Lodged at Mr. Falcom's; was known, and kindly entertained. I laboured to make Mrs. Falcom sensible of her danger, and hope not in vain. Prayed evening and morning in the family. *Tues.* Rode by Miller's Cross-roads—a rough way, but got safe along. Stopped at Sandy Creek, where I found a kind old man with whom I lodged. *Wed.* Set out to Green Hills; but with difficulty I got along. On account of the waters, I have ridden about thirty miles out of my way. *Thurs.* Rode twenty-six miles. My horse suffered greatly. About seventy people. *Fri.* A day of fasting. I was weak, and lodging on the floor was uncomfortable. *Sat.* Rode to Cypress Chapel; about 100 people. Spoke at Ross's.

"*Sun.* Preached at Green Hills to about 400 souls: dead Gospel-slighters. *Mon.* Made my journey to Jones's. About sixty people; God was with us. *Tues.* Had a heavy night; slept in pain. Rose at four o'clock; set off at six. After riding five or six hours, spoke to about 100 people. *Wed.* Rode to Cooper's. Had about 120 people. Rode to a friend's, and had great difficulty on the way, but am kept from murmuring. While labouring for other souls my own is blessed. *Thurs.* Rode to the chapel. Laboured hard to preach. *Fri.* God was with me. I was much comforted in the preaching-house this morning. I suffered much for want of a place of retirement. I cannot go into the woods: there are so many ticks, chiegoes, and such insects at this season upon the ground. Retired into the chapel; it has been a Bethel to me. *Sat.* After spending some time in the chapel alone, I set out to Paschal's, about six o'clock; came in before twelve, and spoke very close and plain to about thirty people. Rode on to B. Hartfield's, about twenty miles, much fatigued with the badness of the road.

"*Sun.* I rose unwell, and somewhat dejected. Spoke on 2 Thess. i. 6—9. *Mon.* I set out about five o'clock, and rode about twenty miles alone. There were many people. *Tues.* Rode sixteen miles—crossed Neuse River. I spoke from Rom. viii. 24—26. After dinner I was alone in the woods for an hour; had sweet meltings. *Wed.* Rode to A. Hill's, and had great liberty in speaking from Heb. iv. 10, &c. *Thurs.* Rode twelve miles: hilly, rocky roads. About eighty people. While I was speaking General Hugine came in, and heard part of the sermon. He is a polite, well-behaved, conversable gentleman. We dined together. After dinner I set out on my journey. We came to a desperate creek where the bridge was carried away by the freshet. We had to go through among rocks, holes, and logs. I was affrighted. *Sat.* We set out for Crump's—over rocks, hills, creeks, and pathless woods and lowlands. With great difficulty we came in about two o'clock, the people looking almost as wild as the deer in the woods. I preached on Titus ii. 10—12.

"*Sun.* We passed Haw River—wide, but shallow; bad going down and coming up. Then we had to travel the pathless woods and rocks again. After much trouble, fear, and dejection, we came to Taylor's, where I spoke on 2 Pet. i. 5—12. I have travelled thirty miles; and could not avoid travelling on Sunday, for I had not where to stay. Rode to Brother Beck's, and was much fatigued. *Mon.* Rose with a sense of God's presence. Have only time to pray. Always *upon the wing,* as the rides are so long—and bad roads. In general I walk my horse. I crossed Rocky River—rocky, sure enough. I can see little else but cabins in these parts, built with poles. I crossed Deep River in a flat-boat, and the poor ferryman-sinner swore because I had not a silver shilling to give him. Rode near six miles to get three, as we were lost. When we came to the place there were about sixty people. I spoke on 1 Pet. v. 9—12. Was glad to get away, for some were drunk and had their guns. *Tues.* Forded Deep River, and rode to a settlement of people from Pennsylvania. Preached to about twenty people. Was very unwell. Then rode sixteen miles to B. Kennon's. It was rainy, and we rode two miles in the dark through the woods. *Wed.* I preached to about 100 people. *Thurs.* I acknowledge the goodness of God in preserving my health, life, and horse from these people. They are very vile; rob, steal, and murder one another with impunity. Rode twelve miles to West's; about 100 people. My trials are great. Riding twenty miles a day, or more; rocky roads, poor entertainment, uncomfortable lodgings; little rest night or day. *Fri.* Rode twelve miles to the chapel and preached to 100 people, on 1 Pet. iv. 18. Exceedingly rough road, through woods, over rocks, through creeks, &c. Rode seven miles to Mr. Trice's; was kindly entertained. Had the pleasure of seeing and conversing with Brother Bailey, from Ireland, a good and sensible man. I slept well, and am better. *Sat.* Rode to Roades's, and preached to about 200 people. Brother Bailey spoke."

Here is a section of the panoramic picture of the evangelist's work, rapidly pencilled by his own hand. Bailey, he found, had capabilities of great usefulness, and in the next day's record we are told that he agreed to go with him as his companion and helper. They travelled together for five weeks during which his experiences were similar to those

just recited, and he then re-entered Virginia, his clothes in
a state which "approached raggedness," and his bodily
frame enfeebled by intermittent fever. For about a week
he tarried among his old friends, while they fitted him out
with a new suit made of "Virginia cloth;"—preaching, as
"this tertian" allowed him, in barns, in private houses,
and once in a chapel "unfinished and one part lying open
to the sun," a company of gay young fellows within sight
diverting themselves the while under the trees. He met
the Societies, which he rejoiced to find in "peace" and
"united in love." He refreshed himself by repeated inter-
views with Mr. Jarratt; and then, in company with Bailey,
started on another tour. But poor Bailey was soon taken
ill, and within a few days removed from him by death. "I
have lost poor Bailey," he exclaims in pensive astonishment—
"so suddenly called away!" "I have great cause to
weep," he adds; "but the Lord hath ordered it. It may
be that I suffer more than those who weep away distress."

No pause. Daily services; long and toilsome rides; poor
accommodation, and indifferent fare; frequent returns of
illness; "pain, pain, pain!"—a few instances of contemp-
tible persecution, as when some "sons of Belial" practised
upon his horse and caused him to run away with him,
though, "by the mercy of the Lord, he stopped near a point
of woods, which, had he entered, I might probably have lost
my life:"—amidst all this, "peace"—a "sweet sense of the
nearness of God," and comfort derived from a confidence,—
wonderfully justified by the event,—that he would hereafter
find fruit of all his labours:—so month after month passed
away.

Immediately after the Conference of 1781 he carried out
his purpose of visiting "the outcasts of the people" in "the
distant wilds" of the Alleghanies, thankful for "health and

peace." William Partridge, who had been a year in the work, accompanied him. He says, " We found some difficulty in crossing Great Capon River. Three men very kindly carried us over in a canoe, and afterwards rode our horses over the stream, without fee or reward. I laid me down to rest on a chest, and, using my clothes for covering, slept pretty well. . . . We had to bear away among the mountains. In some places the breaks in the slate served for steps : in other parts of the ascent there were none. We at length reached the place appointed, and preached to about twenty, as I think, prayerless people. . . . I came to a Dutch settlement. Could we get a Dutch preacher or two I am persuaded we should have a good work. . . . I was led to wonder at myself when I considered the fatigue I went through—travelling in the rain ; sleeping without beds, too. . . . Brother Partridge and myself kept on until night overtook us in the mountains among rocks and woods, and dangers on all sides surrounding us. We concluded it most safe to secure our horses, and quietly await the return of day. So we lay down and slept among the rocks, although much annoyed by the gnats. . . . I have been obliged to sleep on the floor every night since I slept in the mountains. Yesterday I rode twenty-seven miles, and to-day thirty. I adore the goodness of God that I am kept in health."

Thus he journeyed on to Leesburg and thus he continued to travel and toil and suffer in Maryland, Pennsylvania, Virginia, and North Carolina ; again on the slope of the western mountains, worshipping " by the side of the stream for want of a house," comforted with the attention shown by " nearly 200 people in this newly-settled country "—but " much fatigued," and his " poor horse so weak from the want of proper food that he fell twice ; " until, after similar records

continued uninterruptedly for three years, we find it a relief
to read :—

"*Sunday, Nov.* 14, 1784: I came to Barratt's Chapel.
Here, to my great joy, I met those dear men of God, Dr.
Coke and Richard Whatcoat.   We were comforted together."

CHAPTER XI.

THE United States having achieved their independence, and the supremacy of the Anglican Church within any of them being abolished, Wesley felt that he could no longer withstand the importunity of his American Societies to provide them with church and pastoral privileges. But, true to his ecclesiastical leanings, his first thoughts were to procure those privileges for them from Episcopal hands. Four years before his own decisive action he applied to the Bishop of London, "to ordain a pious man who might officiate as their minister." But his lordship refused to recognize piety as a qualification for the office, and preferred to send " other persons, who knew something of Greek and Latin, but who knew no more of saving souls than of catching whales." Wesley was distressed, yet utterly at a loss how to act. He was impelled by an ever-deepening sense of duty to do something, but feared to stir. " I mourn for poor America," he exclaimed ; " for the sheep scattered up and down therein. Part of them have no shepherds at all, particularly in the southern colonies ; and the case of the rest is little better, for their own shepherds pity them not. They cannot, for they have no pity upon themselves."

He felt that the most suitable men to administer the

sacraments to the Methodist people were the preachers who
had won their allegiance to Christ. But might he declare
them at liberty to exercise this function? "Not until they
were regularly ordained," was his prompt and natural reply.
On this point his views were perfectly identical with those
expressed by his brother Charles: "Let a man be proved first,
and then let him exercise the office of a deacon, which was
to baptize; of a presbyter, which was to administer the
other sacrament. Ye *have* been proved. Ye are therefore *fit
persons* to receive commission to seal the covenants. But ye
have not a right to do this without any ordination at all, Episcopal or Presbyterian. No church in Christendom allows its
members to take upon them this office merely upon their own
judgment. What confusion would follow if they might!"*

How, then, was this official authority to be obtained?
Wesley pondered the problem continually and with earnest
prayer. He conferred with the best informed and most experienced of his preachers; he took counsel of Fletcher;
and at length his hopes of a solution of the difficulty centred
in Dr. Coke, a clergyman who for eight years had been
more intimately associated with him in labour than Fletcher
himself. Slowly, but with growing confidence, he came to
the resolution which he felt to be the gravest of his whole
career,—not simply to provide the American Societies with
what they requested, the regular administration of the
sacraments,—but to form them, through Dr. Coke, into an
independent church, with Coke and Asbury for its chief
ministers. And, as most suitable to the exigencies of the
vast country over which his people were scattered; as most
agreeable with the existing relations of the several Societies
to each other, under a common government; as most con-

---

* See *Methodist Magazine*, 1867, p. 622.

ducive to the purposes of indefinite aggression ; and as most in harmony with the convictions and preferences of his education,—he determined that the new organization should be Episcopal in form, while differing from every other form of Episcopacy, except that of the primitive Church, by ignoring a distinction of order between bishops and presbyters.

The first to whom he explained this great conception was Dr. Coke himself. Taking him into his study in the newly-built house in the City Road, he reminded him that the English Church had ceased to exist in the States of America, except as a voluntary and imperfectly regulated institution, and that, in consequence, the Methodists there were destitute of the holy sacraments. He told him that he had been requested by Mr. Asbury, in the name of the devout and patient people under his superintendence, to make provision for these necessary rites being regularly administered to them ; and that, having long and prayerfully weighed the subject in his mind, he had resolved to adopt a plan which he would submit to his consideration. He said he had been for many years convinced that a distinction of orders in the Christian ministry was not of Divine authority ; that he especially admired the mode of setting apart a presbyter to be a bishop, which the church of Alexandria had practised for about two hundred years, the bishop or superintendent being ordained to this office (that office not being a distinct order) by his brother presbyters ; and that, being himself a presbyter, he desired Dr. Coke to accept ordination to this office at his hands, and to go out to America, ordain the American preachers, and, in conjunction with Asbury, take the oversight of the entire American Societies.*

* Etheridge (in substance), on the authority of Mr. Drew, who, he believes, obtained the account from Dr. Coke himself. ("Life of Coke," p. 100.

Coke was taken by surprise and shrunk from the project; but promised to consider it, as Mr. Wesley had desired. He forthwith gave himself up to the study of the Scriptures and of the Fathers with reference to it; and, at the expiration of two months, wrote to Mr. Wesley, apparently in reply to some inquiry or appeal from him, to suggest that, before anything was finally decided, some competent person should be sent to America to gather and bring home further information respecting the condition and wants of the Societies. Mr. Wesley, however, thought that the time was come to take immediate steps rather than any further preliminary action, and the doctor thereupon placed himself unreservedly at his service.

In July they met again at Leeds, where the Conference was to be held, and resumed the discussion of the proposal in person. Then, as was usual in matters of great importance, the plan was laid before Mr. Wesley's Select Committee of Consultation, where he was once more confronted with expressions of surprise and objection. "To a man," says the Rev. Luke Tyerman, on the authority of Mr. Pawson, who was one of them, "they opposed it,"—so contrary was it to their habits of thought, and so truly did they breathe the spirit of their leader ! Ultimately, however, they unanimously concurred in the measure, as did also the Conference, and an affirmative resolution was solemnly agreed to—Mr. Fletcher, who was present, giving it his hearty approval.

With Dr. Coke two other preachers were appointed as his companions and assistants, namely, Thomas Vasey, a man of great strength of character, who had been in the Methodist itinerancy about nine years; and Richard Whatcoat, the humble, holy, and self-devoted man, whom Asbury had known as a fellow class-leader at Wednesbury, so many years previously. Mr. Wesley arranged to meet them all at Bristol, on the eve of their embarkation, and there to set them apart for the high functions they were called to exercise. In the interim Dr. Coke submitted to Mr. Wesley his views of the manner in which this should be done, being in effect probably what they had already considered together. He said :—

"The more maturely I consider the subject, the more expedient it seems to me that the power of ordaining others should be received by me from you, by the imposition of your hands ; and that you should lay hands on Brother Whatcoat and Brother Vasey, for the following reasons : (1) It seems to me the most scriptural way, and most agreeable to the practice of the primitive churches ; (2) I may want all the influence in America which you can throw into my scale ; . . . (3) In respect of my Brethren Whatcoat and Vasey, it is very uncertain indeed whether any of the clergy mentioned by Brother Rankin will stir with me in the work, except Mr. Jarratt, and it is by no means certain he will choose to join me in ordaining ; and propriety and universal practice make it expedient that I should have two presbyters with me in this work. In short, it appears to me that everything should be prepared, and everything proper be done, that can possibly be done this side the water. You can do all this ; and afterwards, according to Mr. Fletcher's advice, give us letters of testimonial of the different offices with which you have been pleased to invest us. For the purpose of laying hands on Brothers Whatcoat and Vasey, I can bring Mr. Creighton down with me, by which you will have two presbyters with you." *

All this Mr. Wesley approved and carried into effect. On the last day of August they met in Bristol, and on the 1st September, in that still-called " New Room " where Asbury had made the offer of his service for America, and which had been the scene of so many memorable events in Methodist history, Mr. Wesley took the step which, he says, " I had long weighed in my mind, and appointed Mr. Whatcoat and Mr. Vasey to go and serve the desolate sheep

* Etheridge's " Life of Coke," pp. 102, 103.

in America." Without any blowing of trumpets,—quietly, privately, and before it was yet day,—assisted by Dr. Coke and the Rev. James Creighton, he set them apart to the office of deacon ; and the next day, assisted by the same presbyters, he further ordained them to the office and ministry of the Word and sacraments, as elders or presbyters. He then, on the same occasion, "being assisted by other ordained ministers," set apart Dr. Coke as a superintendent, "by the imposition of my hands and prayer."

Never previously had Wesley innovated so seriously on church order, and no act in his whole history was equally momentous in its inevitable results. It was naturally succeeded, the next year, by the ordination, in the same solemn and impressive manner, of three preachers for Scotland ; the following year (again in the "New Room") by the ordination of five for Scotland and the West Indies ; and eventually—the principle now being fully conceded,—by the ordination of at least three,—Alexander Mather, Thomas Rankin, and Henry Moore—for England. As necessarily, Methodism drifted, after the death of its founder, by a slow and faltering but natural process, into its present definite position as an independent church. Others discerned the logical issues of the act at the time, as Wesley did not. They saw and declared that "ordination was separation." His brother Charles could scarcely believe, he said, that, in his eighty-second year, his "old, intimate friend and companion should have assumed the episcopal character, ordained elders, consecrated a bishop, and sent him to ordain our lay-preachers in America." But how different from these plaintive regrets, and from the bitter reproaches of less friendly critics, is the voice of history !

No man, in our time, who closely studies the whole transaction, with true conceptions of Wesley's character, will be able to avoid the conclusion respecting it to which Miss Wedgewood was brought with reference to the earlier innovation of field-preaching, that "he was led to it by a Wisdom that was not his own." He was dragged into the fields "reluctantly, as he was afterwards, with equal reluctance, led to sanction lay-preaching, by the urgency of his mother." Yet it was this "which gave the whole movement that aggressive character which fitted it to cope with the evils of that turbulent evil age in which it arose, and it was exactly this which gave the clergy of the day the most offence." In the same manner he was driven by the force of events, and by the urgent appeals of those whose judgments he respected, to devise a measure for the relief and profit of his people in America, in contravention of his most cherished prepossessions, which has produced results such as he had not powers to foresee. In both cases we are compelled to recognize the inscrutable agency of the Supreme Will; both alike came "forth from the LORD of Hosts, who is wonderful in counsel and excellent in working !"

CHAPTER XII.

THE NEW CHURCH ORGANIZED.

Coke in America—Meeting in Barrett's Chapel—Coke's Estimate of
Asbury—The Scheme explained—Asbury's Resolution respecting it—
Seeks Divine Guidance—At Perry Hall—Conference opens at Balti-
more—Characters of some of its Members—Message of Wesley—
Resolutions of the Conference—Ordination of Asbury—Ordination of
Elders—Importance of the New Arrangements—Signs of Divine
Approval.

THE elect three, duly equipped, set apart, and dismissed
for their great embassy, set sail from Bristol on the
18th September, 1784, and landed at New York on Wednesday the 3rd November. John Dickins, the preacher
in charge at that city, welcomed them on their arrival, and
heard Dr. Coke's account of the purpose of their mission
with unbounded satisfaction. The doctor preached three
times at New York; then proceeded with his companions to
Philadelphia, where he arrived on Saturday the 6th. The
next day he preached in the morning at St. Paul's Church,
on the invitation of the vicar, Dr. McGaw, the minister previously mentioned as one of Asbury's influential friends in
Delaware; and in the evening in the Methodist Chapel. By
the succeeding Saturday, the 13th, he and Whatcoat had
reached the house of Senator Bassett, at Dover, now one of
the most generous supporters of Methodism, and at that
very time engaged in the erection of a chapel in the city.
The next morning at six Mr. Whatcoat preached in the
Court-house, and at ten o'clock Dr. Coke preached in Bar-

rett's Chapel, so-called, says Coke, "from the name of our
friend who built it, and who went to Heaven a few days ago."
Here he and Asbury first met. The doctor was just ending
his discourse when Asbury, way-worn and weary after a
long journey, presented himself unexpectedly within the doors.
"A plain, robust man," says the preacher, "came up to me
in the pulpit and kissed me. I thought it could be no other
than Mr. Asbury, and I was not deceived." The Rev.
Ezekiel Cooper, an eye-witness of the scene, states that
"a solemn pause and deep silence took place, as an interval
for introduction and salutation. Asbury and Coke, with hearts
full of brotherly love, approached, embraced, and saluted each
other. The other preachers at the same time were melted
into sympathy and tears; the congregation also caught the
glowing emotion, and the whole assembly, as if struck with
a shock of heavenly electricity, burst into a flood of tears." *

The public service ended, Dr. Coke, assisted by Mr.
Whatcoat, administered the Lord's Supper to five or six
hundred communicants, and afterwards held a Lovefeast.
He then retired with Asbury to lay before him Mr. Wesley's
scheme of church organization. His own account of this
interview is given in these words: "Mr. Asbury informed
me that he had received some intimations of my arrival on
the continent, and had collected a considerable number of
the preachers to form a Council; and that, if they were of
opinion that it would be expedient immediately to call a
Conference, it should be done. They were accordingly
sent for, and, after debate, were unanimously of that
opinion. . . . I exceedingly reverence Mr. Asbury; he has
so much wisdom and consideration, so much meekness and
love; and, under all this, though hardly to be perceived, so

* "Stevens," ii. 172.

much command and authority." Asbury himself says, "I
was shocked when first informed of the intention of these
my brethren in coming to this country : it may be of God.
My answer then was,—' *If the preachers unanimously choose
me*, I shall not act in the capacity I have hitherto done, by
Mr. Wesley's appointment.' The design of organizing the
Methodists into an independent Episcopal Church was
opened to the preachers present, and it was agreed to call
a General Conference, to meet at Baltimore the ensuing
Christmas ; as also that Brother Garrettson go off to Virginia to give notice thereof to our brethren in the South."

The condition of taking the office assigned to him by
Wesley, which Asbury here specifies,—namely, the unanimous concurrence of his brethren,—is to be specially noted
as a mark of his surprising legislative ability. Placing
himself as by instinct at their point of view, he saw
that they might justly claim the power of electing to their
chief office as their right ; he also saw that to cede this
right would be necessary to secure the influence which
ought to belong to the office ; and he saw, with equal
clearness and certainty, that to exercise it would effectually
prevent the office of General Superintendent from becoming
identified eventually with the notion of a higher order of
ministers. Had he accepted it simply in virtue of Mr.
Wesley's appointment, it would naturally have fallen to
him and Dr. Coke to appoint and ordain colleagues or
successors to themselves, and gradually, there can be little
doubt, a superior rank of ministers would have been
established. Another thing notable in Asbury's records of
this crisis is the character of his phraseology. It is clear
that Coke had explained to him the nature of the proposed
new *régime* by the use of ecclesiastical terms : the new Church
is to be *Episcopal*, therefore, under the government of *bishops*.

There was an interval of about six weeks prior to the assembling of the Conference. This Dr. Coke spent in visiting places along the route of about 1,000 miles which Asbury had just taken; and Asbury, himself, in various new preaching excursions, and in earnest prayer for Divine guidance with reference to the projected new church. On the following Tuesday he wrote, " Rode to Bohemia, where I met with Thomas Vasey, who came over with the Doctor and R. Whatcoat. My soul is deeply engaged with God, to know His will in this business." On Thursday he says, " Brother Poythross and myself had much talk about the new plan "; and again, on Friday, " I observed this day as a day of fasting and prayer, that I might know the will of God in the matter that is shortly to come before our Conference. The preachers and people seem to be much pleased with the projected plan. I, myself, am led to think it is of the Lord. I am not tickled with the honour to be gained—I see danger in the way. My soul waits upon God. O that He may lead us in the way we should go! " In his next record he mentions an interesting conversation between him and the Rev. M. Weems, " on the subject of the Episcopal mode of Church-government."

From Saturday, the 18th, to Friday, the 24th December, he spent at the magnificent residence of his friend, Mr. Gough, "preparing for Conference." Dr. Coke had previously arrived there with Mr. Black, an English preacher, then stationed in Nova Scotia, who had come into the States to obtain ministerial recruits for that province, together with four other preachers. Coke speaks of it as "a most elegant house," and adds, " I have a noble room to myself where Mr. Asbury and I may, in the course of the week, mature everything for the Conference."

Early in the morning of the 24th,—the day looked forward to with so much solemnity of feeling,—the visitors set out together from Perry Hall to Baltimore, a ride of about twelve miles, where the Conference was appointed to be held. The preachers, sixty-four in number, out of the eighty-four then in the work, assembled in Lovely Lane Chapel. The Conference opened at 10 o'clock: Dr. Coke presided.

Who compose this Conference? Who are these men so strangely convened, without canonical authority, for the organization of a church? A little while ago they were all unknown to the world and to each other. Some of them were living in retired corners or recesses of that broad continent, as plain, simple, and comparatively illiterate peasants; some were rough mechanics in the towns; a few of them were men of social and educational advantages; and one or two of them owners of considerable wealth. But all distinctions are here merged and absorbed in one. Every man in that Council has been brought, through the agency of Methodism, under the action of ennobling and transforming spiritual influences. All have been made partakers of life in Christ; and spiritual life has quickened and enlarged their mental powers, endowed them with force of moral character, and impelled them to devote their renewed energies to the task of seeking, in order that they might save, that which is lost. They are a brotherhood of earnest and honest spiritual men, assembled under a consciousness that they are called to labour together in, with, and for Christ, and for the salvation of the world. Here they are, in the freshness and vigour of early manhood,—their hearts unworn, their spirits buoyant, their strength firm, their souls fired with holy love,—ready to go forth with eager haste, at the bidding and under the protection of their Lord, on any enterprise of toil and hardship for the extension of His kingdom. They are men of that character precisely who, in all ages, have most directly worked-out the purposes of Christ in the institution of His Church.

To Asbury the scene displayed within that chapel,—itself a monument of his successful early labours,—on an occasion so peculiarly solemn and sacred, must have been overwhelmingly impressive. Every man present is well known to him; all are debtors to him, more or less directly, to a greater or more limited extent, for the best elements of their character; some of them are his personal converts. Here is John Dickins, a Londoner by birth, who came to America at about the beginning of the Revolutionary war, and who, having found Christ and salvation under the guidance of the Methodists, entered into the itinerant ministry about seven years ago. He was educated at Eton College, is a proficient classical scholar, and conducts himself with the quiet tact and self-possession which bespeak the gentleman. Asbury described him soon after he came into the work as " a man of great piety, great skill in learning, drinks in Greek and Latin swiftly; yet prays much, and walks close with God." Here are William Phœbus, a man of literary attainments, like Dickins, a careful student of the Bible, and a trustworthy expositor; William Gill, a man of philosophical cast of mind, a deep and calm thinker, yet a man of fervid spiritual aspirations,—a native of Delaware, and probably a child of Asbury's " bonds ; " Freeborn Garrettson, distressingly self-diffident, yet full of fiery heroism, of whom Asbury said, he " will let 'no person escape a lecture that comes in his way; " John Haggerty, robust alike in mind and body; Reuben Ellis,—cautious, taciturn,—expressing himself when necessary in a few well-chosen and weighty words which always command respect; Francis Poythress,

who, like Garrettson, had " great possessions," which he
gladly abandoned that he might carry the Gospel over the
frowning Alleghanies into "the great and terrible wilderness ; " and here are two, strangely linked together by what
might seem a mere casual incident, whose names are Caleb B.
Pedicord and Thomas Ware. Pedicord, a man of distinguished piety and zeal, was also noted for his fine tenor
voice and his skill in singing. He was labouring in New
Jersey in 1781, when, one day, " while riding slowly on the
highway to an appointment at Mount Holly, he was singing,—

> "'I cannot, I cannot forbear
> These passionate longings for home;
> O! when shall my spirit be there?
> O! when will the messenger come?'

A young soldier of the Revolution, wandering in a neighbouring forest, heard him, and was deeply touched, not
only with the melody of his voice, which was among the
best he ever heard, but with the words, especially with the
last couplet. 'After he ceased,' writes the listener, 'I
went out and followed him a great distance, hoping he
would begin again.   He, however, stopped at the house of a
Methodist and dismounted.   I then concluded he must be a
Methodist preacher, and would probably preach that evening.' That evening the youthful soldier heard him, and
Caleb B. Pedicord thus became the spiritual father of
Thomas Ware, one of the most pure-minded and successful
of early Methodist itinerants, for fifty years a founder of the
denomination from New Jersey to Tennessee,—from Massachusetts to the Carolinas,—and by his pen the best contributor
to its early history."*

---

* "Stevens," ii. 31. A week or two after this Conference, Pedicord
reached the "home" for which he sighed.

All these were certainly present, as were probably Joseph Everett, said to have been "rude in speech, yet not in knowledge," and raised, through Asbury's labours, out of a state of deep degradation to be included in the first rank of successful pioneers; Wilson Lee, another of the brave mountain and western wilderness band; William Jessup, also converted under Asbury's ministry in Delaware, who had been greatly persecuted by his ungodly father, a large landholder, but who gladly sacrificed all his worldly interests to "go and preach the Gospel;" and William Partridge, before mentioned as a companion of Asbury, and who is declared to have "not only professed sanctification, but had it." These,—and men of whom these are examples,— were the constituents of that memorable Council. "Perhaps," says the visitor, Mr. Black, "such a number of holy, zealous, godly men never before met together in Maryland." Perhaps,—may we not respond ?—rarely in Christendom.

The proceedings were introduced by reading the following official document :—

"BRISTOL, *Sept.* 10, 1784.

"To Dr. COKE, Mr. ASBURY, and our Brethren in North America :-

"1. By a very uncommon train of providences, many of the provinces of North America are totally disjoined from their mother country, and erected into independent States. The English Government has no authority over them, either civil or ecclesiastical, any more than over the States of Holland. A civil authority is exercised over them, partly by the Congress—partly by the Provincial Assemblies. But no one either exercises or claims any ecclesiastical authority at all. In this peculiar situation, some thousands of the inhabitants of these States desire my advice ; and, in compliance with their desire, I have drawn up a little sketch.

"2. Lord King's "Account of the Primitive Church " convinced me many years ago, that Bishops and Presbyters are the same order, and consequently have the same right to ordain. For many years I have been importuned, from time to time, to exercise this right, by ordaining part of our Travelling Preachers. But I have still refused, not only for peace' sake, but because I was determined as little as possible to violate the established order of the National Church to which I belong.

"3. But the case is widely different between England and North America. Here there are bishops who have a legal jurisdiction. In America there are none—neither any parish ministers. So that for some hundred miles together there is none either to baptize or to administer the Lord's Supper. Here therefore my scruples are at an end; and I conceive myself at full liberty, as I violate no order and invade no man's right, to appoint and send labourers into the harvest.

"4. I have accordingly appointed Dr. COKE and Mr. FRANCIS ASBURY to be joint *Superintendents* over our brethren in North America: as also RICHARD WHATCOAT and THOMAS VASEY to act as *Elders* among them, by baptizing and administering the Lord's Supper. And I have prepared a Liturgy, little differing from that of the Church of England (I think, the best constituted National Church in the world), which I advise all the Travelling Preachers to use, on the Lord's-day, in all the congregations, reading the Litany only on Wednesdays and Fridays, and praying extempore on all other days. I also advise the Elders to administer the Supper of the Lord on every Lord's-day.

"5. If any one will point out a more rational and scriptural way of feeding and guiding those poor sheep in the wilderness, I will gladly embrace it. At present I cannot see any better method than that I have taken.

"6. It has indeed been proposed to desire the English Bishops to ordain part of our Preachers for America. But to this I object—(1) I desired the Bishop of London to ordain only one, but could not prevail; (2) if they consented, we know the slowness of their proceedings—but the matter admits of no delay; (3) if they would ordain them now, they would likewise expect to govern them—and how grievously would this entangle us? (4) as our American brethren are now totally disentangled, both from the State and from the English hierarchy, we dare not entangle them again, either with the one or the other: they are now at full liberty simply to follow the Scriptures, and the primitive Church; and we judge it best that they should stand fast in that liberty wherewith God has so strangely made them free.

                                        "JOHN WESLEY."

The first act of the Conference was to receive this Letter as the basis of its gravest deliberation; the next, to adopt its principle and general plan. This, as stated by William

Watters, the first of the native itinerants, was done " in a regular formal way, with not one dissenting voice." "It was agreed," says Asbury, "to form ourselves into an Episcopal Church, and to have Superintendents, Elders, and Deacons." The question of a *title* was next considered, and John Dickins is said to have proposed that by which it has ever since been designated,—THE METHODIST EPISCOPAL CHURCH IN THE UNITED STATES OF AMERICA; which, after a free discussion, was also unanimously adopted. Then followed the question arising out of Asbury's resolution not to take the office unless with the declared concurrence of his brethren. The Conference would have been perfectly content to recognize the appointment of Mr. Wesley in this instance, as in all cases heretofore; but, in deference to the strongly-expressed determination of Asbury, it unhesitatingly took the responsibility upon itself. "Dr. Coke and myself," he says, "were unanimously *elected* to the superintendency of the Church, and," he adds, "my ordination followed, after being previously ordained deacon and elder, as by the following certificate may be seen:—

"'KNOW ALL MEN BY THESE PRESENTS that I, Thomas Coke, Doctor of Civil Law, late of Jesus College, in the University of Oxford, Presbyter of the Church of England, and Superintendent of the Methodist Episcopal Church in America, under the protection of Almighty God, and with a single eye to His glory, by the imposition of my hands, and prayer (being assisted by two ordained elders), did on the twenty-fifth day of this month, December, set apart FRANCIS ASBURY for the office of a Deacon in the aforesaid Methodist Episcopal Church. And also, on the twenty-sixth day of the said month, did, by the imposition of my hands and prayer (being assisted by the said elders), set apart the said FRANCIS ASBURY for the office of Elder in the said Methodist Episcopal Church. And, on this twenty-seventh day of the said month, being the day of the date hereof, have, by the imposition of my hands, and prayer (being assisted by the said elders), set apart the said FRANCIS ASBURY for the office of a Superintendent in the said Methodist Epis-

copal Church, a man whom I judge to be well qualified for that great
work.   And I do hereby recommend him to all whom it may concern,
as a fit person to preside over the flock of Christ.   In testimony where-
of I have hereunto set my hand and seal this twenty-seventh day of
December. in the year of our Lord 1784.—THOMAS COKE.' "

In the rite of consecration to the office of "Superintendent," Asbury's early Lutheran friend, the Rev. W. P.
Otterbein, was associated with Coke, Whatcoat, and Vasey.*
Dr. Coke preached on the occasion on the great character-
istics of the Christian ministry, and maintained that "of all
forms of Church-government a moderate Episcopacy is the
best, the executive power being lodged in the hands of one,
or at least a few, whereby vigour and activity are given to
the resolves of the body, and those two essential requisites
for any great undertaking are sweetly united, calmness and
wisdom in deliberating, and acting with expedition and
force."   The last act of the Conference was to elect and set
apart, by ordination, twelve preachers as *elders* (having been
previously ordained " deacons ") "to serve our Societies
in the United States, one (Jeremiah Lambert) for Antigua,
and two (Garrettson and James O. Cromwell) for Nova
Scotia," in compliance with the appeal made by Mr. Black.
Whatcoat's account of the proceedings is succinctly given in
these words : " We agreed to form a Methodist Episcopal
Church, in which the Liturgy, as presented by the Rev.
John Wesley, should be read, and the Sacraments be administered by a superintendent, elders, and deacons, who shall

* "I will tell the world," says Asbury, with reference to certain
cavils about apostolic succession, "on what I depend—(1) Divine
authority ; (2) seniority in America ; (3) the election of the Conference ; (4) my ordination by Thomas Coke, William Philip Otterbein,
German Presbyterian minister, Richard Whatcoat, and Thomas Vasey;
(5) the signs of an apostle which have been seen in me."

be ordained by a presbytery, using the Episcopal form, as prescribed by the Rev. Mr. Wesley's Prayer-book. Persons to be ordained are to be nominated by the superintendent, elected by the Conference, and ordained by imposition of the hands of the superintendent and elders; the superintendent has a negative voice " (power of *veto*).

Thus, then, after much inquiry, deliberation, and prayer on both sides of the Atlantic, was the Methodist Episcopal Church solemnly instituted and organized. The importance of the transaction in its bearing upon the spiritual, and even the political, well-being of the American Republic, it would be scarcely possible to exaggerate. No other church was at that time in a condition to supply to the people their lack of spiritual privileges. The Anglican Church was a wreck; the Presbyterians were too much shackled and restrained to undertake the aggressive operations which the times required; and the Independent and Baptist were too exclusive in both theory and practice, and too limited in their resources, to give such a movement their serious thoughts. But for Methodist agency, henceforth to be maintained in a state of impressive completeness, and of redoubled energy and effectiveness; taking the place of the English Church in many places where that had ceased to exist; following the people where they emigrated and forming settlements in new territory; and multiplying itself with the increase of population,—the spiritual destitution of the country must have been appalling. Even aside from purely spiritual results, the service which the new Church rendered to the cause of civilization, public order, and social progress, was incalculably valuable. Looking at the measure comprehensively, at this distance of time; considering its immediate influence on the new-born Republic, and its influence on all classes of society subsequently; considering its marvellous growth, its pre-

sent powerful position in relation to all the other Protestant
Churches of Christendom, it being the largest and mightiest
of them all ; considering also the work it has accomplished,
and is now successfully carrying on by its missionary
agencies, all over the world,—it is scarcely too much to say
that the acts of that Council of sixty devout, unselfish,
and pure-minded men at that Christmas-tide of 1784, are
not surpassed in grandeur and importance by any act of any
assembly of men in the whole history of the Church of
Christ.

Here are its unchallengeable credentials—here is the heavenly impress, which condemns all forms of objection to the
measure,—it has succeeded beyond all other examples of
success : it was therefore suitable to the wants of the people
and the times, and has been attended with the blessing
of God.

An apostle to whom "the keys of the kingdom of Heaven"
were committed, acting in violation of the Law to which he
continued to acknowledge allegiance, "opened the door of
faith " to uncircumcised Gentiles, and even admitted them
to social intercourse with him. He did this with great
personal reluctance, but in obedience to what he was made
to understand was the Divine Will ; and his brethren, per-
plexed and scandalized, called him to account for his
inconsistency. But his ready reply was, "Forasmuch as
God gave them the like gift as He did unto us who believed
on the Lord Jesus Christ, what was I that I could withstand God ? "   And " *they held their peace.*"

CHAPTER XIII.

THE Title "Bishop"—Overruling of Providence—New Duties—Asbury mounted again—Ordination of Willis—North Carolina—South Carolina—Mr. Wayne—Methodism introduced into Charleston—Conversion of Mr. Wells—New Chapel—Virginia—The Bishops wait on Washington—Conference of 1785—Coke's Departure—Asbury "Overdone"—Climbs the Alleghanies—The Dismal Swamp—Georgia—Conference of 1786—The Hudson—New Jersey—Mobbing at Charleston.

DID not Dr. Coke, however, exceed the powers delegated to him by Wesley? Probably, yes; but not to the extent which has been alleged against him, and, through the timely resolution of Asbury to make his brethren responsible for his taking a chief place among them, with ultimate results of a beneficial, and not of an injurious character. His great error—if it was an error—consisted in assuming the canonical title of *Bishop*. This Wesley did not authorize, but disapproved and condemned.

It is perfectly certain that Wesley intended the Church to be Episcopal in its structure. But the kind of Episcopacy which he desired it to take was not the "diocesan"* or modern, but that of the primitive Church, which recognized a difference of rank, though not a distinction of orders, in the ministry.

---

* "If any one is minded to dispute concerning diocesan episcopacy, he may dispute. But I have better work."—*Minutes of Conference,* 1785.

But the title "bishop" had been appropriated for many ages
to a separate *order* which mediæval credulity had held to be
traceable in regular succession to the apostles, and to be
rightfully endowed, in virtue of that succession, with powers
and prerogatives exclusively its own. Used simply with
reference to its etymology, the name was not inconsistent
with Wesley's design ; but it was commonly used and
understood in its acquired, and not in its derivative, meaning, and, moreover, was invested with unapostolic notions
of worldly dignity and importance. Wesley, therefore,
with his nice sense of congruity and fitness, adopted the
title of synonymous meaning, "*Superintendent.*" But Coke,
more vehement and aspiring—perhaps more "ambitious,"
although as far as Wesley himself .from a self-seeking and
pernicious assertion of priestly power—ventured to sanction
—perhaps to suggest—the use of the name " *Bishop.*"

And was there not a guiding or overruling Providence in
this, just as in the prior anomaly committed by Wesley ?
He had declared himself "determined to violate as little
as possible the established order to which he belonged ;"
yet, in despite of this determination, he set up a system of
church polity in independence and implied condemnation of
it—and we recognize in this the purpose and agency of God.
And now, Coke, who is commissioned by Wesley to carry
out his plans,—acting strangely in disregard of his wishes,
if he knew them, and, on other grounds, acting with obvious
inconsistency,—adopts an ecclesiastical title pertaining to an
" order " which the entire scheme ignores. Yet is it possible
to contemplate the whole proceeding and its results, without
perceiving how truly this also contributed to the working
out of the will of Providence ? Coke may have desired to
avail himself of any additional influence which a venerated
name attached to his office might command ; he may have

discerned in the conditions of American society a favourable opportunity for divesting an apostolic word of its worldly and vain-glorious attributes, and of restoring it, together with a restored system of primitive episcopacy, to its primeval use; he may have been moved by the aim to raise the church system he had come to establish upon a true basis of thought and conception ; or he may have been merely carried away, by his ardent temperament and his intense religious zeal, to the use of means which he never strictly scrutinized.   But a practical man will not waste his energies in speculating on the particular motive of an individual agent : he will rather fix attention upon the great principles of his operations, and their *fruit*.

Asbury's new office devolved upon him new duties and responsibilities.   The mere administration of the sacraments was a heavy immediate addition to his labours ; for, the people having been so long deprived of them, offered themselves or presented their children for baptism everywhere, and came in extraordinary numbers to the Lord's Table.

The Conference adjourned on Monday, Jan. 3, 1785, and the same day Asbury preached his first sermon since his consecration.   His text was Ephes. iii. 8, " Unto me, who am less than the least of all saints, is this grace given, that I should preach among the Gentiles the unsearchable riches of Christ."   He was experiencing a reaction of depression from the state of mental strain and excitement through which he had passed, and says, " My mind was unsettled, and I was but low in my testimony."   The next day he rode on horseback about fifty miles " through frost and snow to Fairfax, Virginia, and got in about seven o'clock." He continued his journey southward to Prince William, then onward to the north branch of the Rappahannock, which

he "found about waist-high and frozen from side to side."
On Sunday he "read prayers, preached, ordained Brother
Willis deacon, and baptized some children, feeling nothing
but love ; but sometimes afraid of being led to think something more of myself in my new station than formerly."

Taking Willis with him, whom a day or two later he
ordained "elder," he pressed forward into North Carolina,
experiencing his usual difficulties and trials. "It was so
dark that we could not find the ford. We rode back a mile,
and engaged a young man who undertook to be our guide,
but he himself was scarcely able to keep the way. We rode
with great pain to Waggoner's Chapel ; and, after pushing on
through deep streams, I had only nine hearers." His horse
failed ; but he borrowed another, and rode off seventeen
miles to preach to "a few poor people" at Fisher's River ;
thence over barren mountains, and across "frequent rivers,"
to minister to other small congregations ; gratified to learn
that the "old Church folks and *Catholic* Presbyterians"
very generally expressed their satisfaction at the recent
action of the Conference. In one place he "plunged four
adults, at their special request, they being persuaded that
this was the proper mode of baptism."

Having ridden his borrowed horse "nearly three hundred
miles in about nine days," he left it to rest, and, borrowing
another, was again mounted and off, in company with
Willis and Jesse Lee, in the direction of Charleston, South
Carolina. Arriving at Georgetown, on his way thither, "a
Mr. Wayne, a nephew of the celebrated Gen. Wayne,"
introduced himself to the Bishop. This gentleman afforded
him entertainment, and in a way not foreseen facilitated the
prosecution of his mission. He gave him letters of introduction to Mr. Wells, an influential merchant in Charleston, which secured him an hospitable reception on his

arrival.   These letters he sent forward by Willis, who was also charged with the duty of making arrangements at one or two places on his way for Asbury to preach.

When Willis presented himself at the door of Mr. Wells, he found him preparing to go to the theatre.   This intention, however, he readily abandoned, and spent the evening with his visitor in conversation and worship.   A day or two later he as cheerfully received Asbury and Lee as his guests. Partly by his aid, an old Baptist meeting-house, some time previously closed, was engaged for a series of services. First Willis, next Lee, and afterwards Asbury, preached. The bishop's text was 2 Cor. v. 20: "Now then we are ambassadors for Christ, as though God did beseech you by us; we pray you, in Christ's stead, be ye reconciled to God." "I told my hearers," he says, "that I expected to stay in the city but seven days; that I should preach every night if they would favour me with their company, and that I should speak on subjects of primary importance, and explain the essential doctrines taught and held by the Methodists." One of the first to give evidence of spiritual concern was his host himself.   On Saturday he writes, "This afternoon Mr. Wells began to experience conviction of sin.   My soul praised the Lord for this fruit of our labours, this answer to our prayers."   The next day he preached to "a large, wild company—his soul in travail for Mr. Wells;" and on Wednesday he says, "I had a good time on Matt. vii. 7. In the evening the clouds about Mr. Wells began to disperse; in the morning he could rejoice in the Lord.   Now we know that God hath brought us here, and have a hope that there will be glorious work among the people."   Mr. Wells was henceforth a steadfast, liberal, and consistent Methodist to the day of his death.

Asbury left at the expiration of a fortnight, and Willis

remained to carry on the work. He was shortly afterwards informed that he could no longer occupy the Baptist chapel, and a lady opened her house for worship. This became inconveniently crowded, and better accommodation was offered by another lady. Then the project of building a chapel was entertained, and exactly two years after Asbury first visited the place a Conference was held there. On that occasion he wrote, " Here we have already a spacious house prepared for us ; and the congregations are crowded and solemn." " This was the house in Cumberland Street, which will long be remembered with affection as the birth-place of many scores of precious souls, who there received awakening and converting grace. The opening of this house was of vast importance to the interests of Methodism. It not only relieved the congregation from great inconvenience, but gave to them an established and permanent character. It was a public declaration that we had driven down our stake, and intended to hold on." *

Asbury returned from his first visit to this maritime city by nearly the same route that he went. Re-arriving at Georgetown, he found the wife of his late host, Mr. Wayne, anxiously inquiring the way of salvation, and not long afterwards could write, " In this place the scene was greatly changed : almost the whole town came together to hear the Word of God." In several places through which he passed he records the baptism of children, and states that the people in their generous ignorance of his principles offered him fees—" The poor mother held out a piece of gold to me ! "

Coming back into Virginia, he met Dr. Coke, who had been extending his labours in a similar manner through that

---

* Bishop Andrews.

State, Maryland, and Delaware. For a while they travelled in company, then took their divergent routes, and on the 26th May met again on the banks of the Potomac, and had the honour of an interview with General Washington, " who," says Asbury, " received us very politely, and gave us his opinion against slavery." Dr. Coke states, more particularly, that the object of their visit was to obtain his signature to a petition which the Conference had agreed to address to the Virginia Assembly, for the emancipation of the slaves, " if the eminence of his station did not render that inexpedient." The General assured them that his sentiments were identical with their own, and that, if he had the opportunity, he would not fail to give expression to them in a letter to the Assembly. They dined with him, and were treated with great consideration and courtesy.

The next regular Conference opened at Baltimore, on the 1st June, 1785. Asbury attended it, although unwell. Coke was on the point of his return to England. On his account the first sitting was continued till midnight. Early the next morning the Conference re-assembled, and at eleven o'clock the Doctor delivered an impressive farewell address, based upon St. Paul's discourse to the elders of Ephesus, and immediately embarked on board the " Olive Branch," for home. Asbury says, " We parted with heavy hearts." The increase of members during this year was 3,612 ; the entire number being 18,000. The number of preachers had become 104. The number of regular hearers is believed to have been greater in proportion to the membership than ever previously or subsequently. This is ascribed partly to the greater influence and attractiveness of the new institution, and partly to the still dilapidated condition of the Anglican Church. They are estimated at not fewer than 200,000.

Alone in the discharge of episcopal duties over a Church

not yet perfectly established, and rapidly extending its borders, Asbury felt more deeply than ever that every moment was precious. The following is a sample of his records at this period: "Preached in Baltimore, on 'Ye know not what manner of spirit ye are of.' In the town I spoke three times, and at the Point once. . . . Rode to the springs called Bath; now under great improvement. I preached in the play-house, and lodged under the same roof with the actors. Some folks, who would not hear me in their own neighbourhood, made now a part of my audience, both night and morning. . . . My congregation was large. Hard labour has almost overdone me. I rode to S——s's, where I found some life among the people. A long dreary ride brought us to Morgantown. I preached and baptized, and was much spent. . . . From preaching so frequently in the evenings, and consequent exposure to night air, I have suffered a relapse, and the inflammation of my throat has returned. It is a school of affliction to me; but I am thankful that in my sufferings I have a skilful physician, and constant attendance from my kind nurses; and I am in a house where prayer is wont to be made. I am taught the necessity of walking more holily and humbly with God; to pray more frequently, and to preach more faithfully."

During the year he traversed the continent from Maryland to New York, back through New Jersey, Delaware, and Maryland, into Virginia; thence onward to North and South Carolina; again northward, into Pennsylvania, and ultimately climbed to the very summit of the lofty Alleghanies. For the first time he took "a peep," as he says, "into the Indian land." In this expedition he found much to gratify him, much to stimulate and sustain his powers of thought and action, as he cast his eyes over the boundless plains of the west; he felt himself amply repaid for the

toil and suffering he endured, in the knowledge that he
ministered comfort to his self-denying brethren who were
stationed on those rugged heights, and in meeting many
"old friends from Maryland" who had settled there. But
he could not forbear writing on his return, "I have been
greatly tempted to impatience and discontent. The roads
are bad; my horse's hind-feet without shoes, and but
little to eat. To this I may add that the lodgings are
unclean and uncomfortable. I have in six days ridden
about one hundred and fifty miles, on as bad roads as any
I have seen on the continent."

At the beginning of 1787 he again journeyed southward.
On the 2nd January he rode fifty miles through the snow,
and continued to ride fifteen or twenty miles a day, preaching and exercising all the other functions of his office;
"indisposed and suffering bodily pain," but "feeling uncommon affection for the people," and gladdened with signs
of their spiritual earnestness. "I had a crowd of careless
sinners at Mrs. Ball's," he says with satisfaction; "she is a
famous heroine for Christ." He met his brethren at their
quarterly-meeting, and "was in their company." "Brother
Poythress frightened me with the idea of the Great Swamp,
the east end of the Dismal. But I could not consent to
ride sixty miles round; so we ventured through, and
neither we nor our horses received any injury. Praise the
Lord! I preached in the new chapel, I hope not in vain.
I am now surrounded with waters and hideous swamps."

At Charleston he welcomed the return of Dr. Coke from
Europe, who arrived in time to assist at the opening of the
new church, and to hold a Conference in it. They ordained
two deacons, and Coke gave "the charge." He expresses
his thankfulness to witness the rapid progress which the
work had made there, and prepared to accompany Asbury

on a tour through that and the adjoining States. Provided
with strong horses, they set out together first for Georgia,
then northward, through the Carolinas, Virginia, and
Maryland, frequently on horseback till midnight, preaching
alternately day by day, and making it a point, says Asbury,
" to pray in the families where we lodge, whether public or
private ; and generally where we stop for refreshment."
In one week they rode three hundred miles.

On the 2nd May they held another Conference at Baltimore. Dr. Coke shortly afterwards re-embarked for England, and Asbury was again left to prosecute his episcopal
labours alone. First he visited Long Island and preached
in a paper-mill, then took the course of the Hudson, " rode
over the mountain, and was gratified with a sight of a
remarkable recess for the Americans, during the late war ; "
and remarks that " the names of André and Arnold, with
which misfortune and treachery are so unhappily blended,
will give celebrity to West Point, had it been less deserving of notice than its wonderful appearance really makes
it." Arriving at Newburgh, he preached, administered the
Lord's Supper, and held a Lovefeast, occupying " nearly
seven hours." The next day he addressed about seven
hundred hearers, baptized several adults and many children, and was entertained by a Dutch lady—" *like a queen*."
He came back to New Jersey, " preached at the stone
church, after riding upwards of thirty miles ; then rode
until ten o'clock in the night through a heavy rain, and had
nothing to eat but a little bread and milk." The next day,
after preaching and sacrament, " another long ride after
night ; " and the next (being Sunday), he held one of those
impressive services which were so frequent at this early
period. " I preached in the woods," he says, " to nearly
a thousand people," many of them having rode considerable

distances, and having tied their horses to the adjoining trees. After the sermon he, " like Jonah, went and sat alone," then administered the Lord's Supper, and " baptized a number of infants and adults, by sprinkling and immersion. I felt my body," he quietly adds, " weary *in*, but my spirit not *of*, the work of God." Again he travelled southward through all the States to South Carolina, and says, " I seldom mount my horse for a ride of less distance than twenty miles on ordinary occasions; and frequently have forty or fifty, in moving from one circuit to another. In travelling thus I suffer much from hunger and cold."

By the middle of March he had again reached Charleston, where the preachers from the neighbouring circuits were summoned to meet him in Conference. But while one of them " was speaking in the morning of the Lord's-day to a very crowded house, and many outside, a man made a riot at the door. A general alarm took place; some of the ladies leaped out of the windows of the church, and a dreadful confusion ensued. Again, whilst I was speaking at night, a stone was thrown against the north side of the church; then another on the south; a third came through the window and struck the pulpit: I, however, continued to speak on ' How beautiful upon the mountains!' "

Leaving Charleston he rode again into Georgia, where he held a Conference with the ten preachers, including four probationers, who were labouring successfully in that State, so recently brought within circuit arrangements. At the end of April he again scaled, and for the first time passed over, the Alleghany mountains.

CHAPTER XIV

CONSTITUTION OF THE CHURCH.

Principles of Episcopacy previously recognized—Their Declaration—
Definition of Offices : Bishop ; Elder ; Deacon ; Preachers—Leaders'
Meeting ; Quarterly - meeting Conference ; Annual Conference ;
General Conference—Picture of Annual Conference—The Discipline :
how improved by Asbury—Notes appended by Coke and Asbury—
The Character of Public Services—Practical Results : how achieved.

THE organization of the Church by the Conference of
1784 is not to be thought of as the institution of an
essentially new system of church polity in all its completeness. It was rather the establishment of the Societies, on
principles which they had already recognized in practice, in
a state of greater unity, consistency, and order ; and with a
definite regard to their peculiar conditions and wants. The
event certainly constituted an epoch in the history of the
Church, just as the political independence of the States was
an epoch in the national history of the country. But it was
not the introduction of anything of a revolutionary character.
The very framework of the organization existed previously
in its rudiments ; for the United Societies, in their common
subjection to the government of the Conference, and under
the administration of a " General Assistant " or Superintendent, were a true embodiment of an episcopacy. This was
the character of Methodism when planted in America, as
obviously as it was its character in this country under Mr.
Wesley ; and this character, modified to answer the demands
of the different conditions of civil life, it continued to preserve

as it extended itself over the continent. Its erection into an orderly Episcopacy was but the act of giving more symmetrical form and greater force to the whole system, as already developing itself in agreement with its external conditions out of its own unconscious energies.

Looking back upon the work of that great Conference, Asbury said, " We debated everything freely, deciding questions by a majority of votes. We were in great haste, and did much business in a little time." The system in all its fulness of detail was no doubt grasped by his own mind, and apprehended more or less completely by the minds of others ; but probably little more was absolutely settled than the principles affirmed in the declaration which was shortly afterwards published, namely, that, "following the counsel of Mr. John Wesley, who recommended the Episcopal mode of government, we thought it best to become an Episcopal Church, making the Episcopal office elective, and the elected Superintendent or Bishop amenable to the body of ministers and preachers."

I subjoin a brief account of the constitution of the Church as then accepted *generally*, and since gradually elaborated and matured. It will show how substantially it is identical with the Methodism of this country, and how natural was its growth out of its previous adaptations to existing circumstances in America.

The " General Assistant " became under the new *régime* a General Superintendent,'Overseer, or Bishop ; the "Assistant " became an Elder or Presbyter ; and the " Helper," a Deacon.

The functions of the *Bishop* are defined to be, besides presiding as moderator in the Conferences, to station the preachers, "and, in the intervals of the Conference, to change, receive, or suspend preachers as necessity may

11

require ; to travel through as many circuits as he can, and
to direct in the spiritual business of the Societies, as also to
ordain bishops, elders, and deacons." He is the *first among
equals*, with the same amount of salary as his brethren.
This was fixed at sixty-four dollars per annum with a portion of his travelling expenses.

The duties of the *Elder* are to administer both sacraments ;
to take charge of the other preachers, the local-preachers,
and exhorters, within the sphere allotted to him ; to change,
receive, or suspend preachers ; and to enforce the several
parts of church-discipline. Elders are of two classes—the
one having charge of a single circuit, or station, only ; the
other, who are distinguished as *Presiding-elders*, being put in
charge of a group of circuits, called a district. It is the
duty of the presiding-elder to visit each circuit in his district once a quarter, and to preside over the Quarterly
Conference.

The duties of *Deacons* are, to preach, to baptize, to assist
the elder in administering the Lord's Supper, to visit the
sick, and to meet the leaders weekly.

Preachers are authorized to preach *only*, whether separated to the ministry as travelling preachers, or engaged in
secular business, as local or occasional preachers.

The *Society* is composed of *classes*, each in charge of its
duly-appointed Leader ; and it has its *Society-meetings* and
Lovefeasts, and its *Stewards*.

The Church-courts are :—

(1) " *The Leaders' Meeting*, which is composed of all the
class-leaders in any one circuit or station, in which the
preacher in charge presides. Here the weekly class-collec-
tions are paid into the hands of the stewards, and inquiry
is made into the state of the classes, delinquents reported,
and the sick and poor inquired after.

(2) " *The Quarterly-meeting Conference*, which is composed of all the travelling and local preachers, exhorters, stewards, and leaders belonging to any particular station or circuit, in which the presiding-elder presides, or, in his absence, the preacher in charge. Here exhorters and local-preachers are licensed, and preachers recommended to an Annual Conference to be received into the travelling ministry; and likewise appeals are heard from any members of the Church who may appeal from the decision of a committee.

(3) " *The Annual Conference*, which is composed of all the travelling preachers, deacons, and elders within a specified district of country. These are executive and judicial bodies, acting under rules prescribed them by the General Conference. Here the characters and conduct of all the travelling preachers within the bounds of the Conference are examined yearly; applications for admission into the travelling ministry, if accounted worthy, are received, continued on trial, or dropped, as the case may be; appeals from local-preachers which may be presented are heard and decided, and those who are eligible to deacon's or elder's orders are elected. An Annual Conference possesses original jurisdiction over all its members, and may therefore try, acquit, suspend, expel, or locate any of them, as the *Discipline* in such cases provides.

(4) " *The General Conference* assembles quadrennially, and is composed of a certain number of delegates, elected by the Annual Conferences. It has power to revise any part of the *Discipline*, not prohibited by the restrictive regulations; to elect the book-agents and editors, and the bishops; to hear and determine appeals of preachers from the decisions of Annual Conferences; to review the acts of those Conferences generally; to examine into the general administration of the bishops for the four preceding years, and, if accused, to

try, censure, acquit, or condemn a bishop. This is the highest judicatory of the Church. It is composed of one member for every twenty-one members of each Annual Conference, to be appointed either by seniority or choice, at the direction of such Annual Conference.''*

"The Christmas Conference was the first *General Conference;* that is to say, all the Annual Conferences were supposed to be there assembled. It was, therefore, the supreme judicatory of the Church. It was not yet a delegated body, but the whole ministry in session. It made no provision for any future session of the kind; but for some years legislative enactments were made, as heretofore, every new measure being submitted to each Annual Conference by the superintendents, and the majority of all being necessary to its validity. Another General Conference was held, however, in 1792, no official *Minutes* of which are extant. The third session was held in 1796, a compendium of the *Minutes* of which was published. Thereafter a session has been held regularly every four years, and the *Minutes* of each preserved. In the session of 1808 a motion was adopted for the better organization of the Conference as a 'delegated' body. In 1812 it met in New York City as a 'Delegated General Conference' under constitutional restrictions, which gave it the character of a renewed organization.

"Until the appointment of stated or regular General Conferences, the Annual Conferences continued to be considered local or sectional meetings of the one undivided ministry, held in different localities for the local convenience of its members, every general or legislative measure being submitted to all the sessions, before it could

---

* Bangs's "History of the Methodist Episcopal Church," i. 245-248.

become law."* The term *Annual Conference* is now used to indicate a certain defined tract of country; it is an ecclesiastical division of territory, of similar meaning to the word "*diocese.*"

The annual gatherings of the preachers from the several circuits which constitute one of these Conferences naturally became, in the early period of the Church's history, occasions of peculiar interest. "A bishop presided. There was preaching in the early morning, in the afternoon, and at night. The daily proceedings were introduced with religious services, and were characterized by an impressive religious spirit. They continued usually a week, and it was a jubilatic week, gathering the war-worn heroes of many distant and hard-fought fields, renewing the intimacies of preachers and people, and crowned alike by social hospitalities and joyous devotions. They had their particular regulations prescribed in the *Minutes* or *Discipline.* 'It is desired,' say their Rules, 'that all things be considered as in the immediate presence of God; that every person speak freely whatever is in his heart. How may we best improve the time of our Conferences? While we are conversing let us have an especial care to set God always before us. In the intermediate hours let us redeem all the time we can for private exercises. Therein let us give ourselves to prayer for one another, and for a blessing on our labour.'

"The presiding bishop made out the appointments to circuits for the next ecclesiastical year, of all the preachers within the territory of the Conference. He had no 'cabinet' of presiding elders; for this office was yet unknown in the Church, as the new elders, ordained at the Christmas Conference, were appointed only to administer the sacraments.

---

* Stevens's "History of the Methodist Episcopal Church," ii. 219, 220.

At the close of the Conference, after singing and prayer, he read to a crowded house, amid breathless stillness and deep solemnity, the 'list of appointments;' most, if not all, of the appointed preachers having had no previous knowledge of the fate thus assigned them for the ensuing year. Many of them were torn up by it from endearing localities, and sent to distant, often to hostile and perilous, fields. The reading of the list was like the announcement of an order of battle. It was heard by the militant itinerants with ejaculations of prayer, with sobs and shouts. Few, if any, revolted. The post of greatest difficulty was considered the post of greatest honour. The list ended, the Doxology, sung to the Old Hundredth by preachers and people, rang through the church, and reverberated through the neighbourhood; the apostolic benediction was pronounced; and, usually before the sun went down, but sometimes at midnight hour, the itinerant band and their bishop, after many an affecting leave-taking, were in the saddle, hasting to their new fields of combat and triumph. Few or no scenes of early Methodism were more heroic or more affecting than its Annual Conferences."*

These stated local Conferences have gradually increased in number with the territorial extension of the Church ever since its formal establishment in 1784. The following year (1785) three were held : ten years later there were twenty. Their present number (1874) is seventy, and the present number of bishops thirteen. These belong equally to the whole Church, and attend the several Conferences according to arrangements of their own. They meet in the autumn of each year, and distribute the duties of their office among them, as judges arrange for the discharge of their duties

* Stevens's " History of the Methodist Episcopal Church," ii. 221, 222.

in their several circuits; and they preside over the Conferences assigned to them with a calmness, self-possession, tact, and delicacy which only men of their natural refinement and large experience can display.

The system of Rules of Life, which the Church has adopted as its "Discipline," was gradually evolved out of plans and principles which originated in the earliest labours of Methodism, in the same manner as its outward order. The basis of the whole are, (1) the tractate known in this country as "The Large Minutes," being minutes relating to life and conduct accepted by successive Conferences, and compiled by Mr. Wesley; and (2) the general "Rules of Society." To these, which the Methodists of America, as elsewhere, recognized as authoritative and obligatory, additions were continuously made by the special enactments of their own Conferences. But, in anticipation of Dr. Coke's arrival, Asbury had carefully revised the various super-additions, and was prepared to submit them in their revised form to the Conference which organized the Church. They were probably read and accepted without debate, and by the time of the next regular Conference in June they had passed through the press. The whole was bound up with the "Sunday Service," or Abridged Liturgy of the English Church, and a "Collection of Psalms and Hymns," which Mr. Wesley had sent over in sheets. Asbury says that the day after this Conference he spent three hours profitably in reading this work, and probably in considering how it might be re-arranged and improved. He was evidently dissatisfied with its want of system. On the 27th December of the same year he writes: "For some time past I had not been quite satisfied with the order and arrangement of our Form of Discipline; and persuaded that it might be improved without difficulty, we (John Dickins and himself) accordingly set about it, and,

during my confinement in James City (through illness), completed the work, arranging the subject-matter thereof under
their proper heads, divisions, and sections."

In this revised form the work was brought before the Conference of 1786, and, in compliance with one of its resolutions,
Asbury and Coke prepared and appended to it a body of Notes
and Illustrations, consisting mostly of Scripture warrants.
This was published with the title, " The General Minutes of
the Conferences of the Methodist Episcopal Church in
America, forming the Constitution of the said Church."   The
next year (1787) this was re-published still further modified,
with the title, " A Form of Discipline for the Ministers,
Preachers, and Members of the Methodist Episcopal Church
in America, considered and approved in a Conference held
in Baltimore, and in which the Rev. Thomas Coke, LL.D.,
and the Rev. Francis Asbury, presided ; arranged under
proper heads, and methodized in a more acceptable and easy
manner." In this edition the word "bishop" was substituted
everywhere for the title " superintendent."   In April of the
year 1788 Asbury says again, " I compiled two sections,
which I shall recommend to be put into our ' Form of Discipline,' in order to remove from our Societies, by regular steps,
either preachers or people that are disorderly." We know
therefore, from his own repeated reference to the manual, how
much it occupied his thoughts, and how greatly it is indebted
to the suggestions of his devout, sagacious, and practical mind.
It is the work of Asbury, based upon " The Large Minutes "
of Wesley, in almost as exclusive a sense as that work was
the production of Wesley himself.   In 1804 the briefer title
was given to it which it still bears, " The Doctrines and
Discipline of the Methodist Episcopal Church."   Its doctrines are those of the Articles of the Church of England,
reduced to twenty-five, and modified in some places in their

phraseology; its rules of discipline, so far as they relate to the ministry, are such as George Herbert and Richard Baxter would have placed next in rank to St. Paul's Epistles to Timothy.

Reference has been made to the Abridged Liturgy, and a Collection of Psalms and Hymns which Mr. Wesley sent over for the use of the new Church, and it may be asked whether they were adopted. The following statement from Dr. Stevens is a reply to this inquiry. He says,—referring to the observation of Whatcoat that the Christmas Conference of 1784 "agreed to form a Methodist Episcopal Church, in which the Liturgy, as presented by the Rev. John Wesley, should be read,"—"This organic provision has never been formally repeated. The General Conference has, indeed, at a later session, directed that for the 'establishment of uniformity in public worship, the morning service shall consist of singing, prayer, the reading of a chapter out of the Old Testament, and another out of the New, and preaching;' but is has not directed what the two lessons shall be, nor what the form of prayer; its prescription would nearly correspond with the original 'Sunday Service,' and, as the latter has never been formally abrogated, any Methodist Society could legally adopt it. Public opinion has, however, silently but effectually rendered it obsolete, and few Methodists now know that their Church was organized with a Liturgical Service by the direction of Wesley himself. It was used for a few years, in both cities and country, in the principal churches; but Sabbath-lovefeasts, or other extra services, frequently preoccupied the time allotted to it, and, from being occasionally omitted, it at last fell into entire disuse. It was published in but two editions, both printed in London. In 1787 the 'General Minutes,' or Discipline proper, was published in a separate pamphlet; the Articles

of Religion, the Sacramental, Ordination, and other administrative forms of the Ritual, or 'Sunday Service,' were subsequently copied into the Discipline, and the Collection of
Psalms and Hymns were changed into 'The Hymn-book.'
But there are traces of recognition of the Liturgy down to
1792, when all allusions to it disappear.   Many, if not most,
of the early Methodists had been brought up in the English
Church ; to these the Prayer-book was not unacceptable ; but
the later extension of Methodism comprehended, doubtless, a
majority of members whose early education had given them
no such predilection.   Gowns and bands were also used for
some time by the superintendents and elders, but passed
away in like manner."

The system of church institutions and agencies which was
established in America in its rudimental state with the
planting of Methodism in that country,—and which had been
more fully developed in 1784, by the organization of the
Societies into an Episcopal Church,—had at the period at
which we have arrived acquired stability and vigour ; and
what has been its practical results ?   The number of members at the Christmas Conference was not quite fifteen
thousand ; ten years later (1794) it was 67,643 ; ten years
after this, 103,134 ; at the time of Bishop Asbury's death
(1816) the number was more than 200,000 ; and now,
ninety years after its formation, the Church constructed,
animated, and extended by the life and activity of which
Francis Asbury was the principal medium, and, in the subordinate sense, the centre and source, numbers, with its
ten off-shoots, nearly 3,000,000 members, and includes in
its congregations about 8,000,000 souls.   And the church
property alone of the Methodist Episcopal Church is estimated at 74,875,000 dollars !

But these prodigious results have not been obtained without self-sacrificing effort. A philosophical analyst of the movement would no doubt point out a vast accumulation of conditions which were more or less favourable to its progress ; but no philosophical principles can adequately account for its unparalleled success, which do not recognize Divine agency as the prime cause of that success, and, subordinately, in union and sympathy with the Divine, the agency of men who, like St. Paul, had *the mind of Christ*, and were self-denying " workers together with Him." The movement was promoted by the combined efforts of many like-minded men, who quickened, aided, and encouraged one another ; and circulating amongst them all, as their life, guide, and " ensample," was FRANCIS ASBURY.

CHAPTER XV.

WE return to the point in the course of our narrative
from which we a little while ago departed. We
left the adventurous Bishop in the western parts of North
Carolina, preparing (April, 1788) for his journey over the
Alleghany mountains into Tennessee, to visit the recently-
formed stations in that region, and hold a Conference with
the few toiling and suffering preachers there. One of these
preachers, the presiding-elder, was John Tunnell; another
was Thomas Ware, who, in an account of the visit, supplies
certain details which Asbury has characteristically omitted.

Speaking of the moral character of the people, Ware says,
" Many were refugees from justice. Some there were who
had borrowed money, or were otherwise in debt, and had
left their creditors and securities to do the best they could ;
some had been guilty of heinous or scandalous crimes, and
had fled from justice ; others had left their wives, and were

living with other women." The country was also infested
with infuriated Indians. Ware stated that he once narrowly
escaped being murdered by one of them. "My course led
through a fine bottom, covered chiefly with the crab-apple
tree. I passed along very slowly, making observations
upon the richness and beauty of the country, and had
thoughts of halting to muse a little in the grove." But,
reminding himself that he was in the region of subtle and
incensed Red men, he quickened his pace. He had not
proceeded far when his horse suddenly stopped and wheeled
about. "The same moment I caught a glimpse," he says,
"of an Indian, but at too great a distance to reach me with
his rifle. I gave my horse the reins, and hastened to the
nearest settlement to give the alarm. I had been told that
some horses were singularly afraid of an Indian. Be that
as it may, I have reason to suppose that the sudden fright
which mine took at seeing one was the means, under God,
of saving me from death or captivity." In further proof of
the reality of the peril in which he and all the preachers
lived, he adds, " I was preaching at the house of a man who
had invited us by letter to visit their settlement, when we
were alarmed with the cry of 'Indians.' The terror this
cry excited at the time none can imagine, except those who
witnessed it. Instantly every man flew to his rifle, and
sallied forth to ascertain the ground of the alarm. On
coming out we saw two lads, running with all speed, and
screaming, 'The Indians have killed mother!' We followed
them about a quarter of a mile, and witnessed the affecting
scene of a woman weltering in her blood. The savages were
concealed in a cane-brake, and, coming up slily behind a
fallen tree, so as not to be discovered by her, they drove
the tomahawk into her head before she knew they were
near. The Indian who did the bloody deed was seen by the

boys just as he struck their mother ; but they were at a sufficient distance to make their escape." This event the preacher turned to account by basing upon it an admonitory funeral sermon, which brought many of his hearers, some of whom had been sadly degraded by immorality, to a better state of mind and life. They entreated him with tears to visit them again, and on his re-arrival there, ten or twelve were found united in fellowship as earnest and humble Christians.

Starting for this district on a Monday morning, with hopeful feelings with reference to his Sunday's labours, Asbury says, " After getting our horses shod, we made a move for Holston, and entered upon the mountains ; the first of which I called Steel, the second Stone, and the third Iron mountain. They are rough and difficult to climb. We were spoken to on our way by most awful thunder and lightning. accompanied by heavy rain. We crept for shelter into a little dirty house, where the filth might have been taken from the floor with a spade. We felt the want of fire, but could get little wood to make it, and what we gathered was wet. At the head of the Watawga we fed, and reached Ward's that night. Coming to the river the next day, we hired a young man to swim over for the canoe, in which we crossed, while our horses swam to the other shore. The waters being up we were compelled to travel an old road over the mountains. Night came on. I was ready to faint with a violent headache. The mountain was steep on both sides : I prayed to the Lord for help. Presently a profuse sweat broke out upon me, and my fever entirely subsided. About nine o'clock we came to Grear's. After taking a little rest here, we set out next morning for Brother Cox's on Holston River. I had trouble enough. Our route lay through the woods, and my pack-horse would neither follow, lead, nor drive, so fond was he of stopping to feed on the green herbage. I tried to lead, and he pulled back. I tied his head up to prevent his grazing, and he ran back. The weather was excessively warm. I was much fatigued, and my temper not a little tried. I took refreshment at I. Smith's, and prayed with the family. Arriving at the river, I was at a loss what to do ; but providentially a man came along who conducted me across. This has been an awful journey to me."

Entertainment had been procured for him at General Russell's, " a most kind family in deed and truth." He arrived there on Saturday, and henceforth his gallant host welcomed to his home—an oasis in the desert—all the preachers who laboured within its reach. The intention of Asbury was to have gone forward without delay to a place called Half Acres, where a Conference was appointed to be held. " But," says Ware, " as the road by which he had to travel was infested with hostile savages, so that it could not be passed over except by considerable companies, he was detained for a week after the time appointed to commence it. But we were not idle ; and the Lord gave us many souls in the place where we were assembled, *among whom were General Russell and lady,* the latter a sister of the illustrious Patrick Henry. I mention these particulars because they were the firstfruits of our labours at this Conference. On the Sabbath we had a crowded audience, and Tunnell preached an excellent sermon, which produced good effect. His discourse was followed by a number of powerful exhortations. The Bishop preached on Phil. ii. 5—9. When the meeting closed Mrs. Russell came to me and said, ' I thought I was a Christian ; but, sir, I am not a Christian ; I am the veriest sinner upon earth. I want you and Mr. Mastin to come with Mr.

Tunnell to our house, and pray for us, and tell us what we must do to be saved.' So we went and spent much of the afternoon in prayer, especially for Mrs. Russell. But she did not obtain comfort. Being much exhausted, the preachers retired to a pleasant grove, near at hand, to spend a short time. On returning to the house, we found Mrs. Russell praising the Lord, and the General walking the floor and weeping bitterly. At length he sat down quite exhausted. This scene was in a high degree interesting to us. To see the old soldier and statesman, the proud opposer of godliness, trembling, and earnestly inquiring what he must do to be saved, was an affecting sight. But the work ended not here. The conversion of Mrs. Russell, whose zeal, good sense, and amiableness of character were proverbial, together with the penitential grief so conspicuous in the General, made a deep impression on the minds of many, and numbers were brought in before the Conference closed. The General rested not until he knew his adoption ; and he continued a faithful and an official member of the Church, constantly adorning the doctrine of God our Saviour, unto the end of his life."

The Conference continued three days, on each of which, besides presiding at the sittings, the Bishop preached. " The weather," he says, " was cold ; the room without fire, and otherwise uncomfortable. We, nevertheless, retained our seats until we had finished the essential parts of our business."

He returned to General Russell's, but only for a night ; and, visiting the distant settlements, he jotted down these notes of his journeys : " *Sun*. Rode to a chapel near New River, where I preached. After eating a morsel, we hasted on our way. A twenty miles' ride through the mountains brought us to our lodgings for the night. *Mon*. We rode about fifty miles, and were weary enough. *Tues.* After riding nearly thirty miles, we came to McKnight's Chapel in North Carolina. Here I preached on Peter's denial of Christ. Thence we went to Hill's. After meeting we proceeded to the neat and well-improved town of Salem. Came to the Quarterly-meeting. The Word appeared to have effect. *Frid.* was a damp, rainy day, and I was unwell with a slow fever and pain in my head. However I rode to Smith's Chapel and preached ; and thence to Brother Harrison's, on Dan River, and preached. In the space of one week we have ridden, through rough mountainous tracts of country, about three hundred miles. Brothers Poythress and Tunnell, and myself, have had serious views of things, and mature counsels together."

In North Carolina he continues his perilous daily rides of twenty or thirty miles, and his daily preachings in barns or newly and roughly-built chapels, until he re-enters Virginia, where he holds a Conference, ordains elders and deacons ; has " a gracious season," and is " much blessed " in preaching ; and, recording that he finds " the town-folks remarkably kind and attentive—the people of God in much love," he again climbs the mountains, and passes over into West Virginia. " And now," says he, " our troubles began.

" *Tues.*, *July* 8, 1788. Reached McNeal's, where almost the whole settlement came together. I found freedom in . preaching from, ' Come unto Me, all ye that labour and are heavy laden.' Our brother Phœbus had to answer questions propounded to him until evening. *Wed.* We rode to a very remote and exposed house, where we found good lodgings, for the place. *Thurs.* We had to cross the Alleghany mountains again, at a bad passage. Our course lay over mountains and through valleys, and the mud and mire were such as might scarcely be expected in December. We came to an

12

old forsaken habitation in Tygart's Valley. Here our horses grazed about while we boiled our meat. Midnight brought us up at Jones's, after riding forty or perhaps fifty miles. The old man, our host, was kind enough to wake us up at four o'clock in the morning. We journeyed on through devious lonely wilds, where no food might be found except what grew in the woods. We met with two women who were going to see their friends, and to attend the Quarterly-meeting at Clarksburg. Near midnight we stopped at A——'s, who hissed his dogs at us; but the women were determined to get to the Quarterly-meeting, so we went in. Our supper was tea. Brothers Phœbus and Cook took to the woods. I lay along the floor on a few deer-skins, with the fleas. That night our poor horses got no corn, and next morning they had to swim across the Monongahela. After a twenty miles' ride we came to Clarksburg, and man and beast were so out-done that it took us ten hours to accomplish it. I lodged with Colonel Jackson. Our meeting was held in a long close room. After administering the sacrament I was well satisfied to take my leave. We rode thirty miles to Father Haymond's after three o'clock on Sunday afternoon, and made it nearly eleven before we came in. About midnight we went to rest, and rose at five o'clock next morning. O how glad should I be of a plain clean plank to lie on, as preferable to most of the beds! The gnats are almost as troublesome here as the mosquitoes in the lowlands of the seaboard. The people are, many of them, of the boldest cast of adventurers."

On the return journey he held a Conference at Union Town, and met Mr. Whatcoat, who had been circulating among the settlements of that tract, preaching and administering the sacrament. Leaving this Conference, which was marked by " great peace, love, and prudence," he and Whatcoat, "both sick," travelled together over the mountains "along a very bad road," and came to the Virginia Baths, where, during heavy rains which obliged them to rest from travelling, he was "closely engaged in reading, writing, and prayer."

In 1790 he and his early friend, Mr. Whatcoat, crossed the mountains together again, to hold the first Conference in the interior of Kentucky. Not many years had elapsed since Colonel Boone first penetrated the wilds and woods of this district, and proclaimed the luxuriant fertility of its soil, and its extraordinary facilities for forming settlements. His reports induced many adventurers, principally Virginians, to pour into it, and settle in groups of families in its rich and beautiful valleys. Some of these hardy men were Methodists—a few of them local-preachers ; and one object of their accompanying their friends was to hold religious services among them. In 1786, six years before this fine region had been made a State of the Union, two preachers were appointed to it, as *the Kentucky Circuit.* This was now divided into three, which numbered thirteen hundred members. The privations and sufferings of the preachers had been extreme ; but they had been sustained under them by extraordinary success. Poythress was the presiding-elder of the district.

The Bishop set out with his companion from the south-east. The first night they slept in "a cabin without a cover, except what a 'few boards supplied ;" and they "had very heavy thunder and lightning, and most hideous yelling of wolves around." The next morning they proceeded on their way "through the rain, and crossed the Stone Mountain. Those who wish to know how rough it is," says the Bishop, "may tread in our path ! We came on to the dismal place called Roan's Creek. Here we took a good breakfast on our tea, bacon, and bread. Reaching

the river we had to swim our horses, and ourselves to cross
in a canoe.   Up the Iron Mountain we ascended, where we
had many a seat to rest and many a weary step to climb.
At length we halted for the night.   Now it is that we must
prepare for danger in going through the wilderness.   I received a faithful letter from brother Poythress in Kentucky,
encouraging me to come.   This letter I think well deserving
of publication.   I found the poor preachers indifferently
clad, with emaciated bodies, and subject to hard fare ; yet I
hope they are rich in faith.''

A day or two afterwards he wrote, '' We came on to
brother Bull's, who wrought for us, *gratis*, what we wanted
in shoeing our horses.   Thence we went on groping through
the woods.   We are now in a house in which a man was
killed by the savages ; and, O poor creatures, they are but
one remove from savages themselves !   I consider myself in
danger ; but my God will keep me.''   They had pushed forward to this spot in the expectation of meeting there an
escort of Kentucky people, but none had arrived ; and,
turning out their horses to graze, they strayed off—'' so
here,'' says Asbury, '' we are anchored indeed ! ''   In a day
or two the horses were found.   '' We then,'' says Mr.
Whatcoat, who also describes this expedition, '' travelled
about the settlement, and held meetings for about a fortnight.   One morning Bishop Asbury told me that he had
dreamed that he saw two men well mounted, who told him
they were come to conduct him to Kentucky, and had left
their company in the Grassy Valley.   So it was.   After
preaching they made their appearance.   We then got our
horses shod, mustered up a little provision, joined our company, and passed through the wilderness, about one hundred
and fifty miles.   The first day we came to the new station.
Here we lay under cover ; but some of the company had to

watch all night.   The next two nights we watched by turns,
—some watching while others lay down.   As there was not a
good understanding between the savages and the white
people, we travelled in jeopardy ; but I think I never
travelled with more solemn awe and serenity of mind.   As
we fed our horses three times a day, so we had prayer three
times."

The Bishop says, " Besides brother Whatcoat and myself,
we were sixteen men, having thirteen guns only.   We
moved on very swiftly, considering the roughness of the
way, travelling, by my computation, thirty-five miles the
first day, forty-five the second, about fifty the third ; also
the next day forty-five, passing the branches of Rock
Castle river.   On our journey we saw the rock whence the
river derives its name.   It is not unlike an old church or
castle in Europe.   I was strangely outdone for want of sleep,
having been greatly deprived of it in my journey through the
wilderness, which is like being at sea, in some respects,
and in others worse.   Our way is over mountains, steep
hills, deep rivers, and muddy creeks ; a thick growth of
reeds for miles together ; and no inhabitants but wild beasts
and savage men.   Sometimes, before I am aware, my ideas
would be leading me to look out ahead for a fence ; and I
would, without reflection, try to recollect the houses we
should have lodged at in the wilderness.   I slept about an
hour the first night, and about two the last.   We ate no
regular meal ; our bread grew short, and I was much spent.
I saw the graves of the slain, twenty-four in one camp.   I
learnt that they had set no guard, and that they were up
late, playing at cards.   A poor woman of the company had
dreamed three times that the Indians had surprised and
killed them all.   She urged her husband to entreat the
people to set a guard, but they only abused him, and cursed

him for his pains. As the poor woman was relating her last dream the Indians came upon the camp; she and her husband sprung away, one east, the other west, and escaped. She afterwards came back and witnessed the carnage. These poor sinners appeared to be ripe for destruction. I received an account of the death of another wicked wretch who was shot through the heart, although he had vaunted, with horrid oaths, that no Creek Indian could kill him. These are some of the melancholy accidents to which the country is subject for the present; as to the land, it is the richest body of fertile soil I have ever beheld."

The Conference was held at the house of Mr. Masterson, near Lexington, where the Bishop was entertained in comfort. The business, he says, was conducted "in great love and harmony. I ordained Wilson Lee, Thomas Williamson, and Barnabas McHenry elders. We had preaching noon and night, and souls were converted, and the fallen restored. My soul has been blessed among these people, and I am exceedingly pleased with them. I would not, for the worth of all the place, have been prevented in this visit, having no doubt that it will be for the good of the present and rising generation. It is true that such exertions of mind and body are trying. But I am supported under them; if souls are saved it is enough. Brother Poythress is much alive to God. We fixed a plan for a school, and called it *Bethel*; and obtained a subscription of upwards of £300, in land and money, towards its establishment."

He spent about a fortnight in visiting the preaching-places under the care of the few heroic men who were stationed in that wild region; was gratified to meet with an old Methodist friend from Virginia who offered him a hundred acres of land for the projected school; preached repeatedly to congregations of varied character; recorded

that under one sermon "four souls professed to be converted
to God;" lodged one night under a tree, "very feverish
and unwell;" then set out with a large and helpless company on his return to Holston.   He says, "We had about
fifty people, twenty of whom were armed, and five of whom
might have stood fire.   To preserve order and harmony we
had articles drawn up for, and signed by, our company; and
I managed the people for travelling according to the regulations agreed upon.   Some disaffected gentlemen, who
would neither sign nor come under discipline, had yet the
impudence to murmur when left behind.   The first night we
lodged some miles beyond the Hazel-patch.   The next day
we discovered signs of Indians, and some thought they
heard voices; we therefore thought it best to travel on, and
did not encamp until three o'clock, halting on the east side
of Cumberland river.   We had gnats enough.   We had an
alarm; but it turned out to be a false alarm.   A young
gentleman, a Mr. Alexander, behaved exceedingly well;
but his tender frame was not adequate to the fatigue to be
endured, and he had well-nigh fainted on the road to Cumberland Gap.   Brother Massie was captain; and, finding I
had gained authority among the people, I acted somewhat in
the capacity of an adjutant and quarter-master amongst
them.   At the foot of the mountain the company separated;
the greater part went with me to Powell's river.   Here we
slept on the earth, and next day made the Grassy Valley.
Several of the company who were not Methodists expressed
their high approbation of our conduct, and most affectionately
invited us to their houses."   The journeys of each day were
as follows :—"Monday, forty-five miles; Tuesday, fifty
miles; Wednesday, sixty miles."

On Thursday he reached Captain Amie's, "where," he
says, with thankfulness, "I had a bed to rest on."   The

next day he returned to the house of General Russell, where
he tarried till Monday, witnessing and rejoicing over the
signs of a spiritual change in Mrs. Russell, preaching on
the Sunday, and ordaining two local-preachers to the office
of deacons; one of them being Mr. Benjamin Van Pelt, a
brother of the Mr. Van Pelt of Staten Island, one of his
earliest friends in America. On Monday, after riding forty-
five or fifty miles, he visited "the pioneer hero," John
Tunnell, now in the last stage of consumption. He found
him "a mere shadow; but very humble and patient under
his affliction." Very shortly afterwards he laid him in his
mountain grave, and preached a funeral sermon on the
occasion, from words not less applicable to him than to the
Apostle who wrote them: "For me to live is Christ, and
to die is gain."

On re-entering North Carolina he hastened to McKnight's
to attend the Conference, which he found had been waiting
for him nearly a fortnight. "We rejoiced together," he
says, "and my brethren received me as one brought from
the jaws of death." A few months after his return he
received a letter from Poythress, in which that fervid
fellow-labourer says, "There is a general revival through
my district. At our last Quarterly-meeting we had, it was
supposed, seven hundred souls. . . . O my dear father, I
think that I am as willing to suffer for my dear Master as
you are. I believe that you feel much for the rising
generation in America. May God bless you with a long
and useful life, and success in all your labours! The
Indians are still doing mischief. Not far from the first
house you came to after you passed through the wilderness.
they killed seven men and wounded one."

These bold and hurriedly-penned descriptions are best
left to produce their own impression. To read them as

they stand, is to be reminded involuntarily of the chief
causes of the success which those consecrated men achieved.
They evidently felt that life was real ; that the spiritual
world on which they verged was a reality ; that the Gospel
was a true message from God, and a real power unto salvation unto every one that believeth ; that none are so
deeply degraded as to be beyond its influence ; and that
their call to preach it was not a sham or a fancy, but a true
call from Him who said, "Lo, I am with you always."
They were men of might, because men of faith.

The Bishop's next journey into Kentucky occurred in the
spring of 1792, and was as eventful, perilous, and trying as
the former. I again give the account of it in his own
words. His companions were immigrants, and a hired
guard. He says, "We took half-a-day in having the
smith's work done, in fitting our horses for the journey.
We have confused accounts of Indians. Our guard rested
on the Sabbath-day within four miles of the wilderness. I
preached to all the people I could collect. On Tuesday we
reached Richland Creek, and were preserved from harm.
After crossing the Lamel river, which we were compelled
to swim, we came to Rock Castle Station, where we found
such a set of sinners as made it next to hell itself. On
Wednesday we again swam the river. My little horse was
ready to fail in the course of the day. I was steeped in the
water up to the waist. About seven o'clock, with hard
pushing, we reached the Crab Orchard. How much I have
suffered in this journey is only known to God and myself.
What added much to its disagreeableness is the extreme
filthiness of the houses. I wrote an address on behalf of
Bethel Schools." Arrived at that place, he met the preachers
and a large concourse of settlers from all parts of the
district. "I found it necessary," he says, "to change the

plan of the school, to make it more comfortable to the scholars in cold weather. I am too much in company, and hear so much about Indians, convention, treaty, killing and scalping, that my attention is drawn more to these things than I could wish. I found it good to get alone in the woods and converse with God. In the Conference I was closely employed with the travelling and local preachers, with the leaders and stewards." And it is not difficult to understand how invaluable his guidance was felt to be by those simple, rustic, and, many of them, inexperienced men; how immense the comfort they found in his sympathy with them; and how greatly his example of self-sacrifice, and his intense ardour of spirit, must have served to sustain them in their work. He adds that "vast crowds of people attended public worship."

On Monday, April 30, he says, "An alarm was spreading of a depredation committed by the Indians, on the east and west frontiers of the settlement. In the former, report says one man was killed. In the latter, many men, with women and children. Everything is in motion. There having been so many about me at Conference, my rest was much broken. I hoped now to repair it, and get refreshed before I set out to return through the wilderness; but the continual arrival of people until midnight, the barking of dogs, and other annoyances, prevented. Next night we reached the Crab Orchard, where thirty or forty people were compelled to crowd into one mean house. We could get no more rest here than we did in the wilderness. We came the old way by Scagg's Creek and Rock Castle, supposing it to be safer, as it was a road less frequented, and therefore less liable to be waylaid by the savages. My body by this time is well tried. I had a violent fever and pain in the head, such as I had not lately felt. I stretched myself on the cold ground, and, borrowing clothes to keep me warm, by the mercy of God I slept four or five hours. Next morning we set off early, and passed beyond Richland Creek. Here we were in danger, if anywhere. I could have slept, but was afraid. Seeing the drowsiness of the company, I walked the encampment, and watched the sentries the whole night. Early next morning we made our way to Robinson's Station. We had the best company I ever met with—thirty-six good travellers, and a few warriors; but we had a pack-horse, some old men, and two tired horses—these were not the best part. On Saturday, May 5th, through infinite mercy we came safe to Crabb's. Rest, poor house of clay, from such exertions! Return, O my soul, to thy rest!"

A few days afterwards he writes: "I am more than ever convinced of the need and propriety of Annual Conferences, and of greater changes among the preachers. I am sensible the Western parts have suffered by my absence. I lament this, and also deplore my loss of strict communion with God, occasioned by the necessity I am under of constant riding, change of place, company, loss of sleep, and the difficulties of clambering over rocks and mountains, and journeying at the rate of seven or eight hundred miles per month, and sometimes forty or fifty miles a day."

Ought it not to have been BISHOP ASBURY whom Wordsworth apostrophized thus—

"To thee, O saintly man,
Patriarch of a wide-spreading family,
Remotest lands and unborn times shall turn,—
To thee,
As one who rightly taught how zeal should burn;
As one who drew from out Faith's holiest urn
The purest stream of *patient energy* "?

CHAPTER XVI.

SCHOOLS AND COLLEGES.

Proposal to build a "Kingswood School"—Coke prefers a College—The name Cokesbury invented—Foundation-stone laid—The Site—The Dimensions—Principles on which to be Conducted—True End of Instruction—The College opened—Other Schools projected—Cokesbury Burnt down—A new College and Church at Baltimore—These also Burnt—School in Georgia—Bethel in Kentucky—Bethel in South Carolina.

REFERENCE has been made to Bethel School in Kentucky. This, however, was not the first or only educational institution that Asbury founded. No man could have felt more deeply than he the value of Christian education as an auxiliary to the work of evangelization; and no man could have been more solicitous that all education should be Christianized. More than four years before the arrival of Dr. Coke he had projected the erection of a seminary, to be conducted on the same principles as that which Mr. Wesley had founded at Kingswood, and to be called *Kingswood School in America.* John Dickins, he tells us, assisted him to procure subscriptions for this purpose: "Gabriel Long and brother Bustion were the first subscribers, which I hope will be for the glory of God and good of thousands." He was not able to undertake this work immediately; but he never lost sight of it as a necessary accessory, took every opportunity of interesting the minds of his people in it, and at his very first interview with Dr. Coke at Barrett's Chapel proposed it as one of the schemes of usefulness to be taken into their consideration.

The Doctor naturally regarded the proposition with favour, and it was agreed to lay it before the approaching Conference. But he enlarged the conception. He looked with sanguine eagerness into the future; saw the Methodist Church becoming a great and efficient power in the country, and the Methodist people becoming numerous, wealthy, and occupiers of high positions in social rank; and suggested that, not a school but a college should be the object of contemplation. This design was duly brought before the Conference, which adopted it by a resolution, and also suggested that, in honour of its projectors, as the first bishops of the Church, the college should bear their name in the compound form of *Cokesbury*. The whole scheme was warmly approved by the people, and nearly five thousand dollars were quickly subscribed towards its execution. In the course of a few months a site was procured, plans were prepared and approved, and on the 5th June, 1785, five months after the proposition had been accepted by the Conference, Asbury wrote: "I rode to Abingdon to preach the foundation sermon of Cokesbury College. I stood on the ground where the building is to be erected, and spoke from Psalm lxxviii. 3—6: 'I will utter dark sayings of old, which we have heard and known and our fathers have told us. We will not hide them from their children, shewing to the generation to come the praises of the Lord, and His strength, and His wonderful works that He hath done. For He established a testimony in Jacob and appointed a law in Israel, which He commanded our fathers, that they should make them known to their children; that the generation to come might know them, even the children which should be born, who should arise and declare them to their children.'"

The site of the college was on rising ground near Abingdon, and is said to have been one of the most commanding spots in Maryland. Dr. Coke was delighted with it. He says, "There is not, I believe, a point of it from whence the eye has not a view of at least twenty miles; and in some parts the prospect extends even fifty miles. The water-part forms one of the most beautiful views in the United States; the Chesapeake Bay in all its grandeur, with a fine navigable river, the Susquehanna, which empties itself into it, lying exposed to sight through a great extent of country."

The building, as described by John Dickins, was "one hundred and eighty feet in length from east to west, and forty feet in breadth from north to south, standing on the summit and centre of six acres of land, with an equal descent and proportion of ground on each side."

The principles on which the college was to be conducted were expounded at large in a prospectus drawn up and circulated by the bishops. This document is worthy of being well considered by a student of the movement as a declaration of their views of the province of education, as a help-meet to godliness. It is impossible to mistake Asbury's conceptions on this subject. His business was to save men by the power of the Gospel; but he believed that where the Gospel was effectual it would give freedom and stimulus to the intellectual faculties, and that these, as developed and energized by the Gospel, would conduce by their action to the more complete accomplishment of its great end. He thought of education as the gift of a new power; and was anxious that this power should be used, under the guidance of Christian principle and of a sense of responsibility, not only for the good of the person in whose individual mind it had been created, but for the benefit of the world. "Our first object," said the promoters, "shall be, to answer the design of Christian education, by forming the minds of the youth, through Divine aid, to wisdom and holiness." The curriculum included mathematics, philosophy, the natural sciences, Hebrew, German, French, and the classics. "In teaching the languages," it was said, "care shall be taken to read those authors, and those only, who join together the purity, the strength, and the elegance of their several tongues. And the utmost caution shall be used that nothing immodest be found in any of our books. But this is not all. We shall take care that our books be not only inoffensive, but useful; that they contain as much strong sense and as much genuine morality as possible."

A preparatory school was established in connection with the premises, while they were in process of completion; and the college was formally opened on the 6th December, 1787. Under this date Asbury says, "We opened our college and admitted twenty-five students. I preached on 'Trust in the LORD, and do good,'"—a text beautifully appropriate to his own experience and life at all times. What led him to the choice of another text from which he preached on the occasion, is not so evident. "On the Sabbath," he adds, "I spoke on, 'O man of God, there is death in the pot;' and on Monday, 'They are the seed of the blessed of the LORD, and their offspring with them.'" The principal of the college was the Rev. Mr. Heath, a catholic and devout clergyman, recommended by Mr. Wesley. Bishop Asbury was *ex officio* the President.

So far all seemed to go on well; and Asbury, actuated by a deep sense of the value of a religious education, promoted the erection of schools of the same character, though of a lower grade, elsewhere. But it imposed upon him an immense additional burden of anxiety. The task of raising the necessary funds at that early period placed him under a

perpetual strain ; and he continually received intelligence
respecting the condition and working of the institution
which filled him with disquietude.   On August 10, 1788,—a
few months after the opening, he writes,—" I received heavy
tidings from the college.   Both our teachers have left—one
for incompetency, and the other to pursue riches and
honours.   Had they cost us nothing, the mistake we made
in employing them might be the less regretted."   On the
9th December he records an attempt to burn the college by
fire, put maliciously by some person into one of the cup-
boards.   And after many other references, most of them of
a sombre cast, we find this sad and regretful note :—" We
have now a second and confirmed account that Cokesbury
College is consumed to ashes—a sacrifice of about £10,000
in about ten years !   The foundation was laid in 1785, and
it was burnt December 7, 1795.   Its enemies may rejoice,
and its friends need not mourn.   Would any man give me
£10,000 per year to do and suffer again what I have done
for that house, I would not do it.   The Lord called not Mr.
Whitefield nor the Methodists to build colleges : I wished
only for schools ; Dr. Coke wanted a college.   I feel distressed at the loss of the library."

Asbury, it is evident, was disheartened, and the sight of
the spot never failed thereafter to rouse within him feelings
of gloom.   Shortly afterwards, however, Dr. Coke had
recrossed the Atlantic, and was again by his side.   He had
not been under the same pressure of care and toil respecting
it as his colleague ; and, undaunted, not only proposed its
immediate restoration, but induced many gentlemen, both at
Abingdon and Baltimore, to subscribe liberally for this purpose.   As it happened, however, that a building at Baltimore was then being offered for sale which could be more
quickly made available for college uses, this was purchased

and suitably fitted up, and the re-erection of Cokesbury abandoned. The friends of the Bishop persistently called this new place *Asbury College* ; but he declined to give it any other designation than the *Academy.* A new church was at the same time wanted and in contemplation ; and, as more land was connected with the premises than they required, it was built upon the same site.

This college was eventually opened with a fairer prospect of success as an educational institute than its predecessor. " The academy," said Asbury, " is crowded. They have five teachers and nearly two hundred scholars." Too soon, however, he was called to refer to this also in a different strain. " Through the imprudence," says Dr. Bangs, " of a few boys who had been making a bonfire with some shavings in an adjoining house, the flames were communicated to the house in which they were assembled, and thence to the church and college, which were, after ineffectual attempts to extinguish the flames, entirely consumed. Thus were the hopes of the friends of education again blasted." " Serious news from Baltimore," exclaimed Asbury ; " the academy, and our church in Light-street, with Brother Hawkins's elegant house, all destroyed by fire! The loss we sustain in the college, academy, and church, I estimate from fifteen to twenty thousand pounds. But I concluded God loveth the people of Baltimore, and He will keep them poor, to make them pure."

His school projects at this period were scarcely more successful, and each of them was a source of intense anxiety to him. In March, 1789, he records the appointment of a committee " to procure five hundred acres of land, for the establishment of a school in the State of Georgia." This was at the first Georgia Conference. Dr. Coke was present, and gives an account of the same transaction. The

13

representations of each writer are sufficiently characteristic. "We agreed," says the Doctor, "to build a college in Georgia, and our principal friends in this State have engaged to purchase at least two thousand acres of good land for its support. For this purpose there were twelve thousand five hundred pounds' weight of tobacco subscribed in one congregation, which will produce, clear of all expenses, about one hundred pounds sterling. We have engaged to erect it, God willing, within five years, and do most humbly entreat Mr. Wesley to permit us to name it *Wesley College*, as a memorial of his affection for poor Georgia, and of our great respect for him."

But Dr. Coke must have misinterpreted the purposes of the people of Georgia, and over-estimated their capabilities, when he wrote this. Asbury, with his better acquaintance with them, had more limited and sober expectations. He saw that the most suitable and the only feasible project was not a collegiate institution, but a school for the children of the poor, to be supported by private charity. This accordingly he zealously promoted. "The school for charity boys," he says in the autumn of the same year, "much occupies my mind. Our annual expenditure will amount to £200, and the aid we get is but trifling. The poverty of the people and the general scarcity of money are the great source of our difficulties. The support of our preachers, who have families, absorbs our collections, so that neither do our elders nor our charity-school get much. We have the poor, but they have no money; and the worldly, wicked rich we do not choose to ask." "I received some relief for my poor orphans," he gratefully subjoins a day or two later; and again, full of hope and satisfaction: "We have a prospect of obtaining a hundred acres of land for every hundred pounds we can raise and pay, for the support of

Wesley and Whitefield School. On Monday we rode out to view three hundred acres of land offered for the same purpose."

It was with this scheme fresh in his mind, and with these prospects of encouragement from the Legislature by grants of land for the endowment of the institution that, two months after the entry just quoted, he proposed to Francis Poythress to endeavour to establish a similar school in Kentucky. A hundred acres of land were offered for this purpose by " an old acquaintance from Leesburg," whom Asbury had met in the newly-settled country, and the work was duly entered upon and completed. But, like the kindred institutions, it imposed upon those with whom rested the responsibility of maintaining it a terrible burden of anxiety. Poor Poythress, as presiding-elder in charge of the Kentucky district, is said to have sunk under the weight of care it imposed upon him into a state of temporary insanity. " Bethel Academy," says Dr. Stevens, " started well, but failed, and in its fall dragged down the noble intellect of Poythress." Asbury struggled hard to raise funds for its support. Three whole days, when in another part of the country, he occupied in writing " subscription papers to be sent abroad for the purpose of collecting one hundred pounds ; but," says he, " my expectations are small, the people generally have so little sense of God and religion." Eventually the Legislature was moved to make a grant of six thousand acres of land for its endowment ; but this, in the condition in which it was given, was like the donation of a stone when the children asked for bread. " It remained for a long time unproductive, and proved rather a bill of expense than otherwise."

It is impossible to contemplate this succession of abortive attempts to provide the country with the sound and healthy education it so urgently needed without admiration of the intelligent zeal and forethought of the noble man who originated and directed the movement, and without sympathy with him and his co-workers in their disappointment. But the institutions, like the men who founded them, were in advance of their time. Failure, in some forms of effort, is incident to all reformers, and most of all to moral and religious reformers. After the pause of a few years the work was resumed and carried forward with almost unexampled unanimity and heartiness by the Conference, the people, and the country alike; and at this day Methodist schools, colleges, and universities stud the whole domain of the States.

As a pleasant set-off against this series of failures, I subjoin the following account of a high-school founded by Asbury in South Carolina, as copied by Dr. Strickland from a paper furnished to the *Southern Advocate* :—

"Edward Finch gave thirty acres of land as a site for the Institution. . . During the year 1794 the building was completed, and was formally dedicated by Bishop Asbury on his next annual visit, on the 20th of March, 1795, with a sermon from 1 Thess. v. 16, and was named Mount Bethel. On the succeeding Sabbath Asbury preached again, and held a Lovefeast, which proved to be a blessed season of spiritual refreshing. The school was for six years under the rectorship of the Rev. Mark Moore, a man eminently qualified for the post, assisted by two other teachers, Messrs. Smith and Hammond. At the close of this term of service Mr. Moore resigned, and took charge of a school in Columbia, where, by his influence and preaching ability, which was of the first order, he materially aided in the permanent establishment of Methodism in that city. On the retirement of Mr. Moore, Mr. Hammond, father of ex-Governor Hammond, took charge of the school, and taught it with signal ability for many years. For a number of years Mount Bethel and Willington Academy (in Abbeville District, under the control of the celebrated Dr. Waddell) were the only schools of high grade in the interior of the State, and did much in the educational training of the young men of South Carolina. Mount Bethel was largely patronized, and had from time to time students from Georgia and North Carolina. A number of the leading men in our own State in subsequent years were prepared for college at Mount Bethel, among whom were the Hon. John Caldwell and Chancellor James J. Caldwell, of Newberry District, Judge Earl, the first ex-Governor Manning, of South Carolina, and William and Wesley Harper, sons of the Rev. John Harper. The first and second classes who graduated in the South Carolina College, received the preparatory training here also. Wesley Harper graduated in the second class of the college, and died soon after. William Harper graduated in the third class in 1808, and subsequently became, as is well known, one of the first jurists in the country."

CHAPTER XVII.

METHODISM has never been forward to build upon another man's foundation, or to obtrude itself where other agencies were doing the work efficiently which it believed itself specially called to prosecute. For this reason probably it extended its operations on the American continent southwards as far as Georgia, and westwards among the scattered settlements in the great valley of the Mississippi, before it made any regular attempt to establish itself in New England. There, it might have been presumed, if anywhere in that vast region, there would be no lack of spiritual labourers, and no religious destitution. Descendants of the "Pilgrim Fathers," or inheritors of the spiritual advantages which they had laboured so hard to secure in Church and State for all generations, what deficiency of holy light and influence could there be to deplore in their behalf?

But men are not spiritual and God-like by natural descent. nor are they made so by creeds, formularies, and elaborate external appliances ; and to become bigotedly attached to particular forms and dogmas, without possessing the clear thought they were intended to express, and without experiencing the spiritual life they were given to feed and guard, is to become narrow, pharisaical, and intolerant. And this, too generally, was at this period the character of New England.   With its religious belief defined, its religious rites formalised, its ordinances of religious worship pre-. scribed and established, its religious dogmas interwoven with its political enactments, and with its towns and villages well supplied with churches, colleges, and schools,—its population had long settled into a dead religious calm ; and, " trusting in lying words," were saying, " The temple of the LORD, the temple of the LORD, the temple of the LORD, are these ! "

At length the duty of endeavouring to rouse these formal and exclusive people to a degree of religious earnestness began to press itself upon the attention of some of the preachers. The first to be appointed to this task was Jesse Lee, whom we last saw with Asbury at Charleston, South Carolina.   He had become well imbued with the spirit of his leader, and, receiving his commission from him at the New York Conference of 1789, he promptly entered upon the work, and for twelve months prosecuted it alone, amidst many discouragements, but with regularity and unfailing energy and persistence.   " I set out," he said, " with prayer to God for His blessing on my endeavours, and with an expectation of many oppositions."   He preached his first sermon under an apple-tree on the public way near the town of Norwalk, in Connecticut, after having been first refused the use of a private house, and afterwards of an old building, for which he had applied.   Taking his lonely stand, he began to sing and pray, and gradually about twenty people gathered around him, to whom he preached from the text, " Ye must be born again."   After the service " I told the people, " he says, "that I intended to be with them again in two weeks; and, if any of them would open their houses to receive me, I should be glad; but, if they were not willing, we would meet at the same place." Thence he hastened to Fairfield, asked for and obtained the use of the court-house, and, with the aid of the schoolmaster and his own lusty singing, succeeded in collecting a congregation of thirty or forty hearers. He went on to New Haven and to Stratford, where also he obtained the use of the court-house. And thus he continued his untiring labours, journeying and preaching, without the aid or sympathy of a single colleague, until the 27th of February, 1790, when he received, at Dantown, the unexpected and joyful intelligence that three preachers were on their way to join him.

These were Jacob Brush, George Roberts, and Daniel Smith. The field had been prepared for these additional labourers by their courageous pioneer; but so few persons had been as yet enrolled as Methodists that their number barely doubled that of the preachers. The four at once distributed themselves over the ground previously traversed by Lee alone, carrying on their work on the evangelistic principles now so well understood; and they shortly welcomed amongst them Freeborn Garrettson, accompanied by the eloquent and effective negro-preacher, called "Black Harry." This man, whose name was Harry Hosier, had now been doing valuable service for about ten years. Asbury first took him, when travelling in the South, to preach to the coloured people, and he afterwards attended Dr. Coke in one or two of his excursions, occasionally preaching to white as well as coloured congregations. He was popular in New England as he had been elsewhere, and contributed to rouse among the staid and stately inhabitants of those States an unwonted interest in the Methodist movement.   But this interest was not unmixed with strong antipathy to Methodist doctrine.   " We have hard work," said Garrettson, " to plant what they call Arminianism in this country.   We stand in need of the wisdom of the serpent and the harmlessness of the dove."

On Monday, October 4th, 1790, Lee " entered the Conference in New York city, to solicit additional labourers for New England.   What could he report of his services since he left the same body in June of the preceding year ? A tale of as hard fare and as hard labours, doubtless, as any one there could relate, except possibly the venerable man who sat in the chair—the unequalled Asbury.   But not of toils and trials alone could he speak.   Much had been achieved.   Connecticut, Rhode Island, and Eastern Massachusetts had been thoroughly surveyed for more definite plans of labour.   He, himself, had proclaimed, the principles of Methodism in all the five New England States.   He had removed much prejudice, and put the whole country more or less in expectation of further efforts.   Prior to his departure from Connecticut to Boston he had formed definitively two circuits, Stamford, or Reading, as it was afterwards called, and New Haven, and subsequently the general outlines of another in Eastern Massachusetts.   His fellow-labourers had also extended their travels in many directions, so that five circuits were recorded on the *Minutes* at the Conference of 1790.   Nearly two hundred souls had been united in classes,—a remarkably large number if we consider the formidable obstacles which obstructed every movement of the few labourers in the field.   Two chapels, at least, had been erected ; one in the parish of Stratfield (town of Stratford) by the Society of Weston (now Easton), called *Lee's Chapel*—the first Methodist one built in New England ; the second, in Dantown, partially built when Lee welcomed

into it his newly-arrived assistants on the 27th February.
Such were the results, thus far; and, with these for his
arguments, he could not fail to intercede successfully for his
new field.   He spent three hours in a private interview with
Asbury, discussing its claims.   That good and far-seeing
man not only complied with his wishes so far as to despatch
with him additional labourers, but resolved to visit the
Eastern States himself in the course of the ensuing year." *

Asbury left New York for the States of New England on
the 1st June, 1791; travelled through heavy rain to New
Rochelle, where he introduced Methodism immediately after
his arrival in the country twenty years before; and where, as
the result, there was now a large Society.   He preached
there in the church; proceeded the next day to White
Plains, and preached in the court-house; the same day to
Northcastle and preached again; the following day he rode
to Bedford, and preached in the town-house to about two
hundred hearers; and on the 4th he came to Wilton, within
the State of Connecticut, where he preached to a serious and
attentive audience in a private house, and then rode forward
to Reading.   " We have travelled about twenty-four miles
this day," he says, " over very rough roads.   This country
is very hilly and open; not unlike that about the Peak of
Derbyshire.   I have confidence in God that this visit to
New England will be blessed to my own soul, and the souls
of others.   We are now in Connecticut, and never out of sight
of a house.   Sometimes we have a view of many churches and
steeples, built very neatly of wood, either for use, orna-
ment, piety, policy, or interest,—or it may be some of all
these.   I do feel as if there had been religion in this country
once, and I apprehend there is a little in form and theory left.

---

* Dr. Stevens.

There may have been a praying ministry and people here ; but I fear they are now spiritually dead, and am persuaded that family and private prayer is very little practised. Could these people be brought to constant, fervent prayer, the Lord would come down and work wonderfully among them."

On the 5th, which was Sunday, he preached in the morning to about three hundred attentive hearers assembled in a barn at Reading, and in the evening to "a multitude of people " in a Presbyterian meeting-house at Newtown,— " the young laughing and playing in the galleries, and the aged below seeming to be heavy and lifeless." He "was sick and weary." On Monday he gave an exhortation to a little gathering in a private house at Stepney ; then moved on to Chestnut-hill, where, as proper notice of his coming had not been given, his congregation was at first but small ; before he had concluded, however, many other persons were added to it, and he began again speaking, he says, for about forty minutes in as pointed a manner as he well could. He concluded the day with "a small family meeting " in a friend's house. On Tuesday he arrived at Stratford, where Mr. Lee had formed the first class in New England. "Time was," he said, as he entered this town, " when I should have thought the prospects here were very great,—the people attend in great multitudes. I find it necessary to guard against painful anxiety, on the one hand, as well as against lukewarmness, on the other. Good news ! They have voted that the town-house shall be shut ! Well, where shall we preach ? Some of the select men,—one, at least,—granted access. I felt unwilling to go, as it is always my way not to push myself into any public-house. We had close work on Isaiah lv. 6, 7. Some smiled, some laughed, some swore, some talked, some prayed, some wept. Had it been a house of our own, I should not have been surprised had the windows been broken. I refused to preach there any more ; and it was well I did—two of the esquires were quite displeased at our admittance. We met the class and found some gracious souls. The Methodists have a Society consisting of about twenty members, some of them converted ; but they have no house of worship. They may now make a benefit of a calamity ; being denied the use of other houses, they will the more earnestly labour to get one of their own." The next day he preached in the house of one of the members. "Finding that most of those who attended were serious, I spoke on our blessed Lord's invitation, Matt. xi. 28—30. It was a time of comfort to the few seekers and believers present."

On Thursday he reached New Haven, where an unusual audience awaited him. His appointments, he found, had been published in the newspapers. "Everything was quiet. We called on the sheriff. We then put up our horses at the Bull Tavern, near the College-yard. I was weary and unwell. I had the honour of having President Styles, Dr. W., and the Rev. Mr. E., with several of the collegians, to hear me. When I had concluded, no man spoke to me. I thought of dear Mr. Whitefield's words to Mr. Boardman and Mr. Pilmore at their first coming over to America : ' Ah,' said he, ' if ye were Calvinists, ye would take the country before ye.' We visited the College-chapel at the hour of prayer : I wished to go through the whole to inspect the interior arrangements, but no one invited me. The divines were grave, and the students were attentive ; they treated me like a fellow-Christian in coming to hear me preach, and like a stranger in other respects. Should Cokesbury or Baltimore ever furnish the opportunity, I, in my turn, will requite their behaviour by treating them as friends, brethren, and gentlemen." Cokesbury, which so soon afterwards perished, did not afford him the opportunity of requiting, in the way he proposed, the attentions shown him at Yale. But other Methodist bishops have had the pleasure of conducting other learned professors and divines of New Haven, over a college situated much nearer that town than Baltimore; and they, in turn, have been equally ready to receive and treat with courtesy bishops of the Methodist Church, and professors of the neighbouring Methodist College at Middletown.

With more love than ever, he says, for his own warm-hearted people, he pressed onward the next day to Wallingford, and preached in a meeting-house belonging to the Separatists, a strange *home feeling* coming over him as he traced resemblances in the country through which he passed to the rural scenery of England. After preaching at five o'clock the next morning "in a large room, to a small company," he rode forward to Wallingford-Farms, and preached on the strait gate and narrow way that leadeth unto life; "then," he says, "I came to Middlefields, and lodged at the house of a niece of David Brainerd. Here we enjoy the quiet use of a meeting-house." He was "very unwell" on the Sunday; but he, notwithstanding, preached three times, —in the morning and afternoon at Middlefields, and in the evening in the Congregational Church at Middletown, "to a very large, serious, and attentive congregation," not one of whom had the considerateness to inquire, "Master, where dwellest thou?" After the service he had to ride a mile out of town to find accommodation for the night; but he reminded himself that "it was to the poorer classes that this preaching was anciently blessed," and was comforted.

On Monday he proceeded down the Connecticut to Hoddam, "where David Brainerd was born," and thence to

Lyme, where he arrived late at night, and was hospitably received by "a free, open-hearted Baptist minister who rose from his bed" to welcome him. Onward he went "over rocks, and through heat and dust, to New London. "My mind," he observes, "has felt but little temptation to impatience until yesterday and to-day. But, through grace, I do not yield thereto. It is both unreasonable and unchristian to murmur. It betters nothing. To deny ourselves, and to take up our cross daily, is our duty. Let us not flee from it." After preaching at New London—his church the court-house, his subject 2 Peter iii. 15—he continued his journey "over a most dreadful road" to Stonington, to Westerly, Rhode Island, to Charleston, and thence, crossing the Narragansett "in a spacious open boat," to Newport. Here, he says, "we stayed two nights. I lectured the second night from Isaiah lxiv. 1—7. There was some life amongst the people, although it was late, and the congregation like our Lord's disciples before His passion. I expect before many years the Methodists will have a house of worship here. I feel the state of this people,—they are settled upon their lees, and want emptying from vessel to vessel to quicken them."

On Saturday, he writes, "We go hence to Providence. On this journey I felt much humbled. I am unknown, and have small congregations, to which I may add, a jar in sentiment; but I do not dispute. My soul is brought into close communion. I should not have felt for these people and for the preachers as I now do, had I not visited them; perhaps I may do something for them on a future day. We came to Bristol, and should have gone further, but Captain G. saw us and took us to his house. At the request of a few persons, I preached in the court-house to about one hundred people, and enforced, 'The Son of man has come to seek and to save that which is lost,' and found a degree of liberty. Some time ago there was the beginning of a work here, but the few souls who began are now discouraged from meeting together. I fear religion is extinguished by confining it too much to church and Sunday service, and reading of sermons. I feel that I am not among my own people, although I believe there are some who fear God." He preached in the town, and was gratified to find a few inquirers, and to meet with " an old disciple," who gave him an account of his conversion under the ministry of Gilbert Tennant, and told him much about Mr. Whitefield and the olden times; and, though under deep depression while there, he left it believing that the Lord would " shortly visit the town again, and that even we shall have something to do in it." He says that he rested a day at Easton, though he preached once and " the people felt the word. We have had a solemn, happy, and solitary retreat, and my soul entered into renewed life."

He arrived at length at Boston. Boardman had once visited this city, and had induced two or three persons to meet together as Methodists. Lee and Garrettson had been recently there, and had preached on the Common. But little of a decisive character had been accomplished, and Asbury entered the city of the Puritans in depression. " I felt much pressed in spirit," he says, " as if the door was not open. As it was Court time, we were put to some difficulty in getting entertainment. It was appointed for me to preach at Murray's Church,—not at all pleasing to me; and that which made it worse was, that I had only about twenty or thirty people to preach to in a large house. It appeared to me that those who professed friendship for us were ashamed to publish us. On Friday evening I preached again; my congregation was somewhat larger. Owing perhaps to the loudness of my voice, the sinners were noisy in the streets.

My subject was Rev. iii. 17, 18.   I was disturbed, and not
at liberty, although I sought it.   I have done with Boston
until we can obtain a lodging, a house to preach in, and
some to join us.   Some things here are to be admired in the
place and among the people ; their bridges are great works,
and none are ashamed of labour.   Of their hospitality I
cannot boast.   In Charleston,—wicked Charleston,—six years
ago, a stranger, I was kindly invited to eat and drink by
many—here by none.   There are, I think, nine meeting-
houses of the Establishment (Congregational Churches), one
Roman Catholic, two Episcopalian ; the Methodists have
none.   But their time may come."   And his faith in the
future has been justified.   "In our day," says Dr. Stevens,
"some ten churches, some of them among the best orna-
ments of the city, are occupied by his sons in the ministry,
and are more numerous than its Puritan churches at that
time."

Leaving Boston, he says, "I preached at Slade's Tavern,
on my way to Lynn.   Here I was agreeably surprised to
find a house raised for the Methodists.   As a town, I think
Lynn the perfection of beauty.   It is seated on a plain,
under a range of craggy hills, and open to the sea.   There
is a promising Society, an exceedingly well-behaved congregation ; these things, doubtless, made all things pleasing
to me.   Here," he adds, with prophetic confidence which
facts have verified, "we shall make a firm stand ; and
from this central point,—from Lynn,—shall the light of
Methodism and of truth radiate through the State."   Respecting Marblehead, which he next visited, he writes,
"When I entered this town, my heart was more melted
towards its inhabitants than to any in these parts, with the
exception of Lynn.   After consultation, and some alterca-
tion among themselves, the Committee invited me to preach

in Mr. Storey's meeting-house, which I did accordingly at four o'clock, on Acts xxiv. 17, 18.   I was led to speak alarmingly, while I pointed out the Gospel as descriptive of their misery and need of mercy.   Brother Lee preached in the evening to a great number of people, in and about Mr. Martin's house.   Next morning, weak as I was, I could not forbear speaking to them on, ' Seek ye first the kingdom of God.'"

He proceeded to Salem, where he found five churches, "two of them on the New Divinity plan,—that is, regeneration the first work—no repentance, prayer, or faith till this is accomplished."   He was refused the use of any of them.   "I lectured, however," he says, "in the court-house, on Romans v. 6—9.   I looked upon the greater part of my congregation as judges ; and I talked until they, becoming weary, began to leave me.   I have done with Salem until we can get a better stand.   I had the curiosity to visit the *Calvary of the Witches*—that is, those who were destroyed on the charge of witchcraft " (in the time of Cotton Mather). "I saw the graves of many innocent, good people, who were put to death, suffering persecution from those who had suffered persecution,—such, and so strangely contradictory, is man." He next visited Manchester ; preached, by permission of "the select men," in the parish church ; was heard with attention, and offered a fee which he respectfully declined to accept; and then returned to Lynn, where he tarried ten days.

In this place a Society had been formed about four months previously, by Jesse Lee.   He had come thither under the discouragement of repeated repulses at Boston, and was comforted by receiving unexpectedly a cordial welcome from a Mr. Johnson, who opened his house for preaching.   The news of his arrival and purposes quickly spread through the village, and a congregation was collected, among whom were several

14

persons who had sat under the ministry of the Methodists in
the South, and who expressed a desire to be united in Christian fellowship.   Mr. Lee did not accede to their proposal
immediately ; but, leaving with them copies of the " General
Rules," returned to Boston to make another attempt to
obtain a preaching-place.   After a month's absence he
came again to Lynn, and formed there the first Methodist
Society in Massachusetts.   It was composed of eight persons.
They met as a Society-class for the first time on the 20th
February, 1791 ; but on the 27th June, when Asbury
arrived, had increased to nearly a hundred persons, and had
already erected a wooden meeting-house, by which he was
greatly surprised and gratified.   During his sojourn in
this place he preached repeatedly in this hastily-built chapel
(a mere shed, probably) to an attentive congregation, enjoy-
ing, he says, sweet peace, and full of confidence that "God
would work in these States, and give us a great harvest."   He
visited and " conversed freely " with the families, baptized,
and administered the Lord's Supper, and met the classes,
and was engaged for a time in " close reading."

On the 13th July he began his return journey, passing
rapidly through several towns which he enumerates in order ;
but without any observation, except that at one of them
where he stopped to dine he was not allowed to preach,
because the people were united, and did not wish to divide
the parish.   "Their fathers," however, he drily subjoins,
" divided the kingdom and the Church too, and, when they
could not obtain liberty of conscience in England, they
sought it here among wild men and beasts."   At Springfield
he preached in a private house, where his hearers " were a
little moved," and one person was under deep conviction.
Re-entering Connecticut, he preached at two places, where
he had "large and very criticising congregations," though

" some present had feeling hearts." At Windsor the minister received him kindly, he says ; " but did not fail to let us know how lightly he thought of us and of our principles." At Hartford he preached in Mr. S——'s meeting-house, and was attended by three ministers ; and at Litchfield preached in the Episcopal Church, remarking, " I think Morse's account of his countrymen is near the truth. Never have I seen any people who would talk so long, so correctly, and so seriously about trifles." By a rocky, mountainous way he journeyed on by Cornwall and New Britain to Albany, and thence to New York, " weak and unwell, yet happy in God."

On estimating the distances he had travelled during the eight weeks of his absence, he says, " I judge that my journey to Lynn, and my rides through the country thereabouts, have made a distance of little less than five hundred miles ; and thence to Albany nearly the same ; and from Albany to New York not much less." And with reference to the influence of Methodist agency upon the Established churches in this part of the continent, he says, " I am led to think the Eastern Church will find this saying hold true in the Methodists, namely, ' I will provoke you to jealousy by a people that were no people ; and by a foolish nation will I anger you.' " He did not look for large numerical gains as the immediate result of efforts put forth in this district. His hope was that the little leaven of evangelistic zeal deposited there would quicken into new life the mass of cold and formal dogmatism with which it came in contact, and that indirectly vaster results would be achieved than could be computed and represented by figures. On the 28th May, 1789, he had written, with reference to his appointment of Jesse Lee * to labour in these States : " New-England

---

* Lee was specially fitted for this difficult mission, by his kindly and

stretcheth out the hand to our ministry, and I trust that
thousands will shortly feel its influence. *My soul shall praise
the Lord.*" And already thousands had felt its influence,
besides the multitudes who had been gathered into its
Societies and congregations. The increase of membership
during this single year of Asbury's tour of inspection and
evangelizing was nearly nine hundred ; and only twelve
months later he had the satisfaction of again visiting Lynn,
to encourage and strengthen the few labourers scattered
over that vast and thorny field, and to give them the benefit
of his personal survey of it, on the first occasion of their
coming together as a Conference. I close this chapter with
his brief but suggestive account of this first New England
Conference.

He says : " *Thursday, August 2nd.* Our Conference met,
consisting of eight preachers, much united, besides myself.
In Lynn we have the outside of a house completed ; and,

---

genial disposition and his irrepressible humour. Nothing discouraged
him, and his ready tact and aptness of repartee never failed. Dr. Stevens
gives the following amusing example as an illustration. When on his
way to Lynn from Boston after his repulse from that city, as related a
page or two forward, he saw two lawyers "hastening after him on horseback, with evident expectations of amusement. They entered into conversation with him on extemporaneous speaking, one on each side of him.
'Don't you often make mistakes ?' 'Yes.' 'Well, what do you do with
them ? Let them go ?' 'Sometimes I do,' replied the preacher, drily :
'if they are very important, I correct them; if not, or if they express the
truth, though differently from what I had designed, I often let them go.
For instance, if, in preaching, I should wish to quote the text which
says, the devil is a liar and the father of it, and should happen to mis-
quote it, and say he was a *lawyer*, etc., why, it is so near the truth I
should probably let it pass.' 'Humph,' exclaimed the lawyer, 'I don't
know whether you are more a knave or a fool.' 'Neither,' replied Lee,
looking from one to the other; 'I believe I am just between the two.'
The gentlemen of the bar looked at each other, and were soon in advance
hasting on their way."

what is best of all, several souls profess to be converted to God. I preached on 1 John iv. 1—6, and had some life. There was preaching every night. *Saturday, 4th*. I preached an ordination sermon to a very serious congregation, from the words, ' Not that we are sufficient of ourselves to think anything as of ourselves ; but our sufficiency is of God.' *Sabbath Morning, 5th*. I preached from the text, ' What, know ye not that your body is the temple of the Holy Ghost, which is in you, which ye have of God, and ye are not your own ? For ye are bought with a price : therefore glorify God in your body, and in your spirit, which are God's.'   In the afternoon Brother Allen preached ; and I afterwards gave them a farewell exhortation, and there were some affectionate feelings excited amongst the people.   Many were moved, and felt a great desire to speak in the Lovefeast, but they had not courage. *Monday, 6th*.   We took leave of the town, making a hasty flight,"—to another and similar gathering elsewhere.

CHAPTER XVIII.

A CONSTITUTIONAL DIFFICULTY.

Gradual Growth of the Organization—Occasional Jars in the Working—
The Alleged Excessive Power of the Bishop—Rights claimed by
Wesley—Bishops his Successors—Objections raised—The Answers to
them—The Rev. James O'Kelly's demands—A "Council" proposed
—O'Kelly's Antagonism—The Bishop's Remonstrance—General Con-
ference demanded—Asbury's Letter—O'Kelly's Resolution—The
Debate—"The Republican Methodists"—Comments of Dr. Coke.

I HAVE already called attention to the gradual growth of
the Methodist Church system in the case alike of the
parent stem in this country, and of its vigorous and fruitful
offshoot in America. This, as before pointed out, affords
the explanation of some parts and provisions of the organization, which outside critics have unsparingly censured.
Had the system been constructed on premeditation for the
promotion of all conceivable ecclesiastical purposes, with
a due regard to all the possible requirements of both
preachers and people, a fairer and more shapely exterior
would probably have been given to it; but, whether in that
case it would have worked more satisfactorily, is not so easy
to determine. But we have to deal with the actual, and
not the problematical. Methodism, in all its incidental
details, if not in its essential principles as a Church institution, is as much the creation of circumstances as is the
British Constitution ; and just as the gradual growth of the
British Constitution accounts for some of its theoretic

anomalies, which, notwithstanding, work very satisfactory
results, so the incongruities which a bystander may detect
in the practical system of Methodism are attributable to its
gradual adaptation to new conditions and wants as they
have successively arisen, and probably fulfil the purposes of
the system more effectually than would a more logically
perfect organization. But the machinery of Methodism, like
that of the British Constitution, has not acquired completeness without an occasional jar or shock, which has led to a
renewed inspection, and, it may be, a readjustment of some
of its parts.

One thing which gave dissatisfaction to some of the
preachers, not long after the formation of the Church, was
the power which the constitution lodged in the hands of the
bishop of appointing them wherever he pleased. Nothing
could have been more natural than the vesting of this power
in the episcopal office, and it was not without constitutional
checks. The election to the office belonged to the Conference itself; and, not only was the bishop responsible to
the Conference for the character of his administration, but
was liable to be deposed or expelled for acts of maladminis-
tration. He occupied Mr. Wesley's seat, but with a limitation of his rights. Mr. Wesley always claimed the power to
appoint his preachers to the kind of work for which he
deemed them most suitable. Godly and zealous men, he
said, came to offer him their services as his sons in the
Gospel, to labour when, how, and where he might desire.
This was the understood condition between them and him,
when he accepted their assistance. If they grew weary of
this condition, they were at liberty to withdraw from him;
and he, if he saw sufficient cause, claimed the liberty to
withdraw from any of them. In continuing with him on
these terms, he said, they did him no favour, except as his

reward was with the Lord. At present it brought upon him nothing but trouble and care.

It was inevitable that men whose habits of thought and feeling had been moulded by their relation to Mr. Wesley on this condition, should think of themselves, when called to act as his representatives, as invested with similar power in relation to the men who by their own election placed them at their head. Nor was the power likely to be abused by such a man as Asbury, any more than by Wesley himself. But it was not long before questions and pleas of expediency with reference to it, began to suggest themselves. Ought any man to be entrusted with almost unrestricted power over his brethren? Apart from all considerations of a partial or an impartial exercise of his functions, was it not hard, however abstractedly regarded, that a body of men, some of whom might be personally equal in all respects to the bishop, should be so completely at his disposal? Besides, was it to be expected that he, however gifted and good, should have so just an acquaintance with the wants of localities, and the special fitness of preachers to satisfy them, as would be a sufficient guarantee against his commission of great and cruel mistakes?

None denied that there was weight in these pleas; but how was the difficulty complained of to be overcome? The present method of stationing was not new, and had hitherto given satisfaction; and much might be pleaded in favour of its continuance among men who were all aiming to promote the same ends, who had at heart the prosperity of the same good work. For, as the bishop had the advantage of being free from local bias, and was possessed of such a knowledge of the whole work as only a man of his opportunities of observation could have, there would be less danger of unsuitable appointments being made by him than

by others ; and, if the number of ministers increased beyond
the possibility of his knowing each of them sufficiently, that
difficulty could be met by an increase in the Episcopate.
Let them beware, it was urged, lest, in the attempt to
obviate one contingent or actual evil, another of equal mag-
nitude was not produced.

To Bishop Asbury, any change shown to be adequate to
the requirements of the work, would have been a coveted
relief ; for the load of responsibility which he willingly bore
for the sake of the cause, was a burden which brought with
it no personal advantage.   But what was to be the nature of
the change demanded ?   The answer returned to this question by the leader of the agitation, a preacher of popular
gifts, whose name was James O'Kelly, was, "Let the
preachers severally have the right of appeal from the act of
the bishop to the Conference over which he presides."   But
how was this right, which implied a change in the constitution, to be conferred ?   For no single Conference had the
power to grant it ; and the number of annual Conferences
was rapidly multiplying with the progress of the work.

On other grounds, the institution of a central and representative body had been found necessary, and at the Conference held at New York, in May, 1789, the two bishops
presented the following scheme for the formation of a
convention to be called a "Council," which the Conference
approved and adopted :—

"Ques. Whereas the holding of General Conferences on
this extensive continent would be attended with a variety of
difficulties, and many inconveniences to the work of God ;
and whereas we judge it expedient that a Council should be
formed of chosen men out of the several districts, as representatives of the whole Connection, to meet at stated times,—
in what manner is this Council to be formed, what shall be

its powers, and what further regulations shall be made concerning it ?

"*Ans.* Our bishops and presiding-elders shall be the
members of this Council ; provided that the members who
form the Council be never fewer than nine. And, if any
unavoidable circumstance prevent the attendance of a presiding-elder at the Council, he shall have authority to send
another elder out of his own district to represent him ; but
the elder so sent by the absenting presiding-elder shall have
no seat in the Council without the approbation of the bishop,
or bishops, and presiding-elders present. And if after the
above-mentioned provisions are complied with, any unavoidable circumstance, or any contingencies, reduce the
number to less than nine, the bishop shall immediately
summon such elders as do not preside to complete the
number.

"(2) These shall have authority to mature everything they
shall judge expedient :—(1) To preserve the general union ;
(2) to render and preserve the external form of worship
similar in all our Societies through the continent ; (3) to
preserve the essentials of the Methodist doctrines and discipline pure and uncorrupted ; (4) to correct all abuses and
disorders ; and, lastly, they are authorized to mature everything they may see necessary for the good of the Church,
and for the promoting and improving our colleges and plan
of education.

"(3) Provided nevertheless that nothing shall be received
as the resolution of the Council, unless it be assented to
unanimously by the Council ; and nothing so assented to by
the Council shall be binding in any district till it has been
agreed upon by a majority of the Conference which is held
for that district.

"(4) The bishops shall have authority to summon the

Council to meet at such times and places as they shall judge expedient.

"(5) The first Council shall be held at Cokesbury, on the 1st day of next December."

It met as appointed, and consisted of Asbury, as bishop, and eleven elders, including O'Kelly. It did not deal with the question of stationing the preachers, and could scarcely have been intended to allay the growing feeling of discontent with reference to that question. It had, in fact, the effect of fomenting and increasing the disaffection. A few days after it met Asbury wrote, "I received a letter from the presiding-elder of this district, James O'Kelly. He makes heavy complaints respecting my power, and bids me pause for one year, or he must use his influence against me." And again a little later, "I have felt grieved in mind that there is a link broken out of twelve that should form a chain of union. I hope God will sanctify some providence to the explanation of this matter, and heal the whole." O'Kelly had at length declared war against what he called the bishop's assumption of power, and against the *Council*, as a concentration and increase, rather than a reduction of it ; and was moving the people wherever he had influence to demand the calling of a General Conference, for inquiring into the matter. Would he be content to abide by the decision of such a Conference ? We shall see.

So intense was the bishop's anxiety to keep the unity of the Spirit in the bond of peace that, to use again his own words, he wrote to O'Kelly to declare his willingness to take his seat in the Council as another member, and, on that point, at least, to waive the claims of Episcopacy ; "yea," said he, "I would lie down and be trodden on, rather than knowingly injure one soul." And if ever utterance was guileless, it was this passionate effusion of a full heart. But O'Kelly was not to be moved from his purpose by a generous appeal to his nobler feelings. The Council reassembled on the 1st December, 1790, as had been arranged, he protesting against it by his absence. But the opposition to it, and the demand for a General Conference became so widespread and violent through his incessant agitation, that though it did not formally dissolve itself, it never met again. On the 23rd March succeeding Asbury records the re-arrival of "long-looked-for Dr. Coke," who had been shipwrecked on his fourth voyage from England. "I found the Doctor's sentiments," he says mournfully, "with regard to the Council, quite changed. James O'Kelly's letters had reached London. I felt perfectly calm, and acceded to a General Conference for the sake of peace."

It was forthwith arranged for, and was duly held, at Baltimore, on the 1st November, 1792. Dr. Coke had meantime again crossed and re-crossed the Atlantic, and was present to preside on the occasion. Asbury, who had looked forward to it with great anxiety, says, "I felt awfully. At my desire they appointed a moderator and preparatory committee to keep order, and bring forward the business with regularity. We had heavy debates on the first, second, and third sections of our Form of Discipline." As the prerogatives of the Episcopacy were the subjects of discussion, Asbury says, "I gave up the whole matter to them (to consider, unembarrassed by his presence), and to Dr. Coke, who presided; and sent them the following letter:—

"My Dear Brethren,—

"Let my absence give you no pain: Dr. Coke presides. I am happily excused from assisting to make laws by which myself am to be governed. I have only to obey and execute. I am happy in the consideration that I never stationed a preacher through enmity, or as a punishment. I have acted for the glory of God, the good of the people,

and to promote the usefulness of the preachers. Are you sure that if
you please yourselves, the people will be as fully satisfied. They often
say, 'Let us have such a preacher,' and sometimes, 'We will not have
such an one.' Perhaps I must say, 'His appeal forced him upon you.'
I am one,—ye are many. I am as willing to serve you as ever. I want
not to sit in any man's way. I scorn to solicit votes. Speak your
minds freely ; but, remember, you are only making laws for the present
time. It may be that, as in some other things, so in this, a future day
may give you further light."

O'Kelly's resolution was in the following terms :—

> "That, after the bishop appoints the preachers at the Conference to
> their several circuits, if any one thinks himself injured by the appoint-
> ment, he shall have liberty to appeal to the Conference and state his
> objections, and, if the Conference approve his objections, the bishop
> shall appoint him to another circuit."

It is easy to understand that much might be said on this
proposition, both for and against ; and we are told that the
debate was protracted over three days, but that the motion
was eventually lost by a large majority. The sequel, in the
case of the leader of the agitation, shall be stated in the calm
words of the Bishop. He says : " Mr. O'Kelly, being disappointed in not obtaining the right of appeal from any station
made by me, withdrew from the Connexion, and went off.
For himself, the Conference well knew that he could not
complain of our regulation. He had been appointed to the
south district of Virginia for about ten succeeding years ;
and upon his plan might have appointed himself, and any
preacher, or set of preachers, to the district, whether the
people wished to have them or not."

Unhappily, as is common with disappointed men of an ambitious and turbulent spirit, Mr. O'Kelly retired from the Conference to continue his opposition without. He had already
gathered around him a body of sympathizers, who, now that
he was defeated, pronounced him an injured man, denounced

the Conference, with Bishop Asbury at its head, as a body of tyrants, appealed to the tribunal of Public Opinion, and, of course, evoked from the multitude, who knew, and could know, nothing of the merits of the case, a decision adverse to the whole Methodist system. The result was, that in South Virginia, where O'Kelly's influence was the greatest, the Societies were rent, decimated, or irrecoverably scattered; a body of seceders, with the popular rallying-cry of *Freedom and Reform*, constituted, under O'Kelly's leadership, " the Republican Methodist Church " ; and the progress of the evangelistic movement was seriously impeded. But the triumph of revolt was of short duration. When the schism and the purposes of its leader were mentioned to Asbury he quietly remarked, " I hear that there was a Conference at Reese's Chapel, in Charlotte County, Virginia, to form what they call a *free constitution* and a pure Church ; and to reject me and my creatures. Only let them settle in congregations, and tax the people, and I know how it will work ! Whenever the people are unwilling to receive us, we will peacefully withdraw from them ; and if those who wish the change can serve them better than we have done,—well. Perhaps some of them can think with ——, that I am the greatest villain on the continent. I bid such adieu, and appeal to the bar of God. I have no time to contend, having better work to do. The Lord judge between me and them." And the new organization was as ephemeral as he foresaw and predicted. The seceders soon began to contend for preeminence among themselves ; and this counsel and work, which was not of God, " came to nought."

This harassing business being disposed of, " the General Conference," says Asbury, " went through the Discipline, Articles of Faith, Forms of Baptism, Matrimony, and Burial of the Dead ; as also the Offices of Ordination. The Conference ended in peace, after voting another General Conference to be held four years hence. By desire of my brethren I preached from the text of St. Peter, ' Finally, be ye all of one mind ; love as brethren, be pitiful, be courteous.' My mind was kept in peace, and my soul enjoyed rest in the Stronghold."

Speaking with reference to the whole session, Dr. Coke says, " I have always entertained very high ideas of the piety and zeal of the American preachers, and of the considerable abilities of many ; but had no expectation, I confess, that the debates would be carried on in so very masterly a manner ; so that, on every question of importance, the subject seemed to be considered in every possible light. Throughout the debates they conducted themselves as the servants of the people ; and therefore never lost sight of them on any question. Indeed, the single eye, and spirit of humility, manifested by the preachers throughout the Conference, were extremely pleasing, and afforded a comfortable prospect of the increase of the work of God in the whole continent."

CHAPTER XIX.

BETWEEN the Christmas Conference of 1784 and the General Conference of 1792—this being the beginning of the quadrennial General Conference, and like so many other of the provisions of Methodism, the answer of Providence to a generally felt want—the Church had gradually increased its auxiliary institutions and appliances. Its *Foreign Missions* may be said to date from the period of its organization, when Garrettson and Cromwell were set apart as Missionaries to Nova Scotia. In 1787 definite arrangements were made for the religious instruction of the children of Methodists. In reply to the question, "What can we do for the rising generation ? " the Baltimore Conference of that year said, " Let the elders, deacons, and helpers place the children of our friends in proper classes, as far as it is practicable, meet them as often as possible, and commit them during their absence to the care of proper persons, who may meet them at least weekly ; and if any of them be *truly awakened*, let them be admitted into Society." In 1789 a Methodist publishing-house was opened in Philadelphia; John Dickins was appointed the Book Steward, and under his editorship the first volume of the *Arminian Magazine*, mainly a reprint of Mr. Wesley's, was issued. Thus began the present gigantic Book Concern, " with its two publishing houses, five depositories, a capital of nearly 800,000 dollars, its twelve editors, its nearly. five hundred clerks and operatives, its more than twenty cylinder and power presses, its nearly thirty thousand different publications, its fourteen periodicals, with an aggregate circulation of over one million copies per month." *

The next year (1790) is rendered memorable by the inauguration of Sunday-schools. Four years prior to this a successful trial of one had been made by Asbury. " In the year 1786, five years before any other person moved in this matter, he organized a school in Hanover county, Virginia, in the house of Thomas Crenshaw, and, as one of its first-fruits, John Charlston was converted to God in that school, and afterwards became a useful and successful minister of the gospel in the Methodist Episcopal Church." † Now (in 1790) it was agreed that the effort to promote their establishment should be systematic and general. " Our Conference," Asbury writes, with satisfaction, " resolved on establishing Sunday-schools for poor children, both white and black." " Let us labour," say the Minutes for that year, " as the heart and soul of one man, to establish Sunday-schools in or near the places of public worship. Let persons be appointed by the bishops, elders, deacons, or preachers, to teach (*gratis*) all that will attend and have a capacity to learn, from six o'clock in the morning till ten, and from two o'clock in the afternoon till six, where it does not interfere with public worship."

* Stevens' His., ii. 500.   † Strickland's Asbury, p. 217.

Stevens remarks on this Minute that it is supposed to be the first recognition of Sunday-schools by any American church. "Only about nine years had passed since they were begun in England. A young Methodist woman (Miss Cooke) afterwards the wife of one of Wesley's most distinguished preachers, Samuel Bradburn, first suggested to Robert Raikes their organization in 1781, at Gloucester. She assisted him in forming the first school, attended with him the procession of ragged children from the school to the parish church, and was one of their most effective teachers. John Wesley was the first man in England to publicly approve Raikes' plan, after the latter had published an account of it in the *Gloucester Journal*, in 1784. Wesley immediately copied the account into his *Arminian Magazine*, and recommended his people to adopt the new institution. In the same year Fletcher, of Madeley, introduced it into his parish, and wrote an essay on 'The Advantages likely to arise from Sunday-schools. . . . The endeavour of 1790 to incorporate the institution into the Church, though for some time feeble, if not defeated, at last succeeded, and in our day there are nearly a million and a half scholars, and nearly two hundred thousand teachers (according to the latest returns) in the various Methodist Sunday-schools of the United States. The Sunday-school Union has become one of the most important auxiliaries of the Book Concern, with its four periodicals, having an aggregate circulation of more than 260,000 per number. Its catalogue of publications includes more than 1,300 different works, with an annual issue of about a million copies, and its Sunday-school libraries report nearly two and a half millions of volumes. More than two hundred and thirty thousand conversions have been reported in its schools in the last fifteen years."

Through the good management of Mr. Dickins, the book

establishment had begun to be remunerative, and the General Conference determined that a portion of its profits should be appropriated to the relief of distressed preachers, and that the bishop should be allowed to devote another fixed sum to the establishment of "district-schools;" that is, day-schools, to be under the supervision of the presiding-elders of the several districts.

The business of this important Conference concluded, Dr. Coke prepared to embark for the West Indies, and Bishop Asbury set out with eagerness on his annual tour of the States. His route lay first southward, as far as Savannah; thence through South and North Carolina, across the mountains to Tennessee and Kentucky; back to the Holston, and along the western slope of the Alleghanies into West Virginia; onward along the rugged mountains into Maryland; then northward to Albany and the States of New England. Under the guidance of his faithful Journal we will follow him over this immense circuit, and look at his character in the light thrown upon it by some of its thickly-set incidents.

Leaving Baltimore the day after the Conference adjourned, he rode forty miles to Alexandria, in Virginia, to preside at a District Conference. Here he ministered to the guidance and encouragement of his brethren by an expository discourse, and by a close sitting with them dispatched the business of the Conference in a single day. Then he is off in company with five of them into Carolina county, riding fifty-three miles before sunset. "So much," he says, playfully, "for an American *episcopos*;" and more seriously adds, "travelling in such haste, I could not be as much in mental prayer as I desired; although I enjoyed many moments of sweet converse with God." By the next Sunday he has arrived at Manchester, where again he

preaches, presides over a District Conference, meets the
preachers "in band," and rejoices over their "union and
love." His next halting-place is Petersburg, where, and
in the surrounding places, he preached repeatedly, spoke
encouragingly to the young people, met the Societies,
comforted a dear dispirited old Christian in his recent
bereavement, and projected and "formed a constitution for
a district-school." Thence he directed his course for
Lewisburg, met about forty preachers in Conference, with
whom he was diligently employed for four days; then
giving thanks to God for the hundreds of conversions
reported from their circuits, presses onward into South
Carolina.

"*Sunday,* Dec. 23. We attended from ten till one
o'clock in a house built of poles; here were light and
ventilators plenty. We rode this evening twenty miles to
Mr. Blakeney's. The rain caught us in the woods, and we
were well steeped. Arriving, we found a good house,
table, and bed, which was some relief to weather-beaten
pilgrims. *Christmas Eve.* We rode in the rain twenty-five
miles to our kind brother Horton's, and found many people
had gathered. *Christmas Day.* Rode forty-five miles to dear
brother Rembert's; kind and good, rich and liberal; who
has done more for the poor Methodists than any man in
South Carolina. The Lord grant that he, with his household, may find mercy in that day. *Wednesday,* 26. Preached
at Quarterly-meeting on the words of St. Peter, ' Rejoice,
inasmuch as ye are partakers of Christ's sufferings; that
when His glory shall be revealed, ye may be glad also with
exceeding joy.' I was pleased to hear the young men after
the sacrament. I felt uncommonly melted; tears involuntarily burst from my eyes. God was there. *Thursday,* 27.
I had a long, cold ride of forty-five miles. The unfinished

state of the houses, lying on the floor, then clothing, and inclement weather, keep me in a state of indisposition. *Friday*, 28. We had to cross the Santee, and ride thirty-five miles to dear sister Browing's. *Saturday*, 29. Rode thirty-three miles to Charleston, and found our little flock in peace, and a small revival amongst them."

At Charleston he lodges in comfort with his hospitable friend, Mr. Wells, who, he thankfully notes, gives evidence of increased spirituality; he preaches on the Sunday on "*the Child born; the Son given;* " he holds a Conference which is prolonged over three days; then, on Friday, starts for G—'s, on the Edisto River, where " unwell, and weary, and sleepy, and very unfit for public exercise," he nevertheless preaches Christ as the wisdom and the power of God. The next day he rode fifty miles, and by Thursday reached Washington, in Georgia, where he again presided at a Conference. On the Sunday he preached, nearly the whole town coming to hear " this man that rambles through the States;" and administered the Lord's-supper, held a lovefeast, and ordained. His next remove is direct to his southernmost bourn, Savannah, " where," said he, on starting for it, " I may see the former walks of dear Wesley and Whitefield, whom I hope to meet in the New Jerusalem."

Making Savannah his head-quarters for a few days, he visited the outlying places, passing in one direction through " rice plantations for nearly two miles," and becoming " entangled in the swamp; " and in another direction, " getting pretty well scratched by the trees." " A wretched country this ! " he remarks, " but there are souls, precious souls, worth worlds." He naturally went out to see the ruins of Whitefield's Orphan-house, and was filled with oppressive emotion as he gazed on the confused heaps, and the dreary walls of the wings, as weird sentinels standing

over them. Of course in that distant district the General
Conference, and the secession of O'Kelly, were freely
commented on; and with reference to the part he took in
conversations on this agitating subject, he enters this characteristic note: "I am not enough in prayer. I have said
more than was for the glory of God concerning those who
have left the American Connexion, and who have reviled
Mr. Wesley, Mr. Fletcher, Dr. Coke, and poor *me*. Oh! that
I could trust the Lord more than I do, and leave His cause
wholly in His own hands!"

On Saturday, February 2nd, 1793, he began to retrace
his course to Charleston. On Sunday, preached at Black-
swamp Church; Monday, at Purisburg, "to a house full."
Was faint and low-spirited; stopped at a bridge to pay his
fare, "but oh! the scent of rum, and men filled with it!"
"Hoped for entertainment at Red Hill; but the gentleman
refused to receive us for love, money, or hospitality's sake.
At length we providentially reached a Mr. C——'s, a schoolmaster and minister. We bought some corn for our horses,
and had tea, and bread and cheese for ourselves." Re-
arrived at Charleston, he writes: "Travelling through
heavy rains, deep swamps in dark nights, makes both man
and beast feel the effects of yesterday's journey of forty-five
miles. My mind has been severely agitated this tour. I
have ridden about six hundred and fifty miles in one month,
wanting one day."

After a few busy days at Charleston, he struck out west-
ward to Columbia, the capital of the State, thence by daily
rides through woods and across rivers and swamps, to "the
multitude of mountains." Coming to T——'s, "in the cove,"
after a ride of thirty miles, he "rested in peace, after getting
a little Indian bread and fried bacon, and drinking some of
our tea. Our lodging was on a bed set upon forks, with

clap-boards laid across, in an earthen-floor cabin. But worse than all the rest was the absence of religion. I feel awfully for the people on this account." Ascending the mountain, he stopped at S—'s, and preached to a few people, hastily brought together, on "The promise to you and to your children." "My soul felt for these neglected people," he writes. "It may be, by my coming this way, Providence will so order it that I shall send them a preacher. We hasted on to Cove's Creek, and invited ourselves to stay at C—'s, where we made our own tea, obtained some butter and milk, and some most excellent Irish potatoes. We were presented with a little flax for our beds, on which we spread our coats and blankets, and three of us slept before a large fire." Early the next morning he began to climb the "iron mountain," which was "steep like the roof of a house, and greatly trying to his lungs;" and, at length, through indescribable difficulties, and oppressed with an intermittent fever, he came to "new territory," in Tennessee, where, as yet, there were but four or five Methodist families, but where the much suffering preachers came joyously together to meet and receive fresh quickening and counsel from their sympathizing bishop. Here he records peace in the Conference, "a melting among the people," "a happy time" in spiritual conversation with an old friend who had settled there, though "pained for his children, who are yet unconverted;" and despite the appearances of danger on the road, he prepared for his journey "through the wilderness."

"*Monday*. Our guard appeared. I found that the reports relative to the Indians were true; they had killed the post and one or two more, and taken some prisoners: I had not much thought or fear about them. *Tuesday*. We came off. I went to Robinson's station, where the soldiers behaved civilly. We gave them two exhortations, and had prayer

with them.   They honoured me with the swinging hammock
(a bear-skin), which was as great a favour to me as the
governor's bed.   Here I slept well.   *Wednesday.*   We hasted
on our way (along the line of the mountains).   Fed on the
banks of Cumberland river, and pushed on to Hood's station.
Here there was high life below stairs.   We had a troop of
poor, very poor sinners.   I gave dreadful offence by a prayer
I made."   By Saturday he had arrived at a settlement in the
interior of Kentucky, where there was a little Methodist
Society.   He attended the Quarterly-meeting; warned its
members of the perils of spiritual declension; "had some
light, life, and liberty in preaching;" and "closed the meeting after several had engaged in prayer," crying, "Lord, let
not Thy faithful word fall to the ground!"   On Sunday he
had a large congregation, to whom he discoursed on the
deliverances vouchsafed to the righteous in times of trouble.
"*Tuesday.*   Rode thirty miles without food for man or beast.
There is a falling away among the people.   Lord, help me
to bear up in the evil day.   *Thursday.*   Rode sixteen miles
to Clarke's station to attend the Quarterly-meeting.   Blessed
be God, I live continually in His presence, and Christ is All
in all to my soul!"

He spent about three weeks visiting the several settlements, preaching daily, and on the Sundays, also administering the sacraments and holding lovefeasts; he held a Conference with the preachers from all parts of the district,
which was characterized by frankness and freedom, and
"ended under the melting, praying, praising power of God;"
and left persuaded that under his last sermon "good was
certainly done among old and young."   With a select company he pushed forward through the wilderness on the
return journey, "under great suspicion of the Indians;" and
on reaching the house of Mr. Van Pelt, in Tennessee, he

wrote, "I have travelled between five and six hundred miles in the last four weeks, and have rested from riding fifteen days for Conference and other duties. I have been much distressed with this night-work, the want of regular meals, and of sleep ; and it is difficult to keep up habits of prayer in such rude companies as we have been obliged to travel with. I have also been severely afflicted through the whole journey."

Here he rested on the Sunday; but the next day rode forty-six miles, and at night narrowly escaped being burnt in the cabin where he lodged. Weary, and in pain, he came at last to the mountain-side mansion, where he had been so often greeted with warm welcomes from his friend, General Russell. Mrs. Russell received him with her wonted courtesy; but she was a widow. "I am very solemn," he says; "I feel the want of the dear man who, I trust, is now in Abraham's bosom, and hope ere long to see him there. He was a general officer in the continental army, where he underwent great fatigues. He was powerfully brought to God, and for a few years past was a living flame, and a blessing to this neighbourhood. Oh that the gospel may continue in this house ! I preached on *the cloud of witnesses*, and there followed several exhortations. We then administered the sacrament. Our exercises lasted about five hours." The next day he was busy planning for the establishment of a district school ; then off for a ride of forty-five miles to a congregation waiting for his ministry, and onward "over the hills with rain without, and hunger within, to Green Briar country, in Virginia, where he held a Conference, and was "greatly comforted."

Rest had become an absolute necessity, and he sought it where he could also use means to alleviate his bodily suffering. He says, "We rode to Bath. Here we continued to

rest ourselves. My public work was a sermon on the
Sabbath. Members of our Society, from various parts, being
here, I have an opportunity of receiving and answering
many letters. I am afraid I shall spend nine or ten days
here to little purpose. I employ myself in reading Thomas
à Kempis, and the Bible. I also have an opportunity of
going alone into the silent grove, and of meditating on the
state of the continent, and examining my own heart. I hope
to find some relief from my rheumatic complaint which has
so oppressed me for six months past." Scarcely allowing
himself the time for rest he had proposed, he hastened forward to Oldtown, in Maryland, where he "had no small
consolation in uniting the brethren of three districts in
Conference." Three successive days he is "very closely
employed;" he preaches from the words, "Pray for the
peace of Jerusalem; they shall prosper that love thee;" addresses a "careless and unfeeling" congregation on David's
charge to Solomon; and, each of the succeeding days, rides
thirty-five miles towards the Juniata. The next day he was
detained a few hours through the straying of his horse, but
this afforded an opportunity of urging a woman, whom he
happened to meet, to begin to pray, which, "with tears, she
promised to do." "Perhaps," he says, "this labour may not
be lost. I have had the happiness to hear that an effort of
this kind at widow N——'s, when there last, was successful."

His next remove was to Northumberland, where he found
"a few kind, respectable friends, whose circumstances are
comfortable," to whom he preached Christ as "the Way, the
Truth, and the Life," and then "wrought up the hills and
narrows to Wyoming." "Being the anniversary of the
American Independence, there was a great noise among the
sinners. A few of us went down to Shawanee; called a
few people from their work, and found it good to be there."

He preached here to a small congregation in a private house, but scarcely knew " where to get a quiet, clean place to lie down ; " and continued his journey the next morning over the mountains, and through the " twelve-miles swamp " to the Delaware ; and thence up the Hudson to Albany, where he met the New England preachers, with whom he had brotherly fellowship in Conference. Here he found himself worn down with fatigue, and in great bodily weakness, which caused him to feel the more deeply the want of hospitality, of which he had to complain. " The people of Albany," he says, " roll in wealth ; yet they have no heart to invite any of the servants of God to their houses."

Coming down from Albany, he crossed into Connecticut, visiting and preaching at every place where an opening had been obtained ; and so forward to Massachusetts to attend a Conference at Lynn ; and back into Connecticut, " lame in both feet," and so completely exhausted that, he says, " I laid myself down on the road side, and felt like Jonah, or Elijah. I took to my bed at Reading." In two days, however, he started again. " Rode ten miles on horseback, and thirteen in a carriage, to Bedford, and rested a day at dear widow Banks', where I was at home. Oh how sweet is one day's rest ! "

On the day after the morrow he started again for New York. " When I came near the White Plains my horse started, and threw me into a mill-race, knee deep in water, my hands and side in the dirt ; my shoulder was hurt by the fall. I stopped at a house, changed my clothes, and prayed with the people. If any of them are awakened by my stopping there, all will be well."

At New York he held a Conference, at which he collected forty pounds for the relief of the suffering preachers in New England, and then proceeded to Philadelphia, notwithstand-

ing accounts from that city, which, he says, made him feel
" too much like a man, and too little like a Christian."

The yellow fever was at that time ravaging the city, and
friends strove to dissuade him from exposing himself to the
infection.   He was never rash ; but he believed it to be his
duty to brave the peril, and he unshrinkingly proceeded.
As he approached the city he met on the road multitudes of
the inhabitants who were fleeing for their lives.   " Ah," said
he, " how the ways mourn ! how low-spirited are the people
while making their escape !   I judge the people die from
fifty to one hundred a day.   Some of our friends are dying,
others flying.   Sunday I preached from the words, ' Cry
aloud, spare not, lift up thy voice like a trumpet, and show
My people their transgressions, and the house of Jacob
their sins ! '   The people are alarmed, and well they may be.
I went down to Ebenezer Church, but my strength was
gone.   However I endeavoured to open, and apply, the
words of the prophet Micah : ' The LORD's voice crieth unto
the city, and the man of wisdom shall see Thy name : hear
ye the rod, and Who hath appointed it.'   The streets are
now depopulated, and the city wears a gloomy aspect.   Poor
Philadelphia !   ' The lofty city, He layeth it low.'   I am very
unwell."   He appointed a day of humiliation ; preached on
the occasion from 1 Kings xiii. 37—40, to a large and im-
pressible congregation ; and then " left the city, solemn as
death," and hastened forward into Maryland.   On his way
thither he stopped to attend a Quarterly-meeting at the Cross-
roads, where he preached to a crowded audience from the
words, " Yea, in the way of Thy judgments have we waited
for Thee."   On his re-arrival at Baltimore he found that a
certificate of health was required before admission into the
city.   This he obtained from the health-officer, and passed
the guard, exclaiming, " Oh the plague of sin !   Would to

God we were more guarded against *its* baleful influence!"
Here he "sounded the alarm" on the words, "Give glory
to the LORD your God, before He cause darkness;" then
hasted to Annapolis, attended a Quarterly-meeting held in a
large tobacco-house, and returned to Baltimore to preside at
the Conference.

This tour of the States he accomplished in a little less
than eleven months. On the 16th of November, 1792, he
left Baltimore for the south, and on the 10th of October,
1793, he re-entered this city from the north, having
travelled in the interval not less, probably, than six thousand miles! Seated beneath our own pleasant vine, or fig-
tree, we have in thought hastily traced his route. We have
glanced at the difficulties he boldly faced and surmounted;
the hardships he cheerfully endured; the perils to which he
unhesitatingly subjected himself. We have perhaps sympathized with him in his weak and suffering physical condition; have admired his self-devotion, and have been
edified with the insight he has occasionally given us into his
inner experiences. But is this all? I do not take upon me
to point out to the reader the lessons, important to himself,
and all within the sphere of his own activities and influence,
to be derived from the facts upon which we have dimly
gazed. I will not pay him so ill a compliment as to assume
that he will neglect to make a suitable use of them for his
own quickening and encouragement. But I ask him to join
with me in glorifying, not Francis Asbury, but the grace of
God that was in him: at the same time remembering that
that grace was given according to an eternal principle of the
Divine administration, which applies equally to us all. "To
him that hath (through diligent use) shall be given (more);
and to him that hath not (as the result of his own diligence),
shall be taken away even that which he hath," by Divine gift.

With varied incidents, the Bishop took the same circuit of
the States from year to year, so far as his enfeebled constitution permitted, until the General Conference held in Baltimore, in 1800. He then signified his inability to discharge
efficiently the multiplied duties of his office, and the Conference proceeded to the election of another bishop, to be his
assistant and colleague, " earnestly entreating a continuation
of his services, so far as his strength would permit." The
minister of their choice was Mr. Whatcoat, his early and
peculiarly attached friend, with whom, until his death, in
1806, the labours of the episcopate were equally shared :
the two bishops sometimes travelling in company, and
dividing the duties of their office between them, but more
frequently taking different routes. On the 8th of July,
1806, Asbury sadly inscribed in his Journal these words :
" I found a letter from Dr. Chandler declaring the death of
Bishop Whatcoat, that father in Israel, *and my faithful friend
for forty years.* . . A man so uniformly good I have not
known in Europe, or America." For two years longer
Bishop Asbury had to prosecute his labours unaided, or
with such assistance as he could himself procure, and at the
General Conference of 1808 another assistant was given to
him in the person of the hardy, lion-hearted, and powerfully
eloquent William McKendree ; and Asbury had the satisfaction of writing, " The burden is now borne by two pairs of
shoulders instead of one : the care is cast upon two hearts
and heads."

HOME OF ASBURY'S CHILDHOOD AND YOUTH (FROM A PHOTOGRAPH).

CHAPTER XX.

PIETY AT HOME.

Asbury's genial Affability—His large Circle of Friends—Reasons for his
Celibacy—His Mother's House a Preaching-place—Remittances of
Money to his Parents—Proposes to them to go out to America—Doubts
the Expediency of this Proposal—Explains to them his Circumstances
—His Father's Death—Letter to his bereaved Mother—Tribute to his
Mother's memory—Proof of the Reality of his Philanthropy.

FEW men have been more remarkable than Bishop
Asbury for the warmth and tenderness of their domestic
affections. We have hitherto regarded him so exclusively
in his official relation to the Church, that a distinct recognition of this fact is necessary to preserve us from taking a
partial and faulty impression of his character. A more
loving and lovable man has rarely occupied an influential
position in public life. His nature was irrepressively suscep-

tive of tender emotion, and the interchange of social affection
was one of the principal enjoyments of his life. Not many
men have ever had so large a circle of firmly attached friends.
His homes in his later years dotted the entire region of the
States, and wherever, after a long and fatiguing journey, or
after the discharge of his exhausting public duties, he joined
the household at the fireside or table, he never failed by his
sweet and easy manners, and his childlike simplicity, play-
fulness, and benignity, to diffuse an air of cheerfulness
through the whole dwelling. If, as so frequently occurred
at the commencement of his career, he had to be indebted
to strangers for temporary accommodation, he was always
welcomed to their hospitalities when he revisited the same
neighbourhood ; and eventually the return of his annual visit
was looked forward to by scores of families as one of the
most jubilant events of the year. As in the case of nearly
every man who has exerted an extended moral influence in
the world, his character was most truly discerned and revered
by godly women, whose kind offices and ministry were never
wanting to supply him with any comfort at their command.

No doubt the most suitable thing for a man of his temperament and character of mind would have been to marry, and
find that scope for the exercise of his affections which is
afforded within the family circle. But there were public
considerations which, in his estimation, far outweighed all
considerations of self, and which inflexibly determined his
choice of a single life. What those considerations were is
best stated in his own words. "If I should die in celibacy,"
he says, "which I think quite probable, I give the following
reasons for what can scarcely be called *my choice*. I was
called in my fourteenth year. I began my public exercises between sixteen and seventeen. At twenty-one I travelled. At
twenty-six I came to America : thus far I had reasons enough

for a single life. It had been my intention to return to Europe; but the war continued, and it was ten years before we had a settled, lasting peace. This was no time to marry or be given in marriage. At forty-nine I was ordained bishop in America. Among the duties imposed upon me by my office was that of travelling extensively, and I could hardly expect to find a woman with grace enough to enable her to live but one week out of the fifty-two with her husband. Besides, what right has any man to take advantage of the affections of a woman, make her his wife, and, by a voluntary absence from her, subvert the whole order and economy of the marriage state, by separating those whom neither God, nature, nor the requirements of civil society, permit long to be *put asunder?* It is neither just nor generous. I may add to this that I had little money, and with this little *I ministered to the necessities of a beloved mother until I was fifty-seven.* If I have done wrong, I trust that God and the sex will forgive me. It is my duty now to bestow the pittance I may have to spare upon the widows and fatherless girls, and poor married men."

This is unanswerable; and so far as it concerns the question to which it refers, may be left without comment. It is clear that if he had married he must have relinquished work to which he believed himself Divinely called, or matrimony must have been to him, and all to whom it brought him into intimate and sacred relations, a bitter practical irony. But one part of this plea calls for more particular attention, as based upon a fact which reveals one of the most beautiful features of his genuine character. His parents in their declining years were in narrow, and even, at times, necessitous circumstances. This was not generally known; and their cottage, always neat and clean, wore from year to year the same appearance of quiet respectability and comfort.

16

For nearly half a century its principal room was used as a
preaching-place, and as such was put in order for worship
punctually at the appointed hour, a cheerful fire always
glowing on the hearth in the winter evenings ; and the
preacher, after the service, was always offered refreshment
before taking his, in some cases, long and dreary walk to his
home.　　But a never-failing contributor to the cost which
this incurred was the distant, but ever-mindful and affectionate, son of the venerable pair who tenanted that well-known
dwelling.　　Throughout his long and perilous travels, and
amidst all his personal trials and his incessant solicitudes in
behalf of the great work he was superintending, that homely
little abode in England, the scene of events which marked
his childhood and youth, and of such social joys as he had
never since experienced ; the scene of his mother's prayers
and anxieties in his behalf, and of the weekly gatherings of
neighbours for public worship, Christian fellowship, and
prayer, was continuously present to his thoughts and his
heart.　　The amount which the Societies placed at his disposal for personal expenses was sixty-four dollars per
annum, occasionally supplemented, as we learn from grateful acknowledgments in his Journal, by small donations
from his friend, Mr. Gough ; and the greater part of this he
carefully laid aside, and, as he had the opportunity, remitted
to his parents, to provide them with a few personal comforts
of which they must otherwise have been deprived, and to
enable them to keep their house open for the religious
benefit of their neighbours.

He had cherished the hope, from the time of his leaving
England, that sooner or later he would return, and had
expressed this to his parents when he took his final leave of
them, though his less sanguine father had passionately "cried
out," in reply, as he tells us, " *Never !*—I shall never see

him again !" He had also repeatedly given intimations to his American friends of his desire to revisit his country and parents, though only for a limited period ; but had uniformly suppressed this desire in deference to their pleadings against even a temporary absence from them, and in obedience to his clear sense of duty. Ultimately it occurred to him to suggest to his parents the alternative of their joining him in America. This suggestion, with reasons for and against it, he put before them sometime during the year 1795, in the following letter :—

"I have received several letters expressive of your paternal love and gratitude toward me. I have often revolved the serious thought of my return to you. I have frequently asked myself if I could retire to a single circuit, step down and act as lay preacher. This, if I know my own heart, is *not* my difficulty. With humility I may say, one hundred thousand respectable citizens of the new world, three hundred travelling and six hundred local preachers, would advise me not to go. I hope the voice of the people is the voice of God. At present we have more work than faithful workmen. I am like Joseph ; I want to have my parents near me. I am not ashamed of your *poverty*, and I hope, after so many years professing religion, you will not be wanting in *piety*. I have considered you have that which is my joy and my glory ; that you have had for forty years open doors for religious exercises, when no other would or even dare do it. It is a serious subject, whether you think it is your duty still to keep a place for preaching, or if on your removal the Gospel will be taken from the place. Yet when I think you have no child with you, nor friend that careth for you, the distress of the land, and the high prices of provisions, I wish to see you, and have you near me. It is true, while I live you will live also, if I keep my place and piety. I study daily what I can do without. One horse, and that sometimes borrowed, one coat, one waistcoat—the last coat and waistcoat I used about fourteen months—four or five shirts, and four or five books. I am in doubt, if I should be called away, you will not be provided for so well in England as in America, among those for whom I have faithfully laboured these twenty-four years. It is true you are not immortal, any more than myself, and judging according to the nature of things, you may go first, one or both of you. All these things I have weighed in my mind. I wish you to consider the matter, and ask much counsel of God, and of your best and most impartial friends. I wish you, after considering it, to send me another letter. Whether I be present or absent, dead or alive, I trust my friends in Baltimore will take care of you by my help. You have spent many pounds upon Christian people, I know, from my childhood. Happy was I when this was done, and I hope it will come home to you in mercy. You must make it a matter of much fasting and prayer before you attempt anything. You must not expect to see me more than twice a year."

A few months afterwards he wrote, "Perhaps I was constrained, from the high sense of filial duty I had, to invite you here. I now think you much better where you are. I sincerely wish I could come to see you ; but I see no way to do so without sinning against God and the Church." With reference to a remittance of money, he adds, " Were it ten thousand per year, if I had it in my possession, you should be welcome, if you had need of it."

In another letter, addressed to them a year or two before his father's death, he says :—

"I have had considerable pain of mind from information received that the money was not paid. I last evening made arrangement for a remittance to you. It will come into your hands in the space of three or four months. My salary is sixty-four dollars. I have sold my watch and library, and would sell my shirts before you should want. I have made a reserve for you. I spend very little on my own account. My friends find me some clothing. The contents of a small pair of saddle-bags will do for me, and one coat a year. Your son Francis is a man of honour and conscience. As my father and my mother never disgraced me by an act of dishonesty, I hope to echo back the same sound of an honest upright man. I am well satisfied that the Lord saw fit you should be my parents rather than the king and queen, or any of the great. I sometimes think you will outlive me. I have made my will, and left my all to you, and that is soon done. While I live and do well, I shall remember you every year. Oh! that your last days may be your best, and that you may not only live long, but live well and die well ! "

June 17th, 1798, he thus expresses himself with

reference to his father's death, " I now feel myself an orphan with respect to my father. Wounded memory recalls to me what took place when I parted from him nearly twenty years ago. For about thirty-nine years my father hath had the Gospel preached in his house. The particulars of his death have not yet come to hand." They were not long delayed, however, and though few and briefly expressed, conveyed all that he most desired to know. " Mr. Phillips, of Birmingham," he says, " writes thus of my father, ' He kept his room six weeks previous to his death. The first month of the time he ate nothing but a little biscuit, and the last fortnight took nothing but a little spirits and water. *He died very happy.*" The following is his letter to his aged mother with reference to her bereavement :—

" From the information I have received I fear my venerable father is no more an inhabitant of this earth. You are a widow and I am an orphan, with respect to my father. I cannot tell how to advise you in this important change. You have made to yourself respectable and extensive friends, who, though they cannot give to you, can comfort you. I have been, as you have heard, afflicted by excessive labours of mind and body. I had to neglect writing, reading, and preaching for a time. I had to stop and lie by in some precious families, where parents and children, in some measure, supplied your absence. I lay by in Virginia. When you hear the name you will love it unseen, for you will say, ' That is the place where my Frank was sick.' I am now much mended. I move in a little carriage, being unable to ride on horseback. Were you to see me, and the colour of my hair—nearly that of your own ! My eyes are weak, even with glasses. When I was a child, and would pry into the Bible by twinkling firelight, you used to say, ' Frank, you will spoil your eyes.' It is a grief to me that I cannot preach as heretofore. I am greatly worn out at fifty-five ; but it is a good cause. God is with me ; my soul exults in God."

As is common with men of healthy and refined moral sensibilities, his affection for his mother was peculiarly strong and tender. She died in January, 1802, and this is his tribute to her memory : " I may speak safely concerning my very dear mother : her character to me is well-known. . . . . She was an afflicted, yet most active woman ; of quick bodily powers and masculine understanding ; nevertheless, ' so kindly all the elements were mixed in her ' that her strong mind was most susceptible to the subduing influences of that Christian sympathy which *weeps with those who weep, and rejoices with them that do rejoice.* As a woman and a wife she was pure-minded, modest, and blameless : as a mother (above all the women of the world would I claim her as my own) she was ardently affectionate : as a *mother in Israel*, few of her sex have done more by a holy walk to live, and by personal labour to support, the Gospel, and to wash the saints' feet : as a friend, she was generous, true, and constant."

A thoughtful reader will dwell with especial satisfaction on the feature of character which is now before him, as an evidence of the genuineness of that spirit of self-renunciation in which he has seen the good Bishop conduct himself as a preacher and chief pastor. Love for the souls of men which prompts to the denial of self is not different in nature from the love of kindred : it is the same affection elevated, expanded, and refined. The one is the true outgrowth of the other under the fostering influences of Divine grace. True charity for the world implies and presupposes charity at home, and that man is under a strange illusion who persuades himself that the fervour of his religious zeal compensates for the neglect of " those of his own household," and most of all for the desertion of aged and dependent parents. " *Let him learn first to show piety at home, and to requite his parents.*" How greatly Asbury's beloved mother needed the aid, which, by the practice of a rigorous self-

denial, he occasionally afforded her, he never fully understood : to what painful straits she was reduced to maintain
her position of self-respect and liberality it was well for him
that he never knew.   He records with astonishment, "I find
that a certain Mr. Emery has taken all her property."   He
had never been informed, therefore, that she had made over
all her effects to Mr. Emery, the brother of a friend of his
youth, as her landlord, by a bill of sale, in lieu of the payment of rent ; and that she thus lived rent free from about
the time of her husband's death !

CHAPTER XXI.

WITH the opening of the present century was instituted, without preconception or design, like so many other of the institutions of Methodism, that peculiar form of evangelistic agency called *the Camp-meeting.* An account of this, as promoted by Bishop Asbury, remains to be given, and we must then hasten onward towards the serene end.

Two brothers, John McGee, a Methodist local-preacher, and the Rev. William McGee, a Presbyterian minister, were settled, the one as an agriculturist, the other in charge of a small congregation, in the west of Tennessee. Though belonging to different churches, they agreed in religious sentiment, and frequently worked together on the same plans for evangelizing the rapidly-increasing, but spiritually careless, populations of the western States. In July, 1799, they set out in company to visit and preach to certain new settlements in Kentucky. At one of them, in Logan county, there was

a small Presbyterian Church, under the care of the Rev. James
M. McGready, which, at the time of their arrival, was holding one of its usual sacramental services. Mr. John McGee
was invited to preach on the occasion, and spoke with extraordinary power and impressiveness. He was followed by
his brother, and by another Presbyterian minister, whose
name was Hodge, under whose discourse a woman gave
expression to feelings beyond her control, in loud and start-
ling ejaculations of praise. Other members of the congregation were simultaneously wrought upon in a similar manner;
and the Presbyterian ministers present, except Mr. William
McGee, embarrassed and overcome with emotion, retired
from the place, leaving the meeting in charge of him and his
brother. For a time they also were overpowered with feeling;
and, seized with a strange tremor, they sat in silence on the
floor. At length John arose and exhorted, "as the Spirit
gave him utterance," his hearers responding involuntarily in
loud sobs and cries. Many previously thoughtless persons
were suddenly filled with spiritual concern: some fell to the
ground as if through a stroke of paralysis. This unlooked-
for manifestation led to the appointment of another meeting
for the Holy Communion and prayer, which was similarly
characterized. The impossibility of tracing the ecstatic and
other phenomena witnessed on these occasions to natural
causes, and the evident change of character experienced by
those who were affected by them, convinced the earnest men
in charge that they proceeded from a superhuman agency;
and in the full confidence that they were acting in agreement
with the will of God, they arranged to hold other and larger
meetings for the same spiritual purposes elsewhere.

Asbury heard that preparations were being made to hold
one of them on the Cumberland River, Tennessee, when
presiding over the Conference in Kentucky, in 1800; and

he, with his companions, Bishop Whatcoat and Mr. McKendree, resolved to attend it. They arrived, the Bishop states, at "the close of the sacramental solemnity, that had been held four days," and each of them, on the invitation of the "Presbyterian officiating ministers," gave an address, Asbury's subject being *the work of God.* "In the intervals between preaching," he says, " the people refreshed themselves and their horses and returned upon the ground. The *stand* was in the open air, embosomed in a wood of lofty beech trees. The ministers of God, Methodists and Presbyterians, united their labours, and mingled with the childlike simplicity of primitive times. Fires blazing here and there dispelled the darkness, and the shouts of the redeemed captives, and the cries of precious souls struggling into life, broke the silence of midnight. The weather was delightful ; as if heaven smiled while mercy flowed in abundant streams of salvation to perishing sinners."

He discerned in the proceedings a new and powerful form of evangelistic action, and at once entered into them with heart and soul. Something of the kind he had long seen to be necessary to bring the sparse and widely-scattered populations of the west under spiritual instruction and quickening ; and this he regarded as a providential interposition to supply the means wanted for this end. He did not expect the work to be carried on by such means without a continuance of the bodily affections, extravagances, and other disadvantages which had marked its first stage. He foresaw in its progress the collateral development of human elements, which would have a tendency to mar the manifestations of Divine working, and to give occasion for the sneers and jibes of profane or sceptical men ; but he was too sagacious and practical, and too much in earnest, to allow this to deter him from adopting what, *if suitably guarded,* might become so immense a power for good ; and henceforth encampments in the wilderness or in forests, for continuous religious services, became one of the recognised forms of Methodist labour. Their immediate popularity and success exceeded all calculation. People thronged to them from the most remote and isolated localities of the neighbourhood in which one was appointed to be held, with their tents, beds, and provision, as to the most attractive public festival. Of course their motives were various. Some came to receive spiritual aid and invigoration ; some to meet distant friends ; some from motives of curiosity ; and some probably to be entertained and amused. But all were brought under the faithful exposition and enforcement of Gospel truth, and more or less under the power of spiritual influences; and many " who came to scoff remained to pray."

Nothing could have afforded more suitable occasion for the exercise of the great gifts of McKendree, and probably he, more than any other preacher, contributed to bring them into repute. A man of commanding presence ; of clear, powerful, and musical voice ; and of great natural eloquence both of speech and action, he drew the strong-minded, though rough and untutored, inhabitants of the western wilds around him in vast crowds, and with every manifestation of unusual interest. The next year he was stationed among them as the presiding-elder of the Kentucky district ; and through his labours in connection with Camp-meetings thousands of persons were brought under the power of the Gospel whom no other human agent had been able to reach. Thus began a new era in the history of the Methodist Episcopal Church : from this period the Camp-meeting was one of its settled institutions.

For some years past, and from this time to the end of life, Asbury had to carry on his episcopal work in almost incessant fightings with disease. His constant exposure to malaria, cold, and rain; his want of suitable food for days together, and his frequent loss of sleep; with consequent exhaustion and continual attacks of fever, sore-throat, and rheumatism, had at length completely shaken and impaired his once healthy constitution. The references in his daily registers to his debilitated and suffering bodily condition are painfully numerous, but are always accompanied with devout acknowledgments of the all-sufficient succours of Divine grace. We envy at the same time that we pity him. "Here let me record the gracious dealings of God to my soul," he writes, after his last journey from Kentucky: "I have had uncommon peace of mind, and spiritual consolations every day, notwithstanding the long rides I have endured, and the frequent privations of good water and proper food to which I have been subjected. To me the wilderness and the solitary places were made as the garden of God." "My soul is at peace," he writes again, shortly after; "Jesus, Jesus is my all. My soul is love to God, to Christ, to His Church, and to all souls." "I have fevers and feebleness, but a soul entirely swallowed up in God." Involuntary utterances such as these, which are of continual recurrence, assure us that he was one of the happiest, as he was one of the most laborious and suffering of men.

In 1801 he records the death of his friend, the Rev. Devereux Jarratt, and writes this tribute to his memory:— "He was a faithful and successful preacher. He had witnessed four or five periodical revivals of religion in his parish. When he began his labours he knew of no other evangelical preacher in all Virginia! He travelled into several counties; and there were very few parish churches within fifty miles of his own in which he had not preached; to which labour of love and zeal he added the preaching of the word of life on solitary plantations and in meeting-houses. He was the first who received our despised preachers. When, strangers and unfriended, they came into his parish, he took them into his house. I have reason to presume that he was instrumentally successful in awakening hundreds of souls to some sense of religion in that dark day and time."

I transcribe another reference to the removal of one of his early friends, on account of its suggestiveness of the untold success of the itinerant labours on which he entered immediately after his arrival in America. On one of his first excursions from New York he visited New Rochelle, and found accommodation at the house of a Mr. Devoue. In June, 1802, he preaches a funeral sermon for one of the daughters of this gentleman, and remarks that he was the first in the city to receive and welcome the Methodist preachers, and that through him New Rochelle " became the gate by which we have had such an abundant and permanent entrance into the State of New York. After sitting under the ministry of the gospel above thirty years, the saint," he says, " the daughter of Mr. Devoue, and his own child in the faith, died very happy in God."

In a paragraph or two I here condense his account of the adventures and experiences which in 1802 marked his annual visit to the Western Conference.

" I have one day to call my own. I write, I read, I think, and refit for the mountains. My mind is in great peace, and has so been kept in all my labours. I rejoice to find the work of God spreading and growing in Frederick circuit. In Fredericktown at last, after more than thirty years' labour, we have a house of worship and thirty souls, or upwards, in fellowship. . . . We passed through Lexington, and being so near, I gratified my curiosity by a view of the Natural Bridge. I walked down the hill to look at the arch thrown, in a regular ellipsis, about 160 feet above a stream, which, in the rainy season, foams and roars beneath. The breadth of the bridge may be 60 feet, and the distance across 160 feet. We have good news,—the work of God revives in all the circuits. . . We came to the Holston. I found the people praising God. A blessed revival had taken place. Fourteen or fifteen times have I toiled over the mighty mountains, and nearly twenty years have we laboured upon Holston ; and lo! the rage of wild and Christian savages is tamed, and God hath glorified himself. Sweet peace fills my mind, and glorious prospects of Zion's prosperity cheer my heart. We have not, shall not, labour in vain. Not unto us, not unto us, but to Jehovah, be all the glory on earth and in heaven for ever !

"I attended a Camp-meeting, which continued to be held four days. From my stand in the woods I spoke from the words, 'Let me go, for the day breaketh.' I felt that the word was given *me* and applied to the hearts of the people. We made towards West Point. In the morning we started in good spirits. We were somewhat shaken in going the old path down Spencer's Hill. I walked, fearing every moment a fall for myself or my horse. It was late when we arrived at Obee's River, and I imprudently lay too far from our encampment fire, and took a cold, which fixed upon my throat. Late the following evening we came into Shaw's, where we lay upon the floor. I was sick indeed. . . . We rode forward to Station Camp, and found the Conference seated. By this time my stomach and speech were pretty well gone. I applied to Mr. William Hodge and to Mr. William McGee, Presbyterian ministers, to supply my lack of public service, which they did with great fervency and fidelity. With great pleasure and pain I heard them both. I was able to ordain, by employing Brother McKendree to examine those who were

presented, and to station the preachers. . . After eight days'
suffering of severely acute pain, the inflammation descended
to my feet. . . I spoke on Heb. iii. 7, 8: some wept, all
were attentive.

"We took our departure at five o'clock, a.m., and continued
on till half-past six o'clock in the evening. We then stopped,
struck a fire, and encamped under a heavy mountain dew,
which, when the wind shook the trees, fell like rain upon
us. Brother McKendree made me a tent of his own and
John Watson's blankets, and happily saved me from taking
cold while I slept about two hours under my grand *marquée*.
Brother McKendree threw his cloak over the limb of a tree ;
and he and his companion took shelter underneath, and slept
also. . . . After riding fifty miles, a part of ninety-three miles
in two days, we came again to West Point. At a rocky
run, in attempting to dismount, my horse gave a sudden
turn, and swung me against the rocks in the stream ; the
rude shock to my tender feet made me cry out bitterly. . . .
I have been sick for twenty-three days. My dear McKendree
had to lift me up and down from my horse, like a helpless
child. . . I have ridden about five thousand five hundred
miles. In the midst of all I am comforted with the prospects
of the Western Conference. We have added three thousand
members there this year; have formed Cumberland into a
district, and have sent a missionary to the Natchez."

On his return from the Kentucky Conference of 1803, he
wrote cheerfully, after mentioning how many hundreds of
emigrants to the west he had seen on the roads : "A man
who is well mounted will scorn to complain of the roads,
when he sees men, women, and children, almost naked,
paddling barefoot and barelegged along, or labouring up
the rocky hills, while those who are best off have only a
horse for two or three children to ride at once. . . . I, too,

have my sufferings; no room to retire to; that in which you
sit, common to all, crowded with women and children, the
fire occupied by cooking, much and long-loved solitude not
to be found, unless you choose to run out into the rain, in
the woods. Six months in the year I have had, for thirty-
two years, occasionally to submit to what will never be
agreeable to me. The people are amongst the kindest in
the world. But kindness will not make a crowded log
cabin, twelve feet by ten, agreeable. Without are cold and
rain, and within six adults, and as many children, one of
them all motion. The dogs, too, must be sometimes admitted.
Amongst my other trials I have taken a foul skin disease;
and considering the filthy houses and filthy beds I have
met with, in coming from the Kentucky Conference, it is
perhaps strange that I have not caught it twenty times.
I do not see that there is any security against it but by
sleeping *in a brimstone shirt.* Poor Bishop! But we must
bear it for the elect's sake!"

A heavy demand on his time, thought, and sympathies
was made in his later years by his ever increasing corre-
spondence. The following letter, written under the pressure
of a mass of business which he was preparing for the Boston
Conference of 1803, may be taken as a sample of the
friendly epistles he was throwing off continually. It is
addressed to the Rev. Charles Atmore :—

Waltham, near Boston, June 3, 1803.
"MY VERY DEAR BROTHER,—

"Not less so by being only known by name. The present
year is marked with great grace to the inhabitants of the United
States. Great things have been done in the Western States of Tennessee, Kentucky, and Ohio, by meetings held by encampments for
several days and nights together. These meetings have obtained in
Georgia, South and North Carolina, Virginia, Maryland, and Delaware.
Some of these meetings have been held four, others six, and one nine

days and nights, with small intermissions. One hundred and seven
have been added in a town in Virginia of about one hundred families,
at a nine days' meeting. The Presbyterians, over half the continent,
are stirred up, and are in church and congregational union with the
Methodists. And they both feed their flocks together, like the ministers
and people of God. We are always pleased to hear from, and honour the
members and ministers of, the ancient Connexion in Europe. We are
one Body. We have one Name, one Gospel, one Christ, one God, one
Holy Spirit, one Heaven. And as it comforteth us (when we find
some barren spots) that there are so many fruitful hills of Zion, you
will rejoice that God is with a branch of the Methodist Connexion in
this country. I hope we shall continue to preach a present and full
salvation, and fill up life to the best of purposes.

"I am now in the 58th year of my age, frequently subject to an
inflammatory rheumatism, sometimes disabled for a season. Then I
revive again, and limp along. Now my constitution is broken, through
heats and colds, and I have grey hairs in abundance upon me. I have
been thirty-seven years in the Connexion, and thirty-two in America.
I hope to hold out a little longer, and then to meet my dear English
brethren, preachers and people, in a better world.

> " ' There all the ship's company meet,
> Who sailed with the Saviour beneath.'

"I thought, when I came to America, four years would be long
enough for me to stay; but the children whom God had given us
asked, 'Will you leave us in our time of distress?' And so here I am.
Give me your prayers, and present Francis Asbury in love to all you
please, as their and your friend and brother in Jesus."

At the General Conference of 1804 Dr. Coke was associated in service with Asbury for the last time. It opened
at Baltimore, on the 7th of May; was the fourth General
Conference; and was distinguished by a further revision of
the *Book of Discipline*, and the fixing of the boundaries of
the several Annual Conferences. At its conclusion Asbury
accompanied Dr. Coke on a visit for a day to their friends
at Perry Hall, and they then finally parted: he to attend
the Conference at Philadelphia, and proceed on his New
England tour; and the Doctor to recross the ocean. But a

17

union of spirit had been established between them which grew stronger with advancing age. " My very dear brother," he wrote to him two years later (May 7th, 1806), " if we should never have the happiness of seeing each other again, can we ever forget the days and nights we have spent comfortably together ? our spirits being sweetly joined, and not a jar existing, unless Diotropheses, here or there, formed for discord, whispered evil. Ah ! my brother, the deep rivers, creeks, swamps, and deserts we have traversed together, glad to see a light, or hear the voice of any human being, or domestic animal ! . . . After riding chiefly on horseback, till last summer, I have bought a very light wagon ; and by this mode of travelling can visit the seven Conferences, with most of the cities and towns, in the year. In five of the Conferences we have an increase of 8,273 members of Society, and of fifty-eight preachers, last year. During the times of sitting of the five past Conferences we calculate that about five hundred persons were made partakers of converting or restoring grace." " My dear Coke," he wrote again, in 1808, " great grace, great peace, great usefulness attend you and your dear wife ! God is gloriously visiting our continent. . . . We visit almost every part within, and over the lines of, the United States. We have, after your example, sent out missionaries into the interior and exterior of Pennsylvania, New York, and Jersey. You need not wonder that I am remiss in writing, since I have to ride on horseback five thousand miles in eight months, and to meet seven Conferences, that comprehend nearly six hundred preachers. . . . I have received your many loving letters, and feel my obligations to you. If I write you one circumstantial letter in a year, well : my eyes, my time, my powers fail. Think how many hours I must be on horseback, when I only ride three, or at most four, miles in an hour. Everlasting love embrace you, my dear brother Coke! The past is gone—with me the present and future are in sight!"

The General Conference of 1808, as before mentioned, was rendered for ever memorable by the adoption of a principle for which Asbury had long earnestly pleaded, by which this, the supreme and only legislative court of the Episcopal Church, became select and strictly representative. Instead of being open to all the members of the several Annual Conferences who choose to attend it, the quadrennial General Conference was to be composed in future of Delegates only, to be elected by the Annual Conferences according to a fixed ratio.

This Conference was further signalised by the election into the episcopate of the first of the native American preachers who filled that office. The vacancy occasioned by the death of "that dear man of God," as he was so justly called, Bishop Whatcoat, had to be supplied; and, by a large majority of votes, Mr. McKendree was chosen to occupy it. On the occasion of his consecration, Asbury preached from St. Paul's charge to Timothy: "Take heed unto thyself and unto the doctrine; continue in them; for by doing this thou shalt both save thyself and them that hear thee;" Messrs. Jesse Lee and Freeborn Garrettson presented the Bishop-elect to the venerable Bishop; and, assisted by four Presbyters, he solemnly set him apart for his responsible functions by the laying on of hands. Asbury then re-ascended the pulpit and delivered a fervid discourse, in which he reviewed the whole history of the Church from its origin in the labours of Embury, Captain Webb, and Robert Shawbridge. "And now," said he, in winding up an impressive peroration amidst general expressions of thanksgiving and praise, "God has, after forty years, raised up a

bishop from among yourselves, a man full of faith and of
the Holy Ghost!"

A day or two before the opening of the Conference,
Asbury's influential friend and convert, Mr. Gough, of Perry
Hall, was removed by death. The event, with the pensive
reminiscences it called up, had a subduing effect on many
minds, and at the funeral several members of the Conference
walked in procession behind the remains and the mourners
to the end of the town. Asbury preached a funeral sermon,
which "was very much a portraiture of his religious experience and character." He "was a man much respected
and beloved," says the Bishop. "As a husband, a father,
and a master, he was well worthy of imitation. His
charities were as numerous as proper objects to a Christian
were likely to make them; and the souls and bodies of the
poor were administered to in the manner of a Christian who
remembered the precepts and followed the example of his
Divine Master."

He remained a few days in Baltimore after the Conference;
preaching in and around the city; and says, after enume-
rating various services in which he had been engaged, "I am
kept at work by my friends. But they do what they can,
Methodists and others, to pay me in affection, in attentions,
in honour. Lord, keep me humble and holy!" They had
learnt to make the most of his too occasional and too brief
visits, though at the cost to himself of continual and un-
relieved weariness. Within a week or two he was again
beyond the reach of their solicitations. Taking with him, as
his companion, Henry Boehm, a German, to preach to the
numerous German settlements in the west, he started on his
annual tour over the Alleghanies; and despite an attack of
inflammatory rheumatism in his feet, which deprived him of
their use, he proceeded to Cincinnati, then a town of about

ten thousand inhabitants, and even as far as Indiana. "We came," he says, "to Lawrenceburgh, the first town in the Indian territory. In this wild there may be twenty thousand souls already. I feel for them."

Returning through Kentucky he held a Camp-meeting in that State in association with Bishop McKendree, who afterwards accompanied him into Tennessee, where the Western Conference was to be held. The preachers, eighty in number, assembled from all parts of that vast region, and formed an encampment in the wilderness, eating and sleeping in their tents. "We sat six hours a day," he says, "stationed eighty-three preachers, and all was peace. On Friday the sacrament was administered, and we hope there were souls converted, strengthened, and sanctified. The increase of the Western Conference for the year will be two thousand five hundred." Boehm, who wrote a narrative of this journey, one of the greatest events of his life, says, "To my great surprise Father Asbury bore up under all the toil and labour of travelling and preaching, together with the care of all the churches, and, notwithstanding, he was a very agreeable companion on the road. He would often indulge in a vein of innocent pleasantry."

From "the Conference ground" in Tennessee the two Bishops travelled in company across the wilderness, over the mountains, and through the Carolinas into Georgia, attending Camp-meetings and Quarterly-meetings, preaching in chapels, private houses, and in the open air, the more aged and infirm of them suffering, yet always rejoicing. "Great news!" he exclaims. "Baltimore taken fire! Bohemia has a great work! Camp-meetings have done this! Glory to the great I AM!" On his way from Augusta to Savannah he says, in his lively and cheery manner, "We are riding in a poor thirty-dollar chaise, in

partnership, two bishops of us ; but it must be confessed it
tallies well with the weight of our purses. What bishops !
Well ; but we have great news, and we have great times.
Each Western, Southern, and the Virginia Conference will
have one thousand souls truly converted to God ; and is not
this an equivalent for a light purse ? And are we not well
paid for starving and toil ? Yes ! Glory be to God ! ''

On the first of May, 1812, the General Conference, convened as a *representative* Assembly, in agreement with the
regulations adopted in 1808, was held in New York. Asbury
had the opportunity of attending it, and of witnessing the
operations of his latest great legislative measure ; and he
refers to it with satisfaction. It was the last General Conference he attended.

In March, 1814, he notes the death of another of his
venerable and beloved friends, '' the holy, the great Otter-
bien. Forty years,'' he says, '' have I known the retiring
modesty of this man of God ; towering majestically above
his fellows in learning, wisdom, and grace, yet seeking to
be known only of God and the people of God. He had
been sixty years a minister, fifty years a *converted* one. I
am at Perry Hall,'' he adds, pathetically, '' where I have
been for three days very ill.''

He endeavoured, notwithstanding, to go forward on his
accustomed tour, at this season of the year, through New
England, *but in vain.* He attended the Conference at Philadelphia, and went on as far as New Jersey, when a violent
fever seized him, and he was laid aside for twelve weeks.
From this attack he never completely rallied. He says with
reference to it, after '' clambering over the rude mountains
to Greensburg,'' '' I would not be loved to death, and so came
down from my sick-room and took to the road, weak enough.
Attentions constant and kindness unceasing have pursued

me to this place, and my strength increases daily. I look back upon a martyr's life of toil, privation, and pain ; and I am ready for a martyr's death. The purity of my intentions ; my diligence in the labours to which God has been pleased to call me ; the unknown sufferings I have endured ;—*what are these ?* The merit, atonement, and righteousness of Christ alone make my plea. My friends in Philadelphia gave me a light, little four-wheeled carriage ; but God and the Baltimore Conference made me a richer present. They gave me John Wesley Bond for a travelling companion. Has he his equal on the earth for excellences of every kind as an aid ? I groan one minute with pain, and shout *Glory* the next."

With the aid of his little carriage and his thoughtful, attentive, and devout travelling companion, he continued his travels and labours in the east, again in the west, and as far as Charleston, in South Carolina. In May, 1815, he attended the New York Conference, which this year was held at Albany, and writes, " *Sunday*, 21*st*. By vote of Conference I preached the funeral sermon for Dr. Coke, of blessed mind and soul, of the third branch of Oxonian Methodists, a gentleman, a scholar, and to us a bishop ; and, as a minister of Christ, in zeal, in labours, and in services, the greatest man of the last century. Poor wheezing, groaning, coughing Francis visited the Conference chamber on Tuesday and Thursday."

A venerable minister now living, the Rev. Daniel De Vinne, who was present at this Conference, and heard the funeral sermon referred to, has lately written his recollections of the appearance of the invalid preacher on the occasion. He says that " time, sickness, and continued hardships had left their indelible marks upon him. He was considerably bent, his steps were slow and feeble, and his hair was thin, and nearly white. He presented the appearance of a man worn out. In ascending the long stairs to the elevated pulpit the venerable man was nearly exhausted. He took with him only Thomas Drummond, a member of the Conference, to assist in the exercises. During the sermon he was supported by a high stool. For one so enfeebled his voice was remarkably strong. It was at once full and distinct, and filled the church. He dwelt briefly on the life and labours of Dr. Coke. In a few days the Conference ended; the preachers went to their respective circuits, and Bishop Asbury went on his northern and last tour.''

CHAPTER XXII.

STARTING from the Conference just mentioned, we will
now follow the tottering but happy patriarch to the
end of his earthly career.

He left Albany, Saturday, May 27th, 1815, to go forward to
the New England Conference, which was to be held at Unity,
Massachusetts, on the 7th of June.   By the following Saturday, June 3rd, he had reached Boston, but was " greatly
outdone " and in much pain.   In the evening of Sunday, however, he preached, though, he states, " in weakness and much
trembling."   Arrived at the Conference, he could do little
more than watch its proceedings and give advice from his
sick-chamber.   " Poor Francis," he says, pleasantly, " was
shut up alone as at Albany."   He " ordained twelve deacons
and twelve elders," but resigned the presidential chair to
George Pickering ; " and," he adds with satisfaction, " our
business progressed well."   At the end of the week he found
it necessary to " reduce his projected tour of sixteen hundred
miles to a straight ride of three hundred and eighty miles to

New York. As I passed through Ashgrove," he says, "I
preached in the chapel." The Society here was formed by
Philip Embury. When Boardman came by Wesley's appointment to New York, in 1769, Embury gave up the work
in that city into his hands, and retired to this remote and,
at that time, uncultivated district; where he, with Paul and
Barbara Heck, a few other "Irish Palatines," and Abraham
Bininger, one of the Moravian Brethren who sailed to Georgia
with Wesley in 1737, formed a settlement, which they called
Ashgrove. Embury for six years was their chaplain and
class-leader. In 1775 he died; but the work continued to
be carried on, and at the time of this last visit of Asbury
Ashgrove was a considerable town, with a good Methodist
church and congregation.

Leaving this interesting and noteworthy spot, Asbury
travelled onward through Troy, to the mansion of his beloved
and hospitable friend, Freeborn Garrettson, at Rhinebeck,—
at this period his favourite retreat. Garrettson, himself a
man of wealth, had married the accomplished and wealthy
daughter of Judge Livingston, who had been won to Christ
and to Methodism by the godly spirit and character of her
servant-maid. He was for many years the presiding-elder
of the Hudson district; and in the decline of life he built
this house on the banks of the noble river, and retired into
it for the remainder of his days. Continuing to labour to
the full extent of his strength, he welcomed to the hospitalities and comforts of his home all his brethren who were
stationed within its reach. Asbury called it *The Travellers'
Rest;* and, as his infirmities increased, occasionally resorted
to it with thankfulness. He describes it as " a good, simply
elegant, useful house for God, His people, and the family.".
" We rested at Travellers' Rest," he says, in one place,
" with my dear friends, Freeborn Garrettson and his prudent

pious wife;" subjoining two days afterwards, "I had to tear myself away from these precious souls; I do believe God dwells in this house." On this occasion he tarried with them five days, including Sunday, when he "preached for them; very feeble." Going on to New York, he warned a large congregation there against the evils of religious formality; preached in "the African Chapel, both colours being present;" proceeded through Burlington to Philadelphia, where he preached in the City Road Chapel; then went forward to Wilmington, to one of the three residences of his friend and spiritual son, Senator Bassett. "Ah, the changes we witness!" he exclaimed. "My long-loved friend, Judge Bassett, some time past a paralytic, is lately re-stricken, and suffers much in his helpless state." One day with his afflicted friend, and he pushes on "across the wide Susquehanna," now spanned by an elegant bridge, to "son Francis Hollingsworth's, Little York." "Here," he says, "I tried to preach, but wanted strength. My audience was partly composed of the respectables of the borough, who were no doubt disappointed."

A Sunday at Carlisle, where he "spoke in the new chapel, and the truth was felt;" and, recording gratefully that his health was better, he advanced with great speed to the mountains, which he crossed to Bloody Run. "The stones of this stream," he explains, "are tinged red as with blood, and the story is, that three men were killed in it by the Indians shortly after Braddock's defeat." Here he preached in the "little chapel in the state in which it was; said a few words to a few people, and lodged at a grand tavern at night." The next day he proceeded to Bedford, and thence to Somerset, where he preached in "the court-house, and the Lord spoke His own truths through a tottering tenement of clay, accompanied with conviction to many minds." The next morning his host, William Ross, "stepped round the town with our mite subscription, and the citizens were liberal,"—this *mite subscription* being in aid of his funds for the relief of the half-starved preachers of the extreme west, whom he expected shortly to see gathered around him. Going forward to Freeport, over the rough "western Pennsylvania roads," which his "poor arms would feel for days to come," he preached for about thirty minutes at Brightwell's, and ordained John Phillips a deacon. Here he forded the Monongahela, and "ascended the dreadful hills to Briggs's, to whom we failed not to give our parting charge. Briggs is a Marylander, and an ancient Methodist. Down went the fence, and through the flax and corn he conducted us, and onward we toiled to Newkirk's mill—a clean house and kind souls. We might not stay. Forward we drove up the valley to Rock meeting-house, a handsome edifice, and thence along the Williamsport-road to Washington. We were lodged like a president at Haslett's. Is it possible?" he continues, characteristically, in a still happier undertone. "Can it be true? A revival at Steubenville! Not far from two hundred converts there, most of them young people! I rejoice exceedingly."

At Washington he preached in the Court-house, and assisted at a kind of Missionary Meeting. As a Baptist Missionary was there, "collecting for foreign lands, I thought," says he, "that I might help with a few words. I related that, a few years past, a London Methodist had complained to me that the kingdom and the Church had given so largely to support distant missions. I observed, in reply, that the Methodist preachers, who had been sent by John Wesley to America, *came as missionaries*. And now behold the consequences of this mission! We have seven hundred travelling-preachers, and three thousand local-preachers ! "

Onward he progressed to West Liberty, on the banks of the Ohio, where he preached on the shortness of time ; to Zanesville, where, immediately on his arrival, he heard that a Camp-meeting was being held five miles from the town, and, proceeding thither in haste, preached from the words, " Knowing the terror of the Lord, we persuade men ; " and thence to Chilicothe, where he first preached in the chapel, and then hasted away to a Camp-meeting nine miles distant, and preached on the repentance of Peter. He had brought with him, in his convenient little carriage, a large quantity of New Testaments, which here, in the far west, he distributed to the poor, his young companion, Mr. Bond, reading a few verses to each person who was asked to accept the gift, and he basing upon them an affectionate exhortation. "On our route," he records, " we called upon many of our old friends, who treated us like presidents."

He was again taken ill, with inflammation of the face, yet presided over the Ohio Conference, and writes concerning it, " Great grace, peace, and success have attended our coming together. We hold in this Conference sixty-eight preachers, sixty-seven of whom are stationed. Ten delegates have been chosen for the General Conference." Bishop McKendree was with him here, and accompanied him to Cincinnati. In this growing town he preached from the words, " Only let your conversation be as it becometh the Gospel of Christ," and distributed copies of the New Testament ; then, going southward, he came to Georgetown, Kentucky, where he preached in the Court-house on, "To you is the word of this salvation sent," and thence proceeded to Lexington. Here he wrote, " My soul is blest with continual consolation and peace, in all my great weak-

ness of body, my labour, and in crowds of company. I am
a debtor to the whole continent, but more especially to the
north-east and south-west. I have visited the south thirty
times in thirty-one years. I wish to visit Mississippi, but
am resigned. I preached in Lexington on, 'I will also
leave in the midst of thee an afflicted and poor people, and
they shall trust in the LORD !' A day or two after he
says, "I took counsel of my elder sons, who advise me *not*
to go to Mississippi this year."

In this town the Kentucky Conference was held, and was
marked by "great peace, great order, and the great deal of business done." Here he wrote, after stating that on the Sunday
he ordained deacons, and preached a sermon with reference
to the death of Dr. Coke, " My eyes fail. I will resign the
stations to Bishop McKendree—*I will take away my feet.*
It is my fifty-fifth year of ministry, and forty-fifth year of
labour in America. My mind enjoys great peace and Divine
consolation. My health is better, which may be owing in
part to my being less deeply engaged in the business of the
Conference. But whether health, life, or death, good is the
will of the Lord. I will trust Him. He is the Strength of
my heart, and my Portion for ever. Glory! glory! glory!"

From Conferences his feet were indeed withdrawn. This
was the last he attended. But he could not refrain from his
loved work of preaching Christ. He was " daily drawing
nearer home," as he was deeply conscious ; but so long as
any measure of strength remained for service on earth he
was anxious to use it. The following Sunday he again
occupied the pulpit, and the next day continued his journey,
still struggling hopelessly against the growing power of
disease. On one day during the preceding week he drove
over roads which he denounces as a disgrace to the State, a
distance of forty-three miles. Arriving two hours after night

at the house of "Father Holt," he says, playfully, with reference to the name, "This will not do; I must *halt* or order my grave." After a day or two here, "very unwell," he set out again, exclaiming, "Oh, what kindness and attention I receive!" and came to the house of Wesley Harrison, in Harrisonburg, Virginia, whose father, he remarks, received him as his guest on his first visit to the town. He and his pious wife, he says, "are, I trust, both in glory."

The next Sunday he attended a Quarterly-meeting, and "bore a feeble, but a faithful testimony to the truth;" and the Sunday following he again preached, his text being Acts xxvi. 17, 18: "Unto whom now I send thee, to open their eyes, and to turn them from darkness to light, and from the power of Satan unto God, that they may receive forgiveness of sins, and inheritance among them that are sanctified by faith that is in Me." Lingering over this, the last text he mentions, when entering the record in his Journal, he says, "Ministers must be *sent;* and to be qualified for their mission must, like Paul, be convicted, converted, and sanctified. Like him, they must be preserved from the violence of the people; but especially from their indulgences and flatteries. And a faithful minister will have the signs following," which the text enumerates. "I die daily," he adds, "I am wasting away with a constant cough," so steadfastly and relentlessly was ulceration of the lungs doing its fatal work! For a day or too the friends with whom he was staying prevailed on him to rest. "My children," he says, "will not let me go out." Once more, however, on the Sunday, he preached, and "we had," he says, "a time of great feeling." On Tuesday he came to the house of "Widow Means. The lady," he says, "was not at home, but the servants are attentive. John Wesley Bond preached in the kitchen."

" *Sunday, December 3rd*, 1815.   Preached at Columbia.
I have passed three nights at Brother Arthur's, two at friend
Alexander McDowell's, and one night at Colonel Hutchin-
son's. *My consolations are great. I live in God from moment
to moment.   Thursday, 7th.*   We met a storm, and stopped
at William Baker's, Granby."

So the wonderful story, so far as it is told by himself,
abruptly ends.   These are the last words of the Journal,
and probably the last the dying saint ever wrote.   His hand
had lost its cunning.   In charge of his faithful and beloved
attendant, Mr. Bond, he continued to travel from place to
place for three months longer, preaching when he thought
his trembling feebleness would permit, though in each case
against the remonstrances of his friends, and without power
to stand for the purpose.   Gently, calmly, and in softened
radiance, did his sun go down.   By the 24th March he had
returned northward as far as Richmond, Virginia, still hoping
to attend the General Conference, to be held at Baltimore on
the 2nd of May.   Here he preached his last sermon.   Without strength to walk into the church, even with the support of
his friends, he was carried into it in their arms, and placed
on a table.   In faltering tones he read for his text Rom. ix.
28: "For He will finish the work, and cut it short in righteousness : because a short work will the Lord make upon the
earth."   His audience, deeply affected, frequently gave vent
to their feelings in loud, choking sobs.   Though unable to
speak many sentences together, he, with frequent pauses to
recover his breath, occupied nearly an hour ; and was then
carried out of the church, as he had been borne into it, in
the arms of loving friends.

Continuing his journey in the direction of Baltimore, he
by Friday, the 29th, reached the house of his friend, Mr.
Arnold, in Spottsylvania, about eighteen miles from Frede-

ricksburg. The next day his watchful companion, Mr. Bond, described his hopeless condition to the Rev. Daniel Hitt, one of his executors, in these words, " Since I wrote last it has been a scene of suffering indeed with our venerable father, Mr. Asbury. His cough almost prevents him from taking rest. He reclines on the bed, but is chiefly propped up with a chair. I find that his appetite has forsaken him, and he is very weak. We have, however, been enabled to travel slowly to this place. The two last Sabbaths our aged father preached, but I fear the exertion he then made was too great for him."

Continuing his letter the next morning, Mr. Bond wrote, " Our dear father appears much worse. He has had a very restless night, and is, I think, in more apparent danger of approaching dissolution than I ever saw him, even in his attack in the State of New Jersey. He says himself that he is apprehensive the scene will soon close." At eleven in the forenoon he requested that the family might be called into his room for worship. Mr. Bond then read the twenty-first chapter of the Book of Revelation, sang a hymn, and offered prayer. During these exercises he appeared to be abstracted in thought, as if by the aid of the imagery used in the chapter read to describe the heavenly Jerusalem, he had already passed to the intended reality. He then looked at his young friend with a smile of unearthly benignity, as if to dispel the expression of distress which his countenance betrayed. In an hour or two Mr. Bond inquired affectionately if Christ continued to be precious, and without power to enunciate a syllable, he simply raised his hands ; and then, reclining his head upon his beloved companion's arm, he calmly entered into rest. " Our dear father," wrote Mr. Bond, " has left us, and has gone to the Church triumphant. He died as he lived,—full of confidence,

18

full of love!—at four o'clock this afternoon." Sunday, March 31st, 1816.

So the redeemed spirit, purified by faith, and, like the Captain of our salvation, made perfect through suffering, passed away to be for ever with the Lord: so the faithful and successful servant entered into his Lord's joy. The transition was the gentlest conceivable. As he approached the heavenly world, and his bodily infirmities increased, his personal meetness for the inheritance of the saints in light had become more and more manifest, and he had realised the earnest in a proportionately increasing measure. The change he experienced was but the putting off this tabernacle to enter into a condition of being where the spiritual activities in which he delighted would be continued without weariness, in the perpetual keeping of a Sabbath reserved for the people of God.

The body was interred in the family vault of Mr. Arnold. It was understood, however, that this was not to be its final resting-place; and when the General Conference assembled in Baltimore, in May, it ordered its removal to that city. A vault, at the request of the Methodist people of Baltimore, was prepared for it beneath the pulpit of Eutaw Street Church; and at the reinterment the funeral was attended by thousands of true mourners. The body was followed from Light Street Church, where the Conference was holding its sittings, by the whole assembly, by many clergymen of other churches, and by a vast concourse of the citizens; the immense procession being headed by Bishop McKendree and the Rev. W. Black, the representative of the British to the American Conference. Bishop McKendree delivered an impressive address to a deeply affected audience, and funeral sermons were afterwards preached throughout the city, and in almost every part of the continent. A marble

monument was erected over the vault, which bears this
inscription :—

𝔖𝔞𝔠𝔯𝔢𝔡 𝔱𝔬 𝔱𝔥𝔢 𝔐𝔢𝔪𝔬𝔯𝔶 of

REV. FRANCIS ASBURY,

BISHOP OF THE METHODIST EPISCOPAL CHURCH.

HE was born in England, August 20, 1745 ;
Entered the Ministry at the age of seventeen ;
Came a Missionary to America 1771 ;
Was ordained Bishop in this city December 27, 1784
Annually visited the Conferences in the United States ;
With much zeal continued to "preach the Word "
For more than half a century ;
and
Literally ended his labours with his life,
Near Fredericksburg, Virginia,
In the full triumph of faith, on the 31st of March, 1816,
Aged 70 years, 7 months, and 11 days.
His remains were deposited in this vault May 10, 1816,
By the General Conference then sitting in this city.
His Journals will exhibit to posterity
His labours, his difficulties, his sufferings,
His patience, his perseverance, his love to God and man.

Two years before his death Asbury made his will,
appointing Bishop McKendree, Daniel Hitt, and Henry
Boehm his executors. With reference to this act he says,
"If I do not in the meantime spend it, I shall leave, when I
die, an estate of two thousand dollars, I believe : I give it
all to the Book Concern. This money, and somewhat more,
I have inherited from dear departed Methodist friends, in the
State of Maryland, who died childless ; besides some legacies
which I have never taken. Let it all return and continue to
aid the cause of piety."

CHAPTER XXIII.

The Author to the Reader—Summary of Asbury's Labours—His Motives not Worldly or Selfish—His great Success—His life Governed by his Aims— Appeal to Preachers—Appeal to Christian Reader.

MY pleasant task is completed; and, by dint of persistent plodding and thrift of time, I trust that I have been able to accomplish it, without, in consequence, omitting or lightly discharging any of the duties which pertain to my official relation to the people of my charge. On account of the great mass of material with which I have had to deal, and the crowding of collateral subjects, as suggested by the facts which have come before me, I have found the work heavier than I at first anticipated, and much heavier than you, my reader, can well conceive. But I have not found it a work of drudgery, but of delight, and I hope also of spiritual profit. And now, on the eve of our parting company, let us glance again for a moment at the picture which we have been contemplating, for one or two immediate practical ends.

We are amazed at the amount of work which Asbury accomplished, and scarcely less so at the spirit of sustained self-abnegation in which it was prosecuted. According to the sober calculation of Dr. Bangs, during the forty-five years of his ministry in America he preached no fewer than sixteen thousand four hundred and twenty-five sermons; travelled over the worst of roads, generally on horseback, not fewer than two hundred and seventy thousand miles; sat in no fewer than two hundred and twenty-four Annual Conferences, their entire business generally devolving upon himself; and probably consecrated, including travelling and local-preachers, more than four thousand persons to the sacred ministry. Yet with all this he was attentive to all the duties of the pastoral office, a diligent reader, and a close and minute observer of the scenes of nature, and the movements of civil and public life.

To what is this unparalleled amount of work done by a single human life to be ascribed ? Under what constraining or impelling power was it steadfastly carried on ? Earthly ambition ? The lust of fame ? The " accursed lust of gold ? " You repel any such suggestion with scorn.

The amount of success which he achieved was proportionate to the extent of his disinterested labours. Thousands of men and women were spiritually enlightened and saved under his personal ministry, and the multitudes more or less benefited by the omnipresent spiritual activities of which he was the mainspring are too vast for computation. To what is his prodigious practical influence to be attributed ? To his extraordinary intellectual endowments, his great scholastic attainments, or his elevated and commanding social position ? The answer is obvious.

But I need not multiply these inquiries. The explanation of the whole is that Francis Asbury ever felt life and its visible and revealed relations to be *real*, and ever lived for a purpose and aim,—an aim and purpose which were never absent from his consciousness ; which gained over him ever increasing governing power ; which gave shape and character to his thoughts, tone to his feelings, a right direction and a true force to his exertions ; which were a well of life within him springing up continually and renewing his sanctified energies day by day. What this life purpose was might be stated in such oft-repeated and passionate utterances as these : " I found my heart led out in prayer for those to whom I cannot preach. The Lord is my Witness, that if my whole body, yea, every hair of my head, could labour and suffer, they should be freely given up for God and souls." "Our total for the year 1803 is 104,070 members. In 1771 there were about 300 Methodists in New York, 250 in Philadelphia, and a few in Jersey. I then longed for 100,000; now I want 200,000—nay, thousands upon thousands." Go through his marvellous life, from the time when, as a mere youth, he exhorted his neighbours to flee from the wrath to come, until, as we have seen, he persisted in setting forth Christ as the Saviour of helpless men in the feebleness of his advanced age and disease, and you will find it radiant throughout with the brightness of this consuming zeal for God and souls.

You admit that the character commands your admiration. Probably, as we have surveyed together the outlines of the wonderful history, you have spontaneously exclaimed to yourself more than once, How noble! How heroic and glorious! How Christ-like! But will you content yourself with this?

Perhaps you are set apart to the same holy work to which Francis Asbury so unreservedly devoted his powers. You are happily free from his heavy trials. But you may thankfully lay aside all considerations with reference to them; for they were but the distressing accidents of the times, and with a will as firmly fixed in its determination for God and the welfare of your fellow-men, you would probably bear up under privation and hardships as heroically as he. But how is it in regard to the will and purpose? Have you a definite aim in your vocation,—such as it so imperiously requires, and so necessarily implies? Is this aim a real and practical thing, and something of which you are clearly conscious?

Supposing your aim *in pulpit preparation* to be the profit of your hearers, and not self-display, it will naturally govern your choice of texts and subjects, with reference to the spiritual condition of your congregation, and will as naturally mould your style of address. A man who does not merely profess to labour for the profit of all, as a thing to be taken for granted in a Christian minister, but is moved by this as his ruling purpose, will pray as Asbury did, "Lord, keep me from preaching empty stuff to please the ear instead of changing the heart;" like him, he will "labour hard to make the people understand," and, like him, will be able to say, "I gave it to them, as the Lord gave it to me--plain enough." Plainness was, in fact, a character of all his compositions, whether written or spoken; clearness and strength of thought, expressed in plain racy English, which told equally on the ear of the educated and the uneducated.

So we might say, with reference to the example we have had before us, that if a preacher is *real* in his views and sentiments, and if his aim is to save himself and those that hear him, evidence of this will appear in his intercourse with his people in their own dwellings;—" in word, in conversation, in charity, in spirit, in faith, in purity;"—in his care for their children, and his wisely directed efforts to win *them* to Christ; in his readiness to use suitable opportunities for dealing with men in their separate individuality, where this is seen to be necessary; in his estimate of the value of time, and his avoidance of habits of listlessness, indolence, and "dawdling"; in the direction of his private studies; and, above all, in his habits of devotion,—his "fellowship with the Father, and with His Son, Jesus Christ."

But you are not set apart to the ministry: if you were you would be as wholly devoted to your work as all this implies! Are you sure that there is no self-deception in this feeling? We are not all called to do spiritual work publicly and officially. "If all were the head, where were the members?" But is it impossible for us to promote that work by noiseless and unostentatious efforts, and by our spirit and general character ? Is it not certain that we shall do this if our hearts are set upon it ?

The first, supreme, and all-important thing for each of us is to come under the great law of holy love, by a true conversion, and, from the moment that we do so, to live for the accomplishment of such a purpose as the Christian conscience approves. For assuredly if you have a life-purpose, your actions and character will be governed by it. Suppose any man, in any station of life, to take the glory of God and the welfare and spiritual salvation of men for his aim and end ; then think how it must influence his intellectual powers, unconsciously, perhaps, moving, guiding, and expanding them ; how it must act upon his natural disposition and temper ; how it must bear upon his conduct in his relation to the individuals or bodies of men with whom he is called to associate in daily life, or within the circle of his friends ; how it would and must govern him in the use of his money, in the employment of his hours of relaxation and recreation, in the choice of his books and companions, in the indulgence of his intellectual tastes ; and how readily it would determine his course of action on those frequent occasions in the history of every man, when two lines of conduct lie before him, the one certainly right, the other doubtful !

Let you and me, my dear reader, *look well to the foundations*, in the first instance. Let us see to it that our relations to God are safe, and let us then keep ourselves in His love ; and, in order to this, live, as Francis Asbury did, in real and unbroken communion with Him. This will give rightness and strength to our purposes, and purity to our motives ; and however obscure our situation in life may be, it will be found hereafter that perhaps in ways unknown to us our lives have been useful to others.

www.ingramcontent.com/pod-product-compliance
Lightning Source LLC
Chambersburg PA
CBHW030626030726
47497CB00006B/1657